T0162375

FALLING HOUR

GEOFFREY D. MORRISON

COACH HOUSE BOOKS, TORONTO

first edition

 Canada Council **Conseil des Arts**
for the Arts du Canada

 ONTARIO ARTS COUNCIL
CONSEIL DES ARTS DE L'ONTARIO
an Ontario government agency
un organisme du gouvernement de l'Ontario

Canadä

Published with the generous assistance of the Canada Council for the Arts and the Ontario Arts Council. Coach House Books also acknowledges the support of the Government of Canada through the Canada Book Fund and the Government of Ontario through the Ontario Book Publishing Tax Credit.

LIBRARY AND ARCHIVES CANADA CATALOGUING IN PUBLICATION

Title: Falling hour / Geoffrey D. Morrison.
Names: Morrison, Geoffrey, author.
Identifiers: Canadiana (print) 20220243972 | Canadiana (ebook) 20220243980 | ISBN 9781552454466 (softcover) | ISBN 9781770567290 (EPUB) | ISBN 9781770567306 (PDF)
Classification: LCC PS8626.O75853 F35 2023 | DDC C813/.6—dc23

Falling Hour is available as an ebook: ISBN 978 1 77056 729 0 (EPUB); ISBN 978 1 77056 730 6 (PDF)

For Robert Wilson Mortimer and Molly Mortimer (née Dalgarno)

Milton produced *Paradise Lost* for the same reason that a silkworm produces silk. It was an activity of his nature.

— Marx, *Theories of Surplus Value*

Green grow the birks on bonnie Ythanside
And low lie the lowlands of Fyvie-o

— 'The Bonny Lass o' Fyvie,' Roud #545

1.

From an airplane, or an out-of-body experience, the town I lived in then would look like someone had scattered a sackful of giant concrete dice in a forest of broadleaf trees. The airline passenger or transmigrating soul would mark that six or seven of the cubes had landed in a huddle around the central lawn of a large public park. The grass was the faded green of an old gaming table.

From the ground, and from inside rather than outside my own body, I could report that the cubes were the colour of sea-damp sand and the grass in the park was steaming. I was sitting on the grass. The seat of my white jeans was wet, as were the palms of my hands. In my lap I held an empty grey picture frame. The pattern around the edges was – well, I don't know if it has a special name. A grey cascade, or a ziggurat, eight steps around each side. Then empty space to put my hands, feet, or head through, if I cared to. I did care to – all of those, so I tried each one in turn. Then I arranged the frame on the grass, stood up, and looked at it. The frame around the grass, the grass around the frame. Blades shivered, stroked harp-like by invisible fingers of air, and a drop of water trailed step-by-step down the ziggurat. Wetness cooled on my hands. The frame remained the frame.

I had found it the previous day on the red hydrant in front of the house I was renting, slung on the diagonal over the hydrant's top and one of its arms like a stiff sash. Kids playing ring toss, I thought. My second thought was that if it wasn't banged up too badly I could sell it on the internet for ten, maybe even fifteen dollars. I did not need the money, exactly, but with this sale I could furnish an hour or more with a purpose, however small. Having a purpose meant I could do something other than reflect on the state of my brain – which, over the past few months, had been the last thing I thought about before I slept most nights, the first thing I thought about in the morning, and the reason I woke up at least once in the hours between, too tired to change the subject but too darkly agitated to rest.

To put it simply, I had begun to think my brain was broken. My thoughts no longer had the geometric neatness I was sure they used to, the reliable line of yellow dashes down the middle of the road: 'and then, and then, and then, and then … ' Now thinking was more like trying to keep a fistful of optical fibres together in one hand while the other was tied behind my back, powerless therefore to stop the strands from splitting away from their neighbours in a superfine fray. A hundred dancing glows, like angel-dusted heads of pins: each one possible, each one possibly important, each one with the power to cancel out all the others if I dared let it veer far enough away on its own. I did not dare, so I made constant minor adjustments and stared, and the bright motes wandered across my face like winter constellations on the ceiling of a planetarium. Gemini, I thought, and Taurus, and Orion's Belt. Orion's Belt especially. The belt of a frozen hunter dead in the sky, like a cosmic-scale version of the kids playing ring toss. The big kids. It was unbearable.

I had taken my discovery to the walk-in clinic, the only adult patient in a roomful of parents with babies who coughed like seals. The GP called my complaint 'intriguing.' Obviously pressed for time, she gave me a number to call to get on the waiting list for group therapy. I called it and truthfully answered their questions about whether I wanted to hurt myself. (I did not. I told you it was unbearable, but evidently some unbearable things can be borne.) They never called me back.

In the meantime, I had tried to feel better by finding things to do. I had a job, but it was in my home, and not hard, and took up little of my time. Perhaps this was part of the problem. My employers owned an online store selling premium bags and accessories to the kind of people who seemed to exist only in photos, who regarded my employers' 'exclusive' pieces as necessary investments in their 'personal brands.' I had never seen anyone wearing them outside of a photo. Certainly not in this town. Officially my function was data entry, but on some days I had no data to enter. I knew my employers were essentially running a doomed vanity business with their parents' money, and at times I suspected I was only on the payroll to create the appearance that this was not so. Likely because I was not being directly supervised, I was paid thirty-six thousand Canadian dollars a year, a figure that occasionally made me feel great and occasionally made me feel guilty. When I felt great it was because I was leeching funds from the idle rich, who had after all 'started it' with their intergenerational theft of surplus value – thereby making my leeching an act of redistributive justice, and me a hero. When I felt guilty, it was not, you understand, because I was being paid a living wage for doing nothing. Rather it was because others were doing worse and harder work for significantly less. Whenever I felt this way, I gave up to a fourth of my paycheque to the Party of Socialist Workers (Marxist-Leninist). I wasn't a member. I didn't even go to their discussion groups. But I had a respect for the organizing abilities of the Bolsheviks in the period leading up to the October Revolution, modest personal tastes, a small rented bungalow in a relatively cheap town, a materialist conception of history, and no one else to spend my money on. I had no pets, or children, or siblings, and I did not know if my parents were living or dead. My guardians, a great-aunt and -uncle, had died seven years before and raised no other children. I lived completely alone, which made the finding of things to do a struggle at times – particularly now that I had decided, in the spirit of a radical therapeutic experiment, to greatly limit my use of the internet (I wanted to delineate exactly how responsible it was for my feeling that I had a broken brain). Sometimes I bought myself clothes. Nothing new, and certainly nothing sold by my employers. I liked thrifted pieces: white denim, nylon shells, acid wash, strange colour combinations. But mostly I read. When I couldn't read, I listened to Japanese ambient music, and when I couldn't do that, I kept my plants alive, a task that required so many mysterious things to go well that it could easily take up most of a day. I watched the advance of a blemish on a bamboo leaf like the spread of an epidemic, tested the soil of my jade plants for pH levels, set aside specially filtered water for a carnivorous butterwort that always seemed on the verge of physically falling apart, reverting to the mush it had sprung from. In the interstitial times between these acts, my memories became the focus of my attention. Playing back the sequences of past events in my mind was almost the only thing that did not make my brain feel broken. I knew I was cheating of course. If I knew already how an event had begun, and developed, and ended, I could pretend it had unfolded with an almost balletic majesty it had not truly had. And once I had locked a coherent sequence of events in place, I could let the chaotic details at the periphery of my memories fall into darkness. The resulting smooth stories were hardly proof that I had not felt broken-brained before – perhaps even the whole time I had been alive. But they were a comfort.

The wet grass shuddered like a slow-moving ocean, waves of blades breaking in confusion against the trees at the great field's edge. I too was at the edge of this ocean, first and foremost because it was hot that day and I wanted to be under a tree. But not coincidentally, the edge of the real ocean had once meant a great deal to me, enough that I will want to say more about it later. I picked up the frame, saw the ghost impression it had made in the grass, saw as well for the first time how the pricing sticker on its back had worn to a jagged, off-white smear so thin it was almost part of the wood. The frame was old, I realized. And heavy. Heavier than the mass-produced ones I was used to, the kind my guardians would have bought to frame the picture postcards of Capri sent them by a better-off second cousin in Dundee, a woman they often told me was 'up hersel' but whose picture postcards they dutifully framed, cheaply. (As working-class Scottish people who had lived as children through the war years and rationing, they did everything as cheaply as possible. The Germans, they often told me, had blown up the ice-skating rink.) The blue of the Tyrrhenian in those picture postcards had been a spectral teal, an aurora hovering unbelievably over the pastel houses that clung like limpets to the coast. I only realized much later that they had been hand-colourized after the fact. But this frame, the grey frame, seemed not only too heavy but too big to have framed picture postcards or any other photo. It must have enclosed a painting.

The depressed wet grass of the ghost impression was imperceptibly rising again. In ten or fifteen minutes it would be as it was before. Far away and behind me across the park I heard a familiar bird call: a low note sliding into a piercing sustained high, cut off by a second, staccato low. The timbre was liquid, like a whistle blown half underwater by a stagehand hidden in the wings. Low-budget Orphic – the sweet burble soaring out to the lovers on the proscenium, silencing the watchers in the pit and the box, and making the set and stage seem for a moment somehow more than that. I first heard this call when I was very young, probably four at the oldest, shortly after my parents had relapsed and my great-aunt and -uncle brought me to Canada. They took me to a park in the town that they lived in and encouraged me to run around on a grassy hillock surrounded by trees. As I had never done something like that before, I remember genuinely needing the encouragement. I remember also having new clean clothes, and the novelty of that. Little grey-blue overalls. It must have been spring or early summer; my mental images are of all-over green and bright light, my abiding sense memory a constant cool wind. They had given me a ball with a strong chemical smell that I liked. I threw it straight up into the blindingly blue sky as hard as I could and tried, through half-opened eyes, to catch it again, feeling small and alive and possible under the sky, shot through with an electric charge I do not think I had ever felt before. It was as I was squinting at the sky on my third or fourth throw that I first heard the call – *dowreeeeeeeeedoo* – from somewhere on the other side of the trees. My head snapped in its direction and I stood completely still; the ball fell back to the ground on its own and rolled away. I could not see the bird. The sound felt less like the work of one beaked mouth and single set of lungs than the voice of the whole green world singing to me at once – the hill, the sky, the distant trees, the black and muddy pools between their roots. In the years afterward I would return to the sound again and again with phantom intimations of what its maker looked like, returning to luxuriate in the freedom of my not knowing, but quietly knowing, at the close of each return, that this freedom could not last. The bird began as a great, plumed, colourful creature in my mind, a peacock or a toucan or a turaco blown north from Brazil and calling forlornly in a language the other birds did not know. As I got older and came to see the unlikelihood of this, I was nevertheless sure it must be a long-legged, graceful bird like a heron or a crane. And the hungry sound, not happy to be only that in my inner world, gathered ever more images to itself, images both of things I had really seen in the outer world and things my inner eye had unravelled from the outer and braided back together anew: a black-and-white picture my guardians owned showing a boy and girl sitting at the rim of a duck pond, a dark curtain of evergreens on the other side of the water preventing me from seeing any further into their world; the strangest scene in the Vanessa Redgrave *Wind in the Willows*, when Mole and Rat meet the Piper at the Gates of Dawn and it is so beautiful that he makes them forget everything they have seen, and the word *forget* echoes as the screen grows dim; a clearing in a park in summertime, where a single red-and-yellow vinyl lounge chair supported a reclining someone I would never know, a person possessing every contradictory feature and quality I wanted to find in another – now a woman, now a man, now neither, but always a beautiful, diamond-sharp spirit – this person holding a cold, clear glass and bringing a straw to their lips, now lifting the sweating glass itself to their forehead, all the while their lips and forehead shimmering alike in sweat with the brilliance of crushed glass.

And then one day when I was twenty-four I saw the bird that made the sound. A perfectly ordinary day in early spring in the riverside Ontario college town I lived in then, and as a matter of fact continued to live in at the time that I visited the park with the picture frame. I did not grow up there, and I do not live there now – or rather, wherever it is I am now, I am not there. There are two nows, by the way. There is the 'now' of the time I visited the park with the picture frame, and the 'now' of wherever it is I am now, and wherever it is I am now is after the park, I know that, I know it because the park is in the past tense and wherever it is I am now is in the present, though the park and its past tense likewise have a 'now,' because there is a 'now' of 'then.' I am aware this is confusing. How do you think I feel? But anyway, then, not now, in the riverside Ontario college town, when I was twenty-four, I saw the bird. I was at a bus stop next to a ditch. The ditch ran in front of a stand of empty trees with leathery bark, like elephant skin, and there were dry grey pebbles on the banks of the ditch and a thin clear trickle of water down its middle like a splintered crystal tether. I had just finished my morning shift at the bowling alley where I liked to tell my co-workers I was 'between lives.' I was on compassionate leave from my master's degree, the reason I had come to this town from the other end of the country in the first place, and I managed to spend most of my workdays reading books and comics under the counter, marking my place with the lace of a men's size 11. The bus home came only every half-hour, on the fifty-seven and the twenty-seven, and because my shifts ended non-negotiably on either the hour or the half-hour exactly, I always had to wait for it. I stood at the stop by the ditch and watched the wind make the slenderer hands of the bare trees draw circles in the air like parking attendants signing for the drivers to keep 'em comin'. The ditchwater came from a PVC pipe covered in what I had always thought of as sandbags but were actually burlap sacks of hardened concrete. The bird was above my head.

I think I saw it before I heard it: a hoppy form in my upper peripherals. Not quite a crow – head too round and beak too short and, yes, epaulettes of red with gold trim, like a circus ringmaster's – but crow-like, and crow-sized, and smart and neat in its movements. It stopped its hopping perfectly in the middle of my field of vision. In one continuous movement my eyes focused, and it opened its beak, and it sang the song, and a colourful and definite room in my inner world turned heavy and grey and burdensome as concrete sacks. There was nothing wrong with this bird except that I had seen and heard it do what it did. But that was enough. Sitting on the bus as it passed the cheque-cashing places and Portuguese pig-roast restaurants and all the little yellow-brick homes and stores set slightly too far apart like in every other small town, I had the pathetic idea that the bird would still prove to possess a beautiful name – whippoorwill, goldeneye, tanager – or at least be exceedingly rare. At home on my roommate's computer – 'Sure, go ahead. I delete my history. But don't fucking sit in my red leather chair' (the leather was fake, very fake, and had peeled in triangular flaps where he rested his thighs) – I would learn that the English name of the black bird with red on its wings was 'red-winged blackbird,' that it was arguably 'the most abundant living land bird in North America,' and that it was also 'among the best-studied wild bird species in the world.' As I learned these things, I felt for neither the first nor the last time that the currents of the world as it really was were washing me into a shape, the shape of something both more painful to contemplate and more true. More painful, I thought, yet more beautiful – in the same way that ice fields are beautiful, or the hard folds of the tundra, or ancient coasts all eaten by the sea, the bases of their sandstone rocks tooled to pegs by the motion of the tides. It only occurred to me later that my insistence that the washing away be beautiful might be as desperate and stubborn in its way as my attachment to the idea that the bird I had seen must have a beautiful name. Not only desperate and stubborn, this insistence on beauty, but less rather than more true; given a truer picture of the world and my relation to it, I had covered it over again immediately with a tasselled woollen blanket, something heavy and fleece-barbed and storm-cloud-coloured. A waft of spices in mysterious amalgam as it billowed out over the true picture, nutmeg, bergamot, caraway, the blanket of cold grey beauty settling over the picture of cold grey truth like sailcloth coming to rest on the seafloor. An aging and apple-wrinkled Donne in his winding sheet. I am already worried my images have taken me too far from what I meant to say, opened the door again to further obscurities of beauty in preference to truth, which felt that at this door it had precedence. But my choice has melted away my other choices in the bundle of shining strands, melted them away or at least banished them to a place where, like Eurydice, they may be rescued only if I do not try to look.

2.

The strand I have chosen among the fibres bundled in my hand glows blue like jellyfish phosphorus, grows bigger, trails out of sight. I follow it hand over hand in the inner darkness like a rope through a cave system, keeping time as I do so with the words that sent me down here in the first place – *beauty, truth, beauty, truth* – and I start to hear the last lines of Keats's poem about the Grecian urn: '"Beauty is truth, truth beauty," – that is all / Ye know on earth, and all ye need to know.' I hear the lines and I see the face of Keats, or more truly a composite of every face of Keats I know, the paintings and sketches and silhouettes, his life mask and death mask, and as I look at them I wonder what possessed this man to write something so obviously wrong. As the first human being whose death I read about in unsparing detail, by accident, in a water-damaged magazine a neighbour gave my great-aunt once she did not want to read it anymore, the face of John Keats haunted my childhood to the extent that I could not look long at a picture of him. By the perverse adulthood alchemy of childhood fear, I now know the precise details of all his portraits and of many things that happened in his life. But as I look through the inner darkness of the cave system, I cannot see Keats write the last lines of his poem. This moment is unknowable to me – even if I think I can see, as through the snow of a scrambled channel, the place he lived when he wrote them: a house with a garden full of fruit-bearing trees, an old shed, and a wine cellar of good claret, a house in a part of London that will soon be as built up as anywhere else in the rapidly growing city but for now is an exurb.

I cannot see him write because I do not understand. All I can see with my own understanding is the writing before the writing: the slow days when the poet unknowingly gathered the words that would turn into the poem and the world inscribed itself upon the writer with its own tools.

We arrive at the house with the garden of fruit-bearing trees in the middle of March in the year 1819. Keats is here. The trees that will bear fruit in the late summer and fall are now showing new buds merely, new buds or nothing. Brittle dark spindles dripping in the rain or flashing dully in pale light, light that is deepening daily but is as yet thin and pale and loitering. It is a time of waiting and a time of the knowledge and memory of death. Tom died in December. Tom, the brother Keats had written to from Scotland the previous summer – letters I must tell you about, but later. Tom was nineteen when he died, of tuberculosis, and Keats the licenced apothecary had been with him for much of this time, suitably trained for the bedside and nursing him but able to do only so much. In the time since the death he has done what he can to keep busy, what any young man with just enough credit to live well on the fringe of the metropole might do. Three days before Tom's funeral he goes off with a group to the West Sussex town of Crawley to bet on a bloody bare-knuckle boxing match that lasts thirty-four rounds. The winner, Jack Randall, is known in the papers as the Prime Irish Lad. Twenty years later, the poet and agricultural labourer John Clare, who will never meet Keats but who will share his publisher, will be confined in an asylum in part because of his delusion that he *is* Jack Randall, who by this point will have died of alcoholism. But that is all to come. Through the first months of the new year Keats has had plenty of society, music, and games with friends; on the eighteenth of March he is hit in the eye with a cricket ball. But on the days without social engagements he often records in his letters that he has done nothing at all. I imagine him staring for hours out the window at the buds on the garden trees, noting each day the barely perceptible changes, thinking too much or too little. His throat hurts. When the good claret from the cellar is not enough to dull the pain, he opts instead for laudanum, which at the start of the nineteenth century is still the only truly reliable painkiller known to English medicine. He may or may not yet know what this pain really means. The biographers tell me that the start of this year 1819 was likewise the beginning of his last sickness unto death. Eighteen nineteen. The numbers beat a rhythm that seduces me, dances me along their strange and interwoven axis, march-step, time-step. That bright blue braid. In the summer of 1818 John writes to Tom, aged eighteen, who dies in December 1818, aged nineteen, not living to see the year 1819 of the nineteenth century. And it is in the beginning of 1819 that John begins his decline from the same disease that killed his brother at the age of nineteen in 1818. And on the eighteenth of March, 1819, he is hit in the eye with a cricket ball. All this could mean nothing. Or on the contrary it could mean *everything* – a seam in the universe, the impress of the tool-and-die company, the aura of unclipped plastic around the cheaply made figurine. Eighteen, nineteen. The bright blue braid.

Within two years Keats will die of the same disease that killed his brother. He will do so in Rome, in the company of a young English painter he does not know very well and who has never before seen someone die. Keats has a medical licence from the Worshipful Society of Apothecaries, and by virtue of his training at Guy's Hospital and attendance at his brother's fatal illness has seen death in many forms. He will use some of his last words on earth to reassure the young painter that he will 'die easy' – telling him 'don't be frightened' and 'be firm' in the same halting breaths. The young painter will shortly afterward record in a letter that, close to the end, Keats 'grieved inwardly' in the mornings when he woke to discover himself still alive. The young painter will stay in Rome for most of the rest of his life, over the long span of which he will imperceptibly cease to be young. He will die at age eighty-five in 1879, the year that Zulu warriors defeat the British at Isandlwana, the first Indian indentured workers arrive in Fiji, Henrik Ibsen premieres *A Doll's House*, and Sandford Fleming proposes his system of standardized time. In the year that the painter dies, millions of babies will be born. Among them will be people named Paul Klee, Margaret Sanger, Emiliano Zapata, Leon Trotsky, Wallace Stevens, Ethel Barrymore, Albert Einstein, and Will Rogers – people who will be more properly thought of as belonging to the twentieth century than the nineteenth. Jeanne Calment, whose hundred and twenty-two years alive still seem unlikely to be far surpassed by anyone, will be four years old when the painter dies; at the time of Calment's death I will be nine, and reading for the first time the terrible article about the last days of Keats. But that is all to come. It is the middle of March 1819, and Keats has been hit in the eye by a cricket ball.

The day afterward he writes a letter to his brother George and sister-in-law Georgiana. The letter will travel a long way to get to them, but I will defer my account of the course of this letter across the world until later. It is too much. Suffice to say that the letter itself is oddly phrased and difficult to follow, probably the fault of the laudanum Keats took for the eye pain. It is in this letter that his Grecian urn first appears to take shape in the paper record of his life, if not yet as a poem then at least as a picture occupant of his mind. 'Neither Poetry,' he writes, 'nor Ambition, nor Love have any alertness of countenance as they pass by me: they seem rather like three figures on a greek vase ... ' But the blue strand I follow through the tunnels of the inner darkness does not want me to become fixed on this vase, to circle it round and round as though there were something further to come on its surface, as though at any moment the figures I have seen turning again and again might change into new ones. It flickers and threatens to die if I do not move on. There is something else in this letter, something written as if for me. The strand brightens and I move through the inner darkness nearly at walking speed, bolder now that I can almost make out the folds of the cavern ceiling, the subtle and gum-like whorls of the floor I had earlier been forced to negotiate so carefully. I am coming to a chapel in the rock, a place where my blue thoughts will have ample room to move and multiply around a brilliant and white-hot object, the ultimate yet unexpected goal of my crawl through the caves. As in a dream, I know that the object is a word, or a cluster of words, or a string of them, but I cannot know or see them yet. I see a dense and fiery knot like a star that wants to go nova. Tapestries hang here, their birds and flowers and leaves blocked out square by square as if by pixels. Soft pixels. My blue strand splits into further, finer strands; they add themselves to the bottoms of the tapestries line after line. The images repeat and variegate – new birds, new flowers, new leaves. The fibres twist and fray. Fibres. That is why we are here in this chamber in the inner dark. I said chapel but I may say also bedchamber, a place where things are known in the night but only nearly remembered on waking, nearly but not actually. Keats sleeps until eleven on the morning he writes his letter. The laudanum, once again. He reports that 'the fibres of the brain are relaxed in common with the rest of the body, and to such a happy degree that pleasure has no show of enticement and pain no unbearable frown.' I know that when Keats uses the word *fibres* in connection with his brain he is not thinking metaphorically, as I am when I use it; he is thinking instead of a nineteenth-century medical theory no one believes anymore. Our term is shared perhaps only in the incidental way that fins are shared by fish and whales, the subject-object-verb structure by Kurdish and Japanese. But I venerate it anyway, this coincidence; I have so little else to go on. I have this and my materialist conception of history, a thing I prefer to think of with images, and so my conception of history is jig dolls, my handmade wooden jig dolls bucking and kicking on the board held in place by my ass. Buck. Kick. Their arms flicking in circles like pinwheels. The flick of red flags on the winds. The dance of the rising of the moon. I see thesis, antithesis, and synthesis turning and swapping places in this papyrus-coloured moonlight; I know these are not Marx's terms, they are not even Hegel's terms, they are Fichte's and Schelling's, but I was poorly taught at first and so when I think about the movement of concepts I use them, I cannot help it, you will just have to deal with it, I set them at play on this brittle board of my own design, and I begin to wonder if our fibres are something more than a coincidence after all.

Two hundred miles from Keats in bed at eleven at Wentworth Place are the textile factories of Manchester, the women bent over the masses of power looms, the children crawling under the taut fibres of the spinning mules to gather waste. They have been here since dawn. I hear the rhythmic wooden smack of the looms in operation, feel the fear and the focus of the hurrying women and children. Somewhere a mill owner quietly accumulates capital without doing anything. Threads bind together. I remember that people of my paternal grandmother's maiden name appear in the Bankrupt Directory in Aberdeen in the 1830s, their profession always listed as 'weaver,' and I understand that they practised the older and humbler (and obsolete, and doomed) trade of weaving by hand. I understand too that, as the focus of British weaving shifted from wool to cotton, the capitalists would support the continuation of American slavery and sympathize with the South in the Civil War, and that when they could not get American cotton they would import it from their colonies in India. The whole shape of that bloody century nineteen was governed by fabrics, fibres, textiles, the machines and the land and the people all yoked together and driven to the absurd ends of ever more elaborate clothes, ever simpler and more mass-reproducible clothes. So that it is perhaps no wonder that doctors of the time would think of human minds and bodies as yet more bundles of fibre.

Why would they not? And within this huge and terrible enterprise, this brutal transcontinental machinery of human bodies, metal mechanisms, and reconstituted plant and animal parts, the genesis of the next terrible process arose almost diffidently and by accident. Joseph Marie Jacquard – a provincial middle-aged debtor, ex-soldier in the army of Revolutionary France, and weaver's son – programmed a pattern on fabric using punch cards.

The English mathematician Charles Babbage would take inspiration from Jacquard's loom as he developed his Analytical Engine, the forerunner of all modern computers and the first germ of the data world they brought into being. Babbage's computer, proposed in 1837 but never completed, was likewise meant to take directions from punch cards. The strange symmetry of this choice was best expressed by his friend and fellow mathematician Ada Lovelace, who so vividly saw the machine's potential and wrote its first algorithm: 'We may say most aptly,' she writes, 'that the Analytical Engine weaves algebraical patterns just as the Jacquard loom weaves flowers and leaves.' Babbage was an unpoetical soul, the kind of placid abacus I have personally always tried to avoid; he hated hoop rolling and organ grinders and allegedly once wrote Tennyson to warn him that his lines 'Every minute dies a man / Every minute one is born' would be better expressed as 'Every moment dies a man / And one and a sixteenth is born.' Lovelace, the daughter of Byron, is much more interesting; her correspondence reveals an irrepressible artist's temperament despite her mathematical mother's wishes that she study only science (her mother feared that if Ada studied poetry she would develop Byron's madness). As she writes to Babbage, 'I do not think you possess half *my* forethoughts, & powers of foreseeing all *possible* contingencies (*probable* & *improbable*, just alike).' Her 'powers of foreseeing,' coupled with her fear of her own madness (something she learned from her mother), made her an early discoverer, ten years before George Boole's *Laws of Thought*, of the new brain, the brain that would come after the nineteenth-century brain of fibres:

> I have my hopes, and very distinct ones too, of one day getting cerebral phenomena such that I can put them into mathematical equations – in short, a law or laws for the mutual actions of the molecules of the brain. I hope to bequeath to the generations a calculus of the nervous system.

This is the punch-card brain, the brain of the data banks – a brain that most people would not realize they had until at least the middle of the twentieth century, when the weaponized calculus of the Second World War brought massive new computers into being, computers that would be used postwar to keep track of census results, polling data, insurance policies, plans for the delivery of thermonuclear weapons by bomber squadron, and tabulations of who or what might survive such a deluge. And in the final decades of that century, brains and computers began to share attributes, qualities, even symptoms. They stored memories, caught viruses (encephalitis or ILOVEYOU, as the case might be), 'processed information,' or said, in so many words, 'I don't want to process this right now.' They froze, died, got wiped, got rebooted. And, just as before, the genesis of the next terrible process inhered in the first like an open secret: over a period of twenty years that century, university research teams and engineers at glassware companies developed hair-fine optical fibres to the degree of attenuation required to send signals across the world. Fibre-optic cable is now the primary hardware infrastructure enabling the internet and the other global computer networks; there are 550,000 miles of it running under the oceans in cold Hadean darkness. 'I don't have enough bandwidth for this,' they are saying now in offices where once they said they could not 'process' it. The simplicity of it terrifies me, the buck and jig of two centuries: fibres; punch cards; finer, frayed fibres. The rising of the moon.

If your brain is fibres, your systems of production are fibres. If your brain is computation and calculus, your systems of production are computation and calculus. If your brain is bright, fraying, sunken fibres, your systems of production are bright, fraying, sunken fibres. If your brain is broken … Well, you understand. Even the straight yellow lines of the highway – those comforting regularities I thought myself to think in earlier on in my life – they too may just have been a memory of the twentieth century's one-and-zero data brain, and the comfort I had retroactively granted them just as much a fakery. But I do not know how knowing any of this will help me. Not only do I still not understand why Keats would write that beauty is the same as truth, I intuit somehow that I never will, just as I will never know the words that burn in the knot in the chapel. It is the middle of March 1819, and Keats has been hit in the eye by a cricket ball, and I think my brain is broken. History may be rumbling all around me like a house that is settling or coming apart, but for me, now (or really then), here (or really there), in the park, with the frame, with my tenuous appointment with a stranger, things are always only ever about to happen.

In the sky a nondescript brown bird circled the open treeless part of the park but did not land. Higher above me a small grey needle of an airliner plowed two white furrows in the sky but did not land. Higher still, the sun quietly exploded but did not land. I saw that in ten minutes the stranger would arrive, if the stranger kept to the timeline we had agreed to, and they would buy the frame for 'twenty dollars or best offer,' which I assumed would be ten, maybe even fifteen dollars, as I have said before. I could see no one else in the park. The benches were empty, and I could have sat on them if I wanted to, but I did not want to. I wanted my ass to be green.

The windows of the concrete cubes across the street were small and rectangular and sepia and obscured by the wide green leaves of the trees at the fringe of the park. There could have been hundreds of people inside. The red-winged blackbird sang again from across the park. I have said already that it makes a liquid sound, but I forgot to tell you that red-winged blackbirds are almost always found near water. I learned that in the red leather chair. The bird was likely calling from one of the trees that shade the cold black water in the pond in the corner of the park farthest away from me, a place where the trees are thicker than the fringe on the perimeter but not as thick as the woods in the other far corner. On June nights, when it is just cool enough to walk in the dark in a sweater, the path echoes with the rasping wooden voices of hundreds of frogs. The rising of the moon. Later in the year, when the leaves change colour and die on the trees that hang over the water, the surface of the pond becomes a spilled jigsaw puzzle, red and yellow predominating – the picture on the puzzle box a fire, a lunar new year, a traditional English-pattern Jack of Hearts. But the cold black water always shows itself in the gaps between the leaves, and one after another the leaves give up and spiral under it. In winter the water freezes, and the thin and lace-like branches of the trees around the pond seem frozen too, like nets caught in the act of being cast into water. Once or twice in March or April I have noticed a curled brown leaf from the previous year, dead but still holding fast to its branch even as the tree starts to bud again, and I have thought about plucking this posthumous leaf and taking it away for myself, placing it on the shelf above my desk among my other dead and ineradicable things: wave-polished seashells, odd-coloured stones. But I never do. I do not trust my hands.

'He got a parcel of people about him at a Cottage door last Evening,' begins a paragraph Keats includes in a letter to his dying brother Tom. 'He' means his friend Charles Brown, with whom Keats travels through Scotland in the summer of 1818, acquiring for the first time an attack of the throat pain that will plague him periodically up to his death. The cottage is on the Isle of Mull – or An t-Eilean Muileach in Gaelic – and, in a pattern that will replicate itself again and again all over the world for over a century afterward, the English visitors like to think themselves celebrities here: men who will be feted for their special modern things. Keats writes of it like they are the first 'civilized' men in the village. He reports that Brown 'chatted with one who had been a Miss Brown, and who I think from a likeness, must have been a Relation – he jawed with the old Woman – flattered a young one – kissed a child who was afraid of his Spectacles and finally drank a pint of Milk.' When I read the conclusion to this part of the letter, I think of my shelf, and my hands: 'They handle his Spectacles,' Keats writes, 'as we do a sensitive leaf.'

3.

I was still waiting, by the way. The drops on the frame ran slickly down
the ziggurat without trailing wetness behind them or sinking down
into the wood. It seemed sealed up in good varnish. And in fact the
more I examined the uniform cuts without error, the sturdiness of the
real wood, the more I believed it had once been expensive, and that it
had once also housed something of great price. Not a poster, a diploma,
a photograph – a painting, I was certain now. And, knowing the tastes
of the few rich people in this town, most likely a terrible painting, something abstract in pastels or earth tones, a piece of hospital art no more
interesting to look at or think about than a stain on a kitchen counter,
or less even, because a stain is at least a spontaneous miracle of nature.
With the subtext, of course, that its owner could afford to spend thousands of dollars on something so bad – so that if they so chose they
could instead have put that money in small bill form and blown it all
over the main street of the town with a leaf blower without feeling the
slightest fiscal pinch, but with the further subtext that they would never
do anything so philanthropic as that, even that small and patronizing
gesture, for the people of the town, a suffering inland post-industrial
town like so many others, and that they would instead lock up that
money forever in a rose and mauve and amber canvas called *Wichita
Sunrise*, steadily appreciating, signifying nothing. It was their special
way of saying 'fuck you' to the people of the town. I felt proud to be
reselling the frame for so little money, and I felt even prouder of the
kids who I imagined had found or stolen it in the first place and slung it
around a hydrant in a lower-middle-class neighbourhood. I liked to

think they had been saying 'fuck you' right back. But they may just have thought it was funny.

The varnish caught hold of the light so that the grass in the empty centre of the frame was bordered by the sun, or rather its residue, the trace of its slow explosion in the distance. Its quiet explosion, as I said before. The residue of sun in a skin of ice. I had not picked this phrase *a skin of ice* by accident. I had in fact been using it in my mind these last few months to describe a phenomenon perhaps related to my broken brain – but if so, a relation whose precise causal order was yet unclear to me. I was not sure if the skin of ice was a symptom, or a sign, or the source of the symptoms, or a warning of something worse to come – perhaps even a 'something worse to come' related to wherever it is I am now.

But I tended to think this phenomenon was most like a fever – an effort from some other zone of my body to hush the worst effects of my broken brain, and like a fever an effort that in the short term just made me feel worse. I had only vague names for the phenomenon. Vagueness appeared to be part of what it was. But the image I kept returning to when I felt this way was that I was sealed in a skin of ice: I could move, but stiffly and at a delay; I could feel, but faintly, as though my nerve endings had been burned away by frost; I could see, but with the soft ocular warp of something clear yet imperfect in front of my eyes. I once had a dream that I went to my regular coffee shop in town and didn't say anything; I just stood in front of the woman at the counter, my mind and face blank, making no gestures, as if any thought or sound or movement would have been enough to destroy me utterly – and yet the coffee appeared, and the woman at the counter coached me through an uncooperative debit machine, and I woke up feeling like I had passed through the eye of a needle. The skin of ice was like this: a brutal protective magic that got me through the day at the cost of everything it deemed unnecessary, up to and including thought and language – an airtight seal ensuring I gave as little as possible to the world. On balance it seemed most like a fever. I wondered if I would feel it when the stranger came for the frame, if I would hand over the item and take the money but say almost nothing. Any minute now, I thought.

In the meantime, a snail had appeared from somewhere dark and cool in the pebbled soil under the leaves of grass, had started to climb the steps of the ziggurat like a Babylonian priest ascending to observe the heavens in a purple robe. I did not mind that it was on the frame. Once it had finished what it meant to do, I could wipe away its trail with my thumb and not tell the stranger about it. Many people are particular about things like this, but I am not. As I see it, the species with the greatest ability to contaminate what it touches is ours. The trace of the snail on the frame was a thin band of silver, and I thought of the stream in the ditch on the day I first saw a red-winged blackbird. Only the snail's silver was beamier, a stream in the light of a rising moon. So that when I watched the snail on the frame, I was watching the slow advance of moonlight across the steps of a temple, the shining steps of a temple catching in its finished stones the slow explosion of the sun. The temple at the wild outer shore of the hesitating sea of green bright blades. The leaves of the tree above me shook in the hot wind and a single leaf detached and fell to the ground seesaw-style. Everything was exploding, and everything that was not exploding was falling down. 'Walking is falling forward,' I read once, our biped movement just a guided fall of odd deliberateness, like the demolition of a condemned building. Slow falling powered by controlled explosion. And this seemed true at either end of cosmic scales of size, complexity, and time. Millions of big and small metabolic systems and reactions and abreactions and chain reactions and dominoes. So that the snail was exploding as surely as I was, and the grass, and the sun, and even the moon has a molten core for all its outward aspect of inertia. Because it was mostly dead matter, I was not quite sure the frame was exploding all that much – though once I heard that wood never dies. In any case, it was falling as the world was.

The snail kept climbing. Its ruffles, a grey the colour of tide-soaked sand, were pitted like dinosaur skin, and they billowed in slow motion, caught at the face of each oncoming step like a damp tablecloth flung outward. Its horns stretched and dipped like cantilevers as it moved. My eyes fixed above all on its shell, the way it twisted like a shepherd's crook in the Book of Kells, one twist a dark mahogany and the other complementary band a honey-white-yellow at the tight nucleus, the yellow of watercolour daffodils, yellow bleaching out steadily as the coil unwound, ending at the opening in an ivory or papyrus off-white. A marvel. This cold grey blanket (again, I thought) was alive, and it lived inside itself in a brittle Fibonacci sequence, smoother inside than almost anything a human hand could make except for plastic, which was after all just a distillation of very old shells. I knew that snails were male and female at the same time, that in their mating they impregnated their partners and were impregnated by them in turn, and the symmetry of this was beautiful to me. Not least because whatever the observer would think about me from my appearance, the world I inhabited inside myself was male, female, and neither all at once, and had been so at least since adolescence, and so the world inside the coils of self I carried with me had felt like an open world, if in many ways also a secret world, and also a world that I myself could hardly understand. When I was fifteen or sixteen I saw a picture of a young, shirtless Javier Bardem in a newspaper review of the Spanish film *The Sea Inside* and felt the beginnings of what I now recognize to have been a crush, and it is perhaps for that reason as well as for the poetry of the title, a poetry I was drawn to naturally as I grew up along the coasts and the estuaries, that the words *the sea inside* remained with me and became an image I could use for the world inside myself, even as I continued to never see the film or learn why it had been titled that way. This inner, open world was a dark sea, a warm sea, a salt sea I still knew only a corner of, could map its currents by only the broadest drifts and streams. The dark sea of myself existed in unclear relation to my brain and its brokenness: was my brain the sea, or a vessel on this sea, or the navigator in the cabin, or her instruments? Or was my brain the wind and rain and bitter crosscurrents that churned the sea's surface like a fearsome avenging hand? I did not know then, in the park. Wherever it is I am now I continue not to know.

'The Scotchman has made up his Mind within himself in a sort of snail shell wisdom. The Irishman is full of strongheaded instinct.' So says Keats as part of a long passage about the difference between Scottish and Irish people in another one of his letters to Tom from his travels. The passage is about as bad as you would expect. I never said I loved the man who haunted me, and in fact I mostly hate the Keats of these letters, who sounds like any other nightmare English tourist to a place that is not England: bitching about the poor quality of the food, moaning about the shabbiness of the lodgings, always trying to get in a dig about the people who 'clatter' or 'gabble away' in Gaelic in the rooms adjacent to his. At times he looks at the world with the eyes of a wretched colonial administrator, weighing and measuring the character traits of the Scottish and Irish peasantry to see how far they might be 'improved' and 'refined.' He was by no means the first. The open secret of each of the modern period's transoceanic empires – certainly in the bloody two centuries after Keats's letter, and just as certainly in the bloody three centuries before – is that they practised their demonic instruments close to home first. Spain to the Conversos and Moriscos, France to the Cathars of Languedoc, England to Scotland, Ireland, and Wales. What had Louis Riel written to the Irish American paper the *Irish World* in 1885?

In their treatment of us, however, the behavior of the English is not singular. Follow those pirates the world over and you will find that everywhere and at all times they adopt the same tactics and operate on the same thievish lines.

Ireland, India, the Highlands of Scotland, Australia, and the isles of the Indian Ocean – all these countries are the sad evidences and their native populations are the witnesses of England's land robberies.

In their own private way, the condescending letters from Keats are incident reports, white papers, intelligence gatherings on behalf of the pirates of the world; he is looking at Ireland and the Highlands of Scotland with a pirate's eyes, even if he fantasizes the next year about joining Simón Bolívar's army of liberation in South America, and even if by some accounts his great poem to autumn is in secret about the pitiless redcoats descending upon the Manchester weavers at Peterloo. So that the man who haunts me is my enemy at the same time that he haunts me, and at the same time that he has written poems that have served the continuation of my life. I see no contradiction. It may all be put to use. The 'snail shell wisdom' he observes in the rural poor of Scotland is a part of his larger view of these people as grave, serious, cautious, stubborn, introverted, and self-contained – superficialities all, but not from nothing. Keats without knowing it was observing the effects of a bone-deep cultural Calvinism, of rural poverty, of subsistence-based tenant farming – of course you would be circumspect with the Kirk and the landlord breathing down your neck all the time. And the trace of these things seemed long. My great-uncle was descended from ex-tenant-farmers and crofters and farm labourers in Aberdeenshire, my great-aunt the product of stonecutters and wool spinners and mill workers in the city proper. While as secular socialists they had firmly rejected the Kirk and all that it stood for, a certain tiny mote of its forms had burrowed into them all the same and reproduced itself, so that by the time they emigrated in their mid-thirties they were hauling the weight of centuries across the ocean and not their own mere decades. If this makes any sense, they repudiated Calvinism in a Calvinist way. Their attacks took on the contours of their targets. And so, by extension, and with all the distortions that came from ostensibly growing up on the West Coast of Canada in the 1990s, with *The Simpsons*, *Calvin and Hobbes*, *Age of Empires II*, 'Rowdy' Roddy Piper, about five hundred illustrated non-fiction science and history books from the library, and Shareef Abdur-Rahim's Vancouver Grizzlies, I too acquired by osmosis my own attenuated version of the snail shell wisdom. From childhood I have tended to get stuck within the spirals in my own head.

At last the snail reached the inner edge of the frame and crawled off it, dropped back into the earth under the grass, and softly muscled the blades aside on its way to wherever it is a snail feels it must go after it has crawled across a frame. I licked my thumb and swiped its trail away. The frame looked good as new. I saw I was still alone in the park – no joggers, no dog walkers, no drinkers or smokers – and saw with a glance at my phone that the stranger was late. I could not ask why, as we had not exchanged numbers. We arranged everything in three or four terse emails. I did not even know their name; their email handle had been the completely unrevealing 'onykx22@hotmail.com.' *Onyx?* Wasn't that a Pokémon or something? And a Hotmail too. I imagined a person of potentially any gender, a bit of a nerd, and probably closer to my age than not, who had for whatever reason kept their first email handle, whether for anonymity or nostalgia or because they had never really changed. We had all loved the letter *x* and random strings of numbers once. And all lowercase. All caps too. My own first forum username back in late 2002 had been WORLDBBALL. My guardians would not set up the internet at home for another two years (we were one of the last families at the school to get it, and only because the teachers, expecting that we all had it, had begun to assign homework that I could not do), but I could use it for forty-five minutes at a time at the public library and I wanted to talk to strangers about Allen Iverson. I could imagine onykx22@hotmail.com at the cheap wooden desk in the kitchen fifteen years ago, after dinner and homework were finished and nobody else in the family needed the computer, waiting for, I don't know, opal44 or jasper55 or chalcedon66 to log on, for the tiny circle next to their profile picture to turn green. The forms of our lives in the Bush years were governed by tools of surveillance, of watching and being watched, right down to the scansions of our first loves. They were training us in the libidinal economy of the stakeout, the techne of the snitch. So that Onyx, unwitting student of that world as much as you or I or anyone, would be waiting with their heart in their mouth for a good twenty minutes before messaging 'hello' to not seem too desperate, only for opal44 or jasper55 or chalcedon66 to log off after eighteen and a half minutes, presumably because nobody had messaged them. And it would be a thousand years until the next time that homework was finished and nobody else needed the computer and the tiny green light came on again. Onyx would dig their nails into the palms of their hands, wake up over and over in the night, not just seem desperate now but truly be so. We had felt time and absence so much more powerfully then, before we learned that distance and slowness are the elemental facts of the lives that get the chance to be long. So that sitting on the grass in the park with the frame and knowing that the stranger was late did not feel like the end of the world. But of course it was, and is, and has been, the whole time. Just not because of the stranger, and not, as yet, for me.

4.

The stranger was late, and this was not the end of the world. But there was distress in my world. All my thoughts these last fifteen minutes had distressed me – not all at once, but slowly, like the proverbial frog in the pot. Without correcting course, I would soon be upside down in my distress, floating in it, silently bloat-white and poaching. But I could not think my way out. You never can. Each of my thoughts had lit up the edges of shadowy paths to things I hadn't thought of yet, things I knew would distress me even more. Midway through the journey of this day I found myself in a forest of archways and colonnades, a Mezquita of twisted design. Jonah sitting on the sea floor and holding his breath in the middle of a thousand open-mouthed whales. Or so it felt. So I decided to get up and move. I often do this when I feel distress creeping into my world – make some stupid uncalculated movement – and I do it even if part of me knows it will badly upset the expected course of things. I have been known to French exit, Irish goodbye, fake sickness, bolt from a room without comment if the ambient distress reaches the right levels. And so almost without knowing what I was doing, I began walking the outside edge of the park. If I saw someone waiting at the place I had mentioned in my email, I would return there with the frame and say the appropriate words. 'Hello,' probably. 'My name is Hugh,' probably. I was not yet sure if I would apologize or even explain why I was not waiting where I said I would. I would play it by ear.

But I did not want to walk too far from the meeting place. The park is fairly large – eighty-five acres, reaching the upper limit of a tenant farm able to be run on a precapitalist subsistence model in the farm country of Northeast Scotland – and walking it all the way around would take thirty or forty minutes. Untenable. Instead I would walk to the willow. The only one, as far as I knew, in the park. It stood at the corner where two streets met, streets with the ridiculous and offensive and improbable names of Wellington and Boyne. Incoherent Anglosphere background noise, unless you knew what they were trying to say by that. I knew what they were trying to say. Fucking Brits. Fucking Prods. Fucking Huns, as they would say in the place where I was born. Wellington, Boyne. French exits. Irish goodbyes. But I will delay these matters just a little longer. For the moment, the willow. A great full willow, billowing like a water-laced cliff face in a classical Chinese landscape painting. Fractals and pixels, braided chains of shimmers and flows. Willows I had known since childhood as 'weeping,' known them growing up in the coastlands and estuarylands as water lovers, or if not lovers (because proximity is not the same as love) then at least as water-mad, water-manic, water-fiending, or if not those things then yoked to water by necessity, terrible necessity, brutal and unwelcome symbiosis – known them, to put it simply, as trees that almost always hung their heavy and doubtful heads over water, and had either put together in my mind or received from someone older than me as authentic folklore the idea that the pools and ponds and flowing ditches the willows hung their shimmering heads over were the pools and ponds and flowing ditches of their tears. Why they were weeping in the first place I did not know then. I must have thought it was simply integral to their nature. Weeping willows wept. Hoot owls hooted. Blue moons blued.

I walked slowly to the willow. Slowly, because once I got there, I did not know what I would do with it. Technically speaking, I could do many things. I could touch its leaves, look at its bark, look for snails or ants or centipedes in the folds of the bark. Harvest the bark for aspirin, and then take the aspirin. Climb the willow and look out at the world beyond the park, the concrete cubes and the yellow-bricked Victorian houses behind them and the main street with its bars and restaurants behind those. Pipe dreams, all these plans. When I reached the willow, I would probably just turn around and walk back again. But I did not want to think about that yet. Nothing is stupider and more humiliating, when you are distressed, than walking to a place you pick purely because it is in your eye line, recognizing that, of course, there is nothing for you to do there, not really, and having to walk back again to the place you started from. So I moved like a procession of Zen monks had moved in a video I had seen once. The walking meditation. I stepped like the surface beneath my feet was made of the thinnest and most breakable panes of glass.

About four metres to my left, or in other words the side of me facing further into the park, and roughly halfway between the willow and the place where I started from, stood several magnolia trees of the low, long-skirted kind. The flowers of this kind of magnolia tree flow right to the ground, when there are flowers, but as this was further into the summer the flowers had already come and gone and the leaves had replaced them. Big green upturned half-woven baskets, weird beehives, sketchy semi-geodesic domes spacious enough to hide in and look out of. Perhaps my tree-climbing idea had primed this thought for me, and so I gave the magnolias my close attention. Leaves jerked and stirred. For a second I truly believed I was being watched.

Correction. I knew I was being watched. Just like you, and everyone. I knew they had their algorithms, keyloggers, trackers, taps on every-body's phones. No need to peep me from the magnolia trees, to keep up the pretense that they did not already know every last thing they needed to. But if, as a little treat for themselves in their boredom, in the tedium of their almost infinite knowledge, they were watching me from closer than normal, I wondered what they would think of me, the slight, tallish man in white pants who had come to the park on his own. Sheer vanity, of course, to wonder this. But I wondered. I had been coming alone to this park for three years, and in that time I had noticed that seven out of ten of the other people who came by themselves were walking their dogs. Two of the remaining three out of ten were jogging.

The joggers and dog walkers were solidly middle-class people, if not upper-middle-class people. Certainly not lower-middle-class people, working-class people, poor people, underclass people. You could tell these people had real money and everything else implied by that. They believed in the mechanistic perfectibility of the world. Their Under Armour clung to their gym-formed bodies like robot skin. Their faces said they would literally kill anyone who interfered with the gambols of their dogs. It seemed to me that the people of these strata were reluctant to do anything alone in a park that could not satisfy one of their 'goals,' be crossed off their 'checklists.' So that myself and the other remaining ones, the one in ten, who came alone to the park without any of the obvious utilitarian motives of the solid and appropriate middle classes were, I assumed, almost automatically suspect in their eyes. Cruisers. Voyeurs. Drunks. I knew I could be any of these things to the watchers in the magnolia trees. What would they think of my apparently purposeless and very slow walk toward the willow? My white pants, now grass-stained on the ass and knees in a way I would have to bleach later? (I did not mind. It filled the time.) The frame, balanced on my right shoulder the way a cowboy holds a coil of rope? I supposed they would think what people had thought when I started university, which was that I was on drugs. But I had not been on drugs then. Not cannabis, like they had thought on the study-intensive floor whenever I said or did something they had not previously seen a person say or do. 'Hugh's stoned,' they would say. Not mescaline, like my friends Pia, Bill, and Atefeh had said in the laundry room when I was bent over folding my clothes and they could not see me. (They had been worried about my grades, which I now recognize to have been sweet of them. But at the time it annoyed me. Despite all appearances, my grades were good.) Not antidepressants or anxiolytics or stimulants or muscle relaxants for non-specific low-back pain. Not Tylenol or Flintstones vitamins. I was on nothing but myself. It was unbearable, I thought at the time. Yes, *unbearable*. The very same word I would later use to describe my broken brain.

But it is of some phenomenological interest to me that I did not think of my brain as broken when I started university. This does not necessarily mean it was not broken. Perhaps it was broken in precisely the same way it was when I discovered the frame, when I sat in the park. Perhaps it was broken to a lesser degree, or in a different way. Perhaps it was even more broken when I started university than it was at the time that I waited in the park, and as a function of this first great breaking, my memories of starting university would from then on be permanently distorted, pocked with gaps like a damaged manuscript, and the metaphor of brokenness would not seem to apply to the way that my brain had operated at that time, even though it did, truly did, apply. But whatever the reason, I had not used that metaphor back then. I had not thought my brain was broken. Rather that sometimes it moved very slowly, the lines in the road going by in their proper order, one after the other after the other, but going at so ridiculously safe a speed that I could reach out my hand and caress them without skinning my knuckles if I wanted to. But I did not want to. I did not see the point. The lines in the road had been painted by rote, painted by municipal employees who hated the work and were not paid enough, who went home to tiny apartments and microwave meals, who woke up at three in the morning with wordless longings and unexplained nerve pain. And the road itself was a strip of crap asphalt, of winter-blasted scar tissue, an offence to the landscape as bad as an open dump or a nickel-orange tailings pond. And the place it would take me was not worth the trip: a shelf in the mountains where I would be alone in the wind and the wind would scream upon the forms of my body and when finished with the life in me would pulverize my bones. So I thought. And so all that I did was hobbled by caltrops of slowness, scattered every-where I went by a hidden enemy always retreating before me. And in place of the often extremely powerful poles of emotion I felt through the years I was in high school, my feelings and attachments at the start of university seemed dulled. Broken brain or no, I believe I recognize the nature of that dullness and slowness now. It was nothing less than the first sustained appearance of the skin of ice.

Though I had not yet reached it, the willow was inexorably filling my field of vision. I had been moving toward it all this time, and now it was bigger! As is normal. As is expected. But less normal or expected was the flash of red I could just make out between its ragged overhanging leaves, a red alternately hidden and exposed as the leaves swayed and shimmered in the wind like strings of green beads across an entryway. Perhaps someone was spying on me after all, if red were not so poor a choice of colour for a spy. Or if not spying per se, then looking in my direction from time to time and forming unkind conclusions about me. I could accept this, I thought. I did not exist to please such people. But a gust parted the leaves just enough to show me the red was a sweater draped across the back of a wooden bench on the other side of the willow, hanging damply on the wood as though it had been there a long time, or long enough at least to soak up a night's worth of dew. So far as I knew, I was still alone and unwatched in this corner of the park. And in fact from the moment I arrived in the park with the frame, I had not seen a single person. Not the stranger of course, but no one else either. Not dog-ball tossers, joggers, parents with small children, truant teens, workers on smoke breaks, solitary walkers. Not Robert Walser, Waldo, William Wallace, Alice in Wonderland, Angela Davis, Jesus, Moses, the Virgin Mary, Mary Magdalene, the Buddha, a Zen monk killing the Buddha, Gilgamesh, the Devil. Not Keats, Trotsky, Zapata, Wallace Stevens, Will Rogers, Ethel Barrymore, Georgiana Drew, John Drew Barrymore, Drew Barrymore. Not Marx, Engels, Luxemburg, Lenin, Stalin, Mao, Hoxha, Sankara, Castro. Not Robert Walser dead in the snow. Not a pinpoint of cosmic darkness collapsing all antipathy and contradiction upon itself.

5.

'I was blown away by a lot of things with the CIA – how incredibly diverse the place was and how apolitical.'

– John Krasinski, actor, 2018

It was strange to see no one for so long. Certainly in what was supposed to be downtown, or whatever it is you call the district next to downtown where people neither eat nor drink nor live but only work – the work done in this case in sandcastle-coloured cubes with small tinted windows at the edge of a large public park with a lawn like a gaming table. Cube-town, I could call it. Dice-town. Craps-town. A place for giants to gamble. I suppose most North American towns of sufficient size and importance have their Craps-towns, their places for the forgettable structures, invisible structures, municipal and boring-corporate structures. 'Boring-corporate' referring here to the old parasitic rent-collecting industries, to insurance, accounting, 'solutions.' Solutions to what problems I never could guess. I imagined the front walls of the cubes falling away for a moment like playsets or dollhouses so I could view the interiors, saw scenes from a trapped-in-amber 1997: dress codes, notice boards, staplers, paper shredders, Cisco phones, gormless IT departments, managers with no plan for the improvement of the equipment. Studious avoidance of expressions of political commitment, sincere belief, human pain or need. No, enough of that. I closed up the cubes again in my mind. This was all wrong, as dishonest as a sitcom meant to acclimatize the workforce of a post-industrial society to the limited horizons of low-stakes clerical work, to train them to love it through jokes. Of which there had been many – many jokes and many sitcoms. The American *Office* of course: Jim and Pam smirking at each other across the room. But all of it dishonest, as I said. It was never really like that at any job, or never only like that. I could not know what was inside the cubes, but I was sure it was even worse than I imagined. They could be auditing, adjusting, foreclosing, collecting, denying claims. They could be resting the accumulated weight of all the capital they possessed on the unprotected heads of millions. They could be like McKinsey & Company, a consulting firm happily collaborating with the intelligence agencies of the world. Why not? Even *Office* Jim is CIA now. John Krasinski speaks of the agency lovingly in his pressers for Tom Clancy's *Jack Ryan*, in which he plays the starring role.

None of this meant to suggest, by the way, that the 'fun' corporate workplaces, all the new parasitic rent-collecting industries in technology, gaming, clickbait media – and luxury limited-run streetwear, of course, of course – were any 'better,' any less exploitative, any less determined to crush political commitment and sincere belief, any more reluctant to silence expressions of human pain or need. Worse, if anything, with their arcade games and ping-pong tables and instant messaging platforms and other things for children. Worse still, the ways they liked to talk. 'Hope you took care of yourself today,' said an HR rep for the town's resident clickbait media company (now defunct), in a follow-up email after laying me off three weeks into my fourteen-dollar-an-hour proof-reading job. But what am I saying? Why is this worse? As if it matters which style of bourgeois capital accumulation is more aesthetically distasteful. These distinctions are for the schools. But as a lapsed school-man and a brain victim of the aesthetic sphere, I gathered that in some way these distinctions were for me too. So I made them, the distinctions, without being able to help myself.

Here is one distinction I made: the bunker-like buildings of Craps-town dated to the seventies and early eighties, after brutalism's first flush of egalitarian optimism had faded and the *ism* at the end of the word had crumbled and worn off in the rain like the edges of most of the buildings. After all that, but before coked-up shoulder-pad guys tripped over their dicks into every Canadian city in the mid-to-late eighties, waving plans for crimes in rose-quartz-finished stone and aquamarine plasticated glass, works still evident everywhere now. My god, what ugly cities this country has. The western cities especially. Those in charge of things always go with the lowest bidders, partly for the same reason they buy ugly paintings. An axiom: working-class and lower-middle-class people, my people, buy the second-cheapest thing. Middle-class and upper-middle-class people buy the expensive thing. Very rich people, as much as they can possibly help it, buy the cheapest thing. How else do you think they stay rich? The only truly beautiful Canadian city, I thought, was Montreal, and for a long time a number of its people had not wanted to be Canadian in the first place. Godspeed, I thought. Me neither. It was possible that Quebec City or Halifax or St. John's were beautiful, but I had never seen them. I could not imagine any reason why I would.

But I was saying how strange it was to see no one. I had not even seen anyone walk by on the sidewalk, or a car drive by. Unless I had seen a car and not noticed it, or heard one, which was all quite possible. Cars were such a part of ambient 'North American life' that I had almost lost my ability to perceive them if they were not about to run me over. They were as invisible as the buildings of Craps-town. And in fact my continuing immersion in 'North American life' had no doubt impeded my ability to perceive many things. It had wrapped itself around me like a skin. Yes, another skin. On top of the skin of ice that covered the frozen sea inside. Frozen sea? I had called it a warm sea, the sea inside me. What was I talking about? I saw that it could be frozen or warm, just as I could be both sealed in a skin of ice and not sealed, and either of these while also sealed in the skin of America, broadly construed, though I lived in Canada. There were skins upon skins in this cosmos, strata on strata, all bending the light and impeding the air and buckling my perception like water damage on the page of a magazine. Explosions and fallings and skins and seas and broken brains.

What could I still perceive in these conditions? My body, probably, or parts of it. My left kidney hurt. Perhaps this meant I would pass a stone one day, a futile little baby of my own creation that could not talk or move. I had seen them in pictures, brass-yellow like pieces of shattered ammonite or smoker's tooth. It saddened me that this was the best I could do in the birthing department. I knew on the day it passed I would not look at it closely, I would immediately throw it away. I could perceive the grass, and that it was steaming. A steady and undulating rise of thin vapours across the whole of the visible grassy field. Odd to still be steaming after noon. I could perceive the beaded curtains of the willow leaves, and through the swaying leaves the wet red sweater draped over the damp brown bench. Heavy and flat red sweater; heavy and flat brown bench. The leaf-bearing strands of the willow bouncing in front of these objects almost as though elasticated. I still had not yet reached the willow. I walked as though at any given step I might fall through the crust of the earth. I could perceive the calls of birds. Many birds all piping and chipping at the same time in the trees above me, so that I could not identify any specific kind of call or determine the sorts of birds that made them. I felt that even if I looked up and saw a bird open its mouth to sing, I would have been hard-pressed to isolate the sound it made from the general cacophony, to say, 'Yes, that is the Bird A that makes Sound B.' But I did not see any at that time and so this hypothesis remained untested. I knew only that they must be small birds because the sounds were small. I had not to my knowledge heard any further call from the red-winged blackbird far away and behind me at the other side of the park. Only the small birds up above me and close I could perceive, and only for the moment by ear. But I could perceive no people. Only the things they had made and scattered in their wake, almost like the residue of the snail along the frame, but worse, so much worse than the innocent film left behind by a snail. My god, in this country they had made and done such terrible things.

I ruled out civic holidays or the departure of the people to something called 'cottage country' as the reason why they were not here. This 'cottage country' thing I have never been able to make sense of, not least because of the word *cottage* itself, doubly confusing to me as a prole who grew up on the West Coast of Canada and a product of unimaginably old Scottish people. As a prole who grew up on the West Coast of Canada because I understood that some people went to 'cabins' in the 'woods,' but that these never had electricity or running water, as the Central Canadian 'cottage' appeared to. (A classmate in third grade, the son of a lumber grader, had brought in a photograph of himself bathing in a twenty-gallon plastic garbage can for show-and-tell. Only his head could be seen over the rim. 'The cabin,' he said.) As the product of unimaginably old Scottish people because I understood a 'cottage' to be a stone building with a thatched or tarred roof where poor rural people lived long ago, possibly with their animals inside. Uncle's grandmother, a farm servant who married a struggling farmer's son, had died in such a place, after some bad years of foot-and-mouth disease had driven her children off the tenant farms and into the industrial cities to become proletarians. So that the rhythms of a Central Canadian summertime in 'cottage country' were completely beyond my comprehension and probably would be forever. But in this suffering inland town that was not Toronto I did not think that many people went to 'cottage country.' And in fact on civic holidays the big public parks of the town hosted food fairs, craft fairs, musicians. I would have known if something like that were going on. Clearly it was not. The people were simply not present. Not even present in secret to spy on me, unless they were looking out at me from the opaque windows of the sand-coloured buildings that bordered the park. CIA Jim, I thought. There could have been hundreds of people inside.

But even if that were true, I would have no way of knowing it. I am not psychic. How can I be psychic if I cannot read even my own mind? Only a corner of the sea inside is known to me. I said it was a warm and an open sea and I said it was covered over with ice and I believe it all to be true but I do not know how – I am functionally illiterate here. I understood therefore that if I wanted to be spied on while also knowing the methods and locations of my spies, I would have to arrange it all myself. I would place recording technicians on the tops of the sand-coloured buildings at the north end of the park and equip them with high-powered microphones and telescopic sights, and I would assign a photographer to take pictures of me from a similarly high vantage. Then I would pay someone to trail me on foot with a wire, coach him to keep close to me but not too close, and pass him any additional instructions through an earpiece that looked like a hearing aid. This someone would preferably be a middle-aged man, his skin and eyes and hair all exactly the same shade of diffident blond-grey. The day before the assignment, I would take him to a second-hand store and buy him an old jacket in a forgettable camel or navy tone. The whole operation would be managed from a nearby glaziers' van with tinted windows, where an able if melancholic manager would refuse his employee's offer to buy him a beer at Al's Transbay. He would seem a man in pain, peering out at the world through unfashionable glasses and wincing from behind a moustache that looked like a brush. He would be Gene Hackman in the role of Harry Caul, and he would be once again recording in a public park as he did before when he taped the restless young adulterers in the opening scene of *The Conversation*.

I had watched this scene over and over by myself in my undergraduate dorm room on the nights when I could not sleep or did not want to. It closely matched my jags of paranoia in my first and only year living on campus, matched and paradoxically smoothed them out – as though two violent wave patterns met in the sea head-on and by some weird math of mirroring left in opposite directions both calmed now and flattened. Beyond such images of flattening and cancelling out, I cannot say exactly how this worked. The sequence is long and strange, the audio fluctuating and burbling into electric nothingness as the couple wander in and out of range of the hidden microphones. It is San Francisco in early December. While not cold enough for breath to fog, it looks cold for Northern California; everyone is bundled into woollens and long coats that further the sense of muffled obscurity, layer upon layer of secret meaning. The time of day approaches the golden hour, but with none of the romance the term would normally imply. Winter golden hours always look sad to me – the distant sunlight mutes all colour, makes the earth anemic and hostile to life. All the more so in this scene thanks to the distinctly flat palette of outdoor shots in movies from the early seventies that cost less than two million dollars to make. Perhaps the flatness was part of the reason Coppola fired his first cinematographer after he finished this scene. I do not know. But I cannot think of Gene Hackman without thinking of off-whites, milk greys, pale yellows, the yolks of overcooked hard-boiled eggs. The bitter winter world of *The Conversation* has almost exactly the same colour palette as the bitter winter world of *The French Connection*.

All very far from the summer world of the park, so luscious and saturated. All colours in the park flashed crisply under the light of the near sun, dazzled as the sunlight ricocheted off tiny gems of evaporating dew. I was caught in a shooting gallery of small prisms. This metaphor suggests that the sun is shooting things, with a gun. No, that is not true. It suggests that sunlight is the thing being shot, like a bullet. Even when I know that my metaphors are wrong I do not grasp correctly why. I am having trouble with metaphor even here, wherever it is I am now. It all comes back to the fibres of my brain. But on the matter of the dew: I still did not understand why it was wet so late. If anything, it seemed wetter than it had been when I first arrived, a thing completely against all expectation and precedent. I had seen enough skies, and days, to know when the ground would be wet or not. And the sky was entirely clear. Strange wet luscious hot saturated day. My clothes were both wet and green, green on the ass and the elbows. A famous rude saying could be made from those words, *ass* and *elbow*, the kind of famous rude saying the brash Canadian men Uncle worked with might say. 'Kid doesn't know his ass from his elbow,' they said about me at the truck terminal, on Take Your Kid to Work Day. It is true, completely true. I do not. I never will.

6.

It has been a while since I mentioned the frame. It hung on my shoulder, as earlier, and dug into the muscles there. The trapezius or something. This hurt, but only if I turned my mind to it, which for some time I had not, neither in the park nor wherever it is I am now. Perhaps it was due therefore to simple negligence that I did not mention the shoulder pain when I said I could still perceive my body and mentioned my kidney only. Or perhaps a pedant's part of me believed the shoulder pain was not strictly speaking a part of my body at all but rather the result of an interaction between my shoulder and the frame, the foam and sizzle that come when acid meets base. Whereas the pain in my kidney had been completely sui generis inside me and could therefore be counted as an observation about my body. But if I thought this, it could hardly have been conscious, and it seemed likelier that when I was not thinking about the pain in my shoulder I was thinking about nothing at all. But they had trained us in the schools to look for unconscious motivations so assiduously, and I, so hungry and dutiful and afraid, had done so, even to the point of rank improbability, so that I had at times completely shattered my ability to know why I had done or thought anything at all, shattered it with the terrible certainty of my doubt. In any case I had forgotten about the frame for a while. I had not turned my mind to it. It was nevertheless still there.

Though it was closer than when I had started, I still had not reached the willow. God, was I slow. As slow as a snail. Ha ha. For thinking something so stupid I should have gone to jail. But I do not really mean that. I hate all jails and guards, hate them as I do armies and missiles, as

I do money and companies. As I do all the legions of the smiling powerful who try to soften the people's instinctive hatred for these things. Many times while thinking in what could never be true seclusion I had wanted to blow them up. I knew they knew. Their keyloggers, as I said before, and their methods for listening through phones. This happened to Gene Hackman in *The Conversation*. Or rather to Harry Caul. He was among the earliest victims of the passive phone listening we all expect to be victims of now, the kind where the phone itself becomes a bugging device and records you whether you are speaking on it or not. Halfway through the film we see this described at a trade show and learn that you can do it without even tampering with the target's own phone. You simply place a call that can never be hung up. It seems to be the only way that Harrison Ford (no one remembers his character's name) could possibly be listening to Harry at home; he tears apart his entire apartment in search of bugs and never finds any, not even in the phone itself. He is at first too uneasy to take down and examine the little rubberized Virgin Mary on his shelf. It is one of the very last things he breaks.

I have begun to describe already the long opening scene of the film, the way the light sits so coldly on every object in the winter square. But I was not finished. And so I return again to winter in San Francisco, to the vantage point of the man on the roof with the high-powered microphone that looks like a gun. He has a chess master's total visual survey of the square, but the audio is compromised by a poor signal-to-noise ratio. We hear a jazz band playing 'When the Red Red Robin (Comes Bob Bob Bobbin' Along),' hear percussionists pounding an intricate polyrhythm on conga drums, hear unclear fragments of dialogue from unintended targets. Cuts to cameras at ground level show us the drummers and the passersby who make these sounds. The distortion persists, but once or twice we can just make out what they say: 'Well, I wanna go over to my place and start, you know, gettin' it on, because I'm just tired as all get-out … ' This moment is so subtle I had to watch the scene several times over to catch it – thereby becoming my own version of Harry Caul, who likewise plays and replays a phrase he never truly hears right. The speaker of this dialogue, a boy with long hair speaking to a girl with long hair, becomes a kind of collateral damage of knowing, his intimate wishes exposed by accident, suggesting that all such privacies are liable to exposure in the world of the film. And, by extension, in ours.

Harry Caul and his associates are not the only ones making a back-up copy of the day's events. The chessboard overhead shots of the square show a mime in whiteface and black velvet jacket imitating people and animals that pass by. He joins a party of old ladies, blocks someone's path while pretending to be encased in glass, and crouches and lifts his leg at stray dogs. The mime is a hack. His gestures are broad if not obnoxious, obnoxious if not offensive. At one point the mime follows two young Black men while doing a 1970s white person's stereotype of a 'cool Black guy walk.' When they notice, the mime runs away, as if he expected them to hurt him, or expected his audience to expect that. I hate this mime. But something strange happens when he trains his attention on Harry Caul. Harry is a man of about forty, beginning to go bald, with the brow-line glasses of the previous decade and a moustache even older – the moustache of Thomas Dewey, a famous loser, famous for nothing but losing, for thinking he had won when he lost. He wears a flimsy nylon raincoat of a dull, translucent grey. My guardians would have called it a 'pakamac.' It looks like it will tear all the way apart if he gets too close to a nail in a wooden bus shelter. It looks like it will tear apart as easily as he tears apart his apartment at the end of the film, as easily as he tears apart the rubberized Virgin Mary after he overcomes his initial reluctance and in panic and despair splits it open to see if there are listening devices inside.

Harry stands in the square by himself and drinks now and again from a paper coffee cup. Even though Harry's neat economy of movement gives the mime almost nothing to work with, he still stands next to Harry and drinks from an imaginary cup of his own. Harry looks at the mime for no more than a second before he begins to walk across the square. The mime follows, continuing to copy Harry's coffee-drinking, and copying additionally the turn of his head as he glances across the park. This solitary glance aside, Harry's eyes are mostly on his cup or down on the ground, and certainly not on the mime, who before long gets bored and gives up on this most withholding of subjects. He clicks his heels – of course, he is a hack, and his repertoire consists solely of familiar gestures – and moves on to someone else. But to me Harry's slight movements are put in the spotlight by the mime's broad ones and come out more meaningfully in contrast. Harry is the real mime in this world, has real pathos, the kind that whiteface and gurning could never achieve so freely. I remember that a film critic once pointed out how a 'caul' refers to both 'a spider's web' and 'the membrane that encloses a fetus.' No wonder, then, that Harry Caul covers his body in a coat both cobweb grey and vaguely see-through. He is more truly trapped by invisible fields of containment than any huckster slapping his white-gloved hand on empty air to create the illusion of substance.

Or so I thought to myself, alone in my room at university, as I watched and rewatched a scene that had doubtless never been meant to sustain this level of scrutiny. So I thought again in the park as I moved so slowly and strangely toward the willow, under the sightlines of the non-existent watchers in the magnolia trees and the possibly existent watchers in the sand-grey buildings with small sepia windows, the CIA Jims. So I think too, wherever it is I am now.

'The perfect operator,' wrote ex-CIA director William Egan Colby, 'is the traditional grey man, so inconspicuous that he can never catch the waiter's eye in a restaurant.' It was quoted in all his obituaries. I recall the words of this spymaster for American empire, best known if known at all for aiding fascist paramilitaries and terrorists in Italy during Operation Gladio and overseeing extrajudicial killings in Vietnam, and I place them parallel to Harry, and his caul, and his movement through the world like a fly who broke free from the web but still stutters stiffly, the spider silk stuck in his joints. Harry in his modest greyness might seem to be a type of the traditional grey man described by Colby, and yet I think I could pick him out in the crowded square even before I was properly introduced to him – as can the mime, even if he soon gets bored. His business rival bugs him easily as a joke, as do his enemies for more serious reasons, and Teri Garr, who plays the woman he has been seeing, states matter-of-factly that she knows he waits alone at the top of the stairs in her building. He is hardly the perfect operator.

A shadow fell across my face. I had reached the willow. How was this possible? Perhaps as I thought about *The Conversation* I had begun walking faster without knowing it. Or perhaps I had been thinking for much longer than it had seemed. In any case I had arrived at the tree and would now have to choose what to do. I chose to step closer. A string of leaves grazed the top of my head. A second string brushed my ear. The willow bark was ash-grey and textured with long, criss-crossed pleats, the bark almost a fossilized version of the pleated strings of leaves that swayed all around me, landed on my head and face, caught at the sun and filtered it yellow-green. I placed my hand against the bark and left it there. I tried to cry, if only to give CIA Jim something to think about through his binoculars, to confuse him, but I could not make any tears. As I looked closer at the pleated grey bark, I began to think of the folds of the vestments of Harry Caul's little rubberized Mary, also pleated, and grey as the light had been in the square at the start of the film, and thinking the word *grey* and the image of CIA Jim made me think again of grey CIA William Colby, who like Harry Caul was a Catholic, but of a very different kind – his colleagues called him a 'warrior priest.' And as I thought these things I began to wonder if there might be distinct Protestant and Catholic concepts of watching other people. Gramsci thought so. In a letter from prison he had said that the empirical, outward-focused methods of Sherlock Holmes were quintessentially Anglican and looked small and stupid next to the deeper psychological insights of Father Brown. Never mind that G. K. Chesterton was born an Anglican and only converted to Catholicism later, and that Sir Arthur Conan Doyle was born a Catholic and converted to Spiritualism, not Anglicanism, and that he was convinced by two little girls that some cardboard cut-outs in a garden were real fairies. There might still be some truth to Gramsci's theory. And in movies informed by Catholic themes I had the example of Coppola's film, but also the work of his contemporaries Scorsese and De Palma, and perhaps most importantly their shared teacher Hitchcock, whose own teachers had been Jesuits. For these filmmakers, themes of voyeurism are accompanied by great moral anguish and doubt: one is always at risk of seeing something one was not supposed to see. God is always watching, which means he is also watching you watch others.

And I had the opposite artistic example in music of the bilious Northern Irish Protestant Van Morrison, whose *Astral Weeks* is anchored by figures who look out of cars or upper-storey windows down into the streets below almost as a matter of course, their gawping an integral mode of their being. And, closer to me and no longer an example from art, I had the suspicion that my forbears, the Scottish Protestant people, had once been some of the nosiest people in the world.

And finally I had the knowledge that my great-aunt and I had shamelessly looked into the windows of a neighbouring house for many months when I was a boy.

7.

Yes, when I was a boy my great-aunt and I would stand on the balcony of the co-op apartment together and look into the windows of the neighbours' house. This was the house of the Hawerchuk family, who, being at least nominally Ukrainian Orthodox, possessed a stance and a cultural inheritance on the question of voyeurism totally unknown to me. Perhaps they had no stance at all other than not liking it done to them personally, which seems like a common enough stance in connection with many things in the world. They were a family of three round-headed boys, a short-haired, clerical-seeming mother – perhaps a school receptionist or a legal secretary – and a barrel-like father whose deep voice could be heard up and down the lane in the morning saying hello to the other fathers as they picked up the mail and the paper. But he greeted the house-dwelling fathers more often than the co-op fathers, and never greeted my great-uncle – being old, 'eccentric,' and in Mr. Hawerchuk's view only tenuously and by fiat alone a father. We knew that Mr. Hawerchuk thought this way because, in the few social settings when he would speak to us, he would tend to say something like, 'Your son – oh, sorry, your *nephew* – ' and shortly afterward excuse himself, most likely to watch hockey and fling out his arms in despair at the TV, as he was a Calgary Flames fan at a time when the team was so bad it was begging people to buy tickets. Which we of course saw him do, fling out his arms, Auntie and I. I cannot say that his hostility toward us prompted us to start spying on him and his family. Nor can I say that the opposite was true. All I know is that it was Auntie's idea.

In the early evenings I liked to go out on the balcony and pretend I was on a ship, a castle tower, or something else I had lately been reading about. I was at the age when this play had acquired a kernel of self-consciousness that would shortly flower into full-bore shame. My great-aunt would sometimes join me out there, very decently never drawing attention to what I was doing, to give me a cup of tea or teach me how to sweep away the dried cedar leaves that covered the balcony in a carpet of brittle auburn barbs. I often had to be retaught. One day in late February, as we swept together, she held a finger to her lips and pointed down into the kitchen window of the Hawerchuk house. The twilit window was just beginning to glow yellow, making the interior of the room faintly visible to us from above. The middle boy (Braden? Brandon? something like that) was sitting at the circular kitchen table with an open Math 4 textbook.

'He's at his maths,' she whispered. 'I wonder what the other boys are doing. Do they work as hard as he does in school? What do you think, Hugh?'

In this way, my great-aunt and I began to build a world, a Hawerchuk world, a quilted world of rumour and speculation, true and untrue stories – conjectures formed from the snatches of evidence at the windows, the tools and toys lying half-buried in the grass in the backyard. I had no consciousness that what we were doing was malicious, or could seem so, and so I watched from the balcony shamelessly. Even though she was more than old enough to know better, my aunt watched shame-lessly too. The Hawerchuk world lasted the better part of the spring – long enough for us to memorize both the background and foreground rhythms of their lives, to feel in some way a part of them. We watched as the mother weeded, watered, pruned, and dug holes for seedlings in the vegetable garden on Mondays, the only day she had completely to herself. She worked the other weekdays, and on Saturdays and Sundays the boys and their father were at home with their difficult and manifold demands. The thick, dirt-caked roots of the weeds would pile up around her like chicken legs or exhumed funereal lace, and I noticed she never wore gloves. This endeared her to me, perhaps because few little boys wear gloves while digging either. Sometimes she would stumble on a grass-covered metal tool or toy and swear under her breath before placing it back in the shed where her husband and sons were supposed to have kept it. Once she was finished she would go inside, wash her hands for a long time in the kitchen sink – so long that she seemed to be praying, or sunk in a fugue from the warmth of the water (we assumed it was warm; we didn't know) – finally dry them, and then sit on the couch with her feet curled underneath her, reading the same paperback novel she had been working through for as long as Auntie and I had been watching. I too loved to read, but the day when I would be good enough to finish a book like that seemed very far away.

From its 'sophisticated' cover alone I knew the words must be packed together in small type, many of them doubtless strange to me. I felt sure that even the ones I knew would relate scenes of subtle adult emotions I could not imagine, realms I was not ready to encounter because I was not yet 'sophisticated.' *Sophisticated* is a word that work-ing-class and lower-middle-class children who grew up in Canada in the 1990s learned from advertisements for things that our families did not buy. The advertisements wanted us to feel that we should buy them, someday, if we wanted the ease and protection enjoyed by the people in the ads. Correlation and causation. I never fully grasped what *soph-isticated* meant, and so in my mind it tended to bring up colours more than ideas. And the colours I saw in my mind when I heard the word *sophisticated* were just the same tawny and sandy colours I saw from far away on Mrs. Hawerchuk's book cover. There was a craze in suburban Canadian restaurants and cafés of the 1990s for a pseudo-naive mural style in these colours, white-aproned waiters and tall-hatted chefs and great swirls of coffee steam all stretched and pulled toward some random focal point up near the ceiling, perhaps with red steel girders or wrought-iron balcony railings in the background, the time and place some vague mid-century transatlantic dream. There used to be one in the Bread Garden. These murals too were 'sophisticated,' and because the image on Mrs. Hawerchuk's book was so far away, I was at liberty to imagine that it too was a sandy and tawny mural of waiters and girders and steam. I imagined as well, as children so often do, that the image on the front of the book was an accurate picture of the story inside, so that Mrs. Hawerchuk was reading a book about waiters – who were, I believed, 'sophisticated' people – and who might feel a secret love for a woman like her, not daring to tell her their secret as they filled and refilled her coffee in a room with a waiter mural of its own, the steam of the real coffee rising like the steam in the mural and forming an ethereal hand around her face, a hand so close to her cheek she could feel the warmth – this close but never quite touching her. I admit I was in a kind of love with Mrs. Hawerchuk, although I did not understand this at the time. I would have met any accusation of it with the strongest denials, not least because I was sure Mr. Hawerchuk would beat me up without the slightest scruple about hitting a little boy.

Mr. Hawerchuk's stiffness toward us I have mentioned already, and his angry devotion to the terrible, pre-Iginla-hitting-his-stride Calgary Flames. It struck me as important intelligence that Mrs. Hawerchuk never joined him for any of the games, perhaps because in addition to flinging his arms he almost certainly yipped and barked at the screen in a way that I had seen some other Canadian fathers do when I played at the houses of my school friends. Whenever I was at the house of a school friend and this happened, an inner voice I barely knew the source of told me to find a pretext to go to another room. Here the mother of the household would often be found likewise waiting for it all to be over. If no such pretext existed, I would simply pretend to be seriously ill until one of my guardians came to collect me. As I got older I would see that this was the essential truth of the country I lived in: a man on a couch barking at a hockey fight, perhaps barking even more if the fight allowed him to play-act some ethnic or sectarian grudge match (if the fighter on the other team was French and the father was Anglo, or Anglo and the father was French, or if the fighter was from Europe, or if the fighter was Black, or if the fighter was someone Don Cherry had insinuated was a 'pansy'), while his son watched him warily from the corner of the room and his wife and his son's 'effeminate' school friend waited it out in the kitchen. What more could be said about this country than that? To what other end could its founding ideals – no, they never had ideals in this country, only myths – to what other end could its founding myths have ever led? But I am getting away from the story at hand. Yes, this is a story, I suppose. It is the first real story I thought of, both while I sat in the park and wherever it is I am now, and it might be the only one – unless the frame and the park are a story, but I tend to believe that they are instead a frame and a park. In any case, now that I have decided that this is a story, I feel certain obligations not to stray.

If the way I looked at Mrs. Hawerchuk was informed by the feelings and images that arose in me when I heard the word *sophisticated*, the way I looked at the boys was informed by the beginnings of the family-centred sitcoms that aired on syndication in the late eighties and early nineties, American shows like *Full House*, which I could not watch at home because we had only three channels. I only ever saw snatches of *Full House* and the other family sitcoms at other children's houses, usually when viewed in a desultory way by an older sister while my schoolmate and I built Lego on the living room floor. There was a way of introducing the characters at the start of these shows that seems difficult to credit now – I am not sure a comparable method could ever be used sincerely again. During the title sequence, each of the principals would get a little segment of three or four seconds meant to explain what they were like as a person. In the case of *Full House* this meant we followed their expensive red car over the big bridge and into the dense-packed off-white city by the water where they were supposed to live – San Francisco on a grey day in wintertime, just like in *The Conversation* (only not really) – and saw Stamos on a park bench with his guitar, Saget spot-cleaning the windshield, Coulier gabbing on the waterfront. We then experienced a jarring switch to interior studio shots, where we saw the kids talking on the phone, throwing a Frisbee for the dog, cracking wise, and doing ballet. We were supposed to know who they were now, a little. These people liked guitars, cleaning, gabbing, phoning, throwing, wisecracking, dancing. And yet as I sorted Lego pieces on the floor with my school friend, I always felt a strange gulf between myself and these people I was now supposed to know – their large, clean house, their evident money, their friendships with celebrities, their witty remarks for every occasion, their lack of any lasting pain. It was as though I were viewing propaganda from an alien culture, which I suppose in a sense I was – the culture of media-class American comfort which is alien even to most Americans. At the time this was more of a feeling than a thought, and I tended to suppress the feeling. I assumed that the people who made television were better than me, and that they knew best. And so even if I somehow knew that the world of the American family sitcoms was an unreal world, I nevertheless began to look at my own, real world with the expectation that things would *mean* in the same way. I was being trained to think of people as *characters* defined by narrow sets of replicable actions and behaviours, and that to be a *character* was the fullest way to be real. Stamos plays, Saget cleans, Coulier gabs.

In my mind the Hawerchuk sons seemed closer to being characters, and therefore real, than I was. I especially remember thinking this when Auntie and I watched them in the kitchen making pysanky eggs for Orthodox Easter, coming as usual a week after we observed it – and by *observed* I mean that my great-aunt would buy me a chocolate rabbit and if prompted enough my great-uncle would very diffidently tell me the story of Jesus, who in his version was a well-intentioned but vain man who loved the poor but told people he was the son of God because he was embarrassed to be the son of a carpenter. (The villains were the Romans, who he always did the voices for, and their accents were always English.) I remember thinking to myself as we watched the boys that the way each one behaved could be filmed for two or three seconds and used as the title sequence for a show called *Hawerchuks' World*, a show that bored older sisters could watch while doing their homework in the family room.

The middle boy – Brendan? Brian? – was the only one who really knew what he was doing. The lines of his egg were as neat as the lines on an official playing field, if a little uninspired in the colour department, and he blew out the yolk and white without a crack. He could almost be a 'knows-what-he-is-doing' character, like Saget. But Bryson-or-Branson's dull competence bored me, and in any case I knew he was unkind to the youngest boy, Michael, a year or so younger than me. He was always changing the rules on the fly when they played games in the yard, declaring in borrowed U11-soccer-referee tones that Michael's goals were offside and didn't count. 'I forgot to tell you that rule earlier,' he would say. He could be a 'know-it-all' character instead, a designation that sounds similar to 'knows-what-he-is-doing' but is not the same.

Michael seemed more like a 'screws up a lot' character. Characters of this type fuelled many of the sicklier episodes of the family shows. They would break something important by accident, hide the evidence, and cry. A character who knew what they were doing would comfort the character who screwed up with a long and boring speech. Then the studio audience would make the sound 'Awww.' I hated these episodes and tried not to look at them as I played Lego. As a person, however, I could almost have liked Michael. He had a certain ambition. His egg was a tragic missed opportunity – he dyed it in colour after rich colour, saffron and crimson and navy and royal purple, and it would have been very beautiful if only he knew how to stop. By the end it was an all-over blackcurrant, almost the exact shine and colour of a beetle shell. The reason I could not like Michael was that he killed my melon. One day I saw him climb the high wooden wall that divided the Hawerchuk backyard from the co-op's communal gardens, swing himself over, and land directly on top of the melon plant I bought with my own money at Plant Land and had been desperate to keep alive. It never recovered, and some of the final vapours of my childhood belief in God were spent wondering if plants went to heaven. My guardians had been unable to console me with a speech.

Halfway through the egg-dyeing, the oldest boy, Joshua, came into the kitchen with his usual gangly insouciance. At best he was a 'they grow up so fast' character. At worst he would be the cause of a very special episode about drugs. He took an egg from the bowl, dropped it without any preparation into the tub of blue dye from high enough that it splashed all over the table, and left again without wiping up, presumably expecting his mother or one of his brothers to do it, and also to fish out his egg when it was ready. Joshua was thirteen or fourteen, but in my eyes already looked like a man – only more frightening than a man, as all teenaged boys were to me then, and probably *rude* and *rough*, transgressions I had gathered from my guardians were fatal. If not for other children, then certainly for me. I believed that if I ever tried to be *rude* or *rough* to someone, I would die.

At this time in the mid-nineties, white suburban Canadian teenaged boys like Joshua wore big flannel shirts and torn-up jeans with wallet chains hanging out the backs. I did not know that they were only wallet chains and attributed all manner of demonic uses to them. Strangling cats maybe. When Auntie and I would go walking to Mr. Grewal's shop, we would sometimes pass teenagers in big groups hanging out in the parking lot outside and I would be afraid. Auntie always seemed less so. Once, as six or seven teenagers came along the sidewalk from the other direction, she told me not to worry because 'there's a girl with them, and sometimes they won't do anything so bad in front of a girl.' She seemed to know what she was talking about, so I asked her if she knew why they had chains hanging out their pants.

'In Aberdeen, in Mastrick,' she said, 'boys would beat each other with chains. In gangs. Not all the gangs did that, mind. But some. There were so many gangs in Scotland. When your uncle and I went to see my people in Glasgow we used to get our parcels knocked out of our hands by a gang called the Billy Boys. They were Protestant. *Rough* boys. They would leave you alone if they knew you were Protestant, but your uncle and I never wanted to give them the satisfaction, so we never told them we were, even though strictly speaking we were, and they knocked our parcels out of our hands. Yes, we were Protestant. Only, I think some of my people might not have been before. We think possibly some of my mother's people came over from Ireland to spin wool in the mills, and married Protestants, and converted for the marriage, or at any rate let their children be raised Protestants. Oh, and some of my people used to be Wee Frees. That's a kind of Protestant. But we were baptized in the Kirk, Uncle and I. Of course we never went to church. If you want to know what we really believed then, we admired the Quakers more than anything. They sent penicillin to North Vietnam. But in a city like Glasgow or Belfast it didn't matter if you went to church or not. It wasn't about that. Even a man like Mr. Grewal – if he lived in that part of Glasgow then, they would have wanted to know if he was a Catholic Sikh or a Protestant Sikh – meaning where did he live, who did he work for, associate with, do business with, vote for, cheer for in the football, and where would he send his children to school? It was the same if you were Jewish, or if you were half Orange and half Green. You could never get away. There was another gang in Glasgow called the Conks, a Catholic gang. They were more *rude* than *rough*. They also wanted to know if we were Catholic or Protestant, so we said we were Protestants with Catholic politics, meaning we knew what was happening to the Catholics was wrong – getting passed over for good jobs and houses, there and in Belfast – and we were all for a United Ireland, and we hated Rangers FC, and unless Aberdeen were playing we cheered Celtic. Everybody hates Rangers in Aberdeen, and twice when the Orangemen tried to march, everybody came out into the street to turn their backs on them. Your uncle and I are very proud of that. But the Conks, they told us to prove we had Catholic politics by saying we would do something *rude* to King Billy, something I can't tell you because you're too young. We didn't care about King Billy, and I have to tell you we thought what they said was funny, there was a flute and everything, so we said we would do it, and we all had a laugh, and they didn't bother us anymore. But then back in Aberdeen, in Mastrick, in the seventies, there was a gang called the Gringo that didn't belong to any cause and bothered everyone. No, I don't know how they got that name. Your uncle thinks it was cowboy movies. They all wore jackets and long hair like Marc Bolan, and they took drugs and started fights in the street with people they didn't know.

And they would spit everywhere. There was no stopping them, nothing you could say. All you could do was wait in the shops until they'd passed. They were one of the gangs who used chains.'

Auntie's stories never made me feel better as a child, but over the years I have tried to remember each one she told me as best as I can. This is how it goes with everything they gave me, and to hold and recount it all makes me feel better now. I have nothing solid, else. All this to say that Joshua, the oldest boy, scared me – scared me with his sharp elbows, his backwards cap, his love, slightly ahead of the curve, of terrible proto-nu metal bands that sounded like wailing souls in hell. We heard them all day from his open bedroom window, saw posters of scowling bald men on his walls. In the days when the Hawerchuks kept their blinds open, that is. Because of course a moment came when my great-aunt and I were caught watching them, and the Hawerchuk world ended forever. I cannot exactly say when they noticed – they may have always quietly known, deep down, and only decided to act when the rattle and knock of that knowledge in the background of their lives became unbearable to them. All I know is that starting sometime in early June, the blinds of the Hawerchuk windows would close practically all at once whenever my great-aunt or I went out on the back balcony to sweep the cedar leaves. This had a powerful shaming effect all on its own, but I felt worse once the stories made it to school.

At lunchtime a couple of days after the Hawerchuks started closing their blinds, Hubert Liu and I built a model of the Maginot Line out of rocks, moss, and twigs in a quiet part of 'the forest' – really just a stand of twenty or so big fir trees at the southeast corner of the school. We had read about the Maginot Line in the library the day before and solemnly pledged to make one of our own. Hubert was a Taiwanese boy who lived with his mother and brother. His father, a doctor, was in Taiwan – but, Hubert told me, this was 'not the same as divorce.' Our friendship began because our first names were so similar and because we both had to field questions about where our fathers were. It deepened from shared temperaments, as in many ways we were like two little old men. Building a Maginot Line was a typical pastime for us. As Hubert placed twigs in the turrets at the correct intervals and I worked on shaping the moss into embankments of the appropriate shape, we became aware of a third person standing over us. It was a boy a grade ahead – Braden-or-Bradley's grade – who always wore a pooka-shell necklace and short-sleeved button-up shirts with blue flames. I had gathered from the way that he skulked around the fringes of his grade's popular crowd that he was low in their pecking order, low but hoping to rise (unlike Hubert and I, who had effectively opted out of the popularity game entirely). All he needed was one good scoop, a tale that would make him the centre of eager questions from those who had paid him no mind before. He stood with his hands on his hips, looked into my eyes, and said, 'You and your grandma are perverts.'

'My grandmother is in Scotland,' I said. 'She might be a pervert, but I don't know. She has dementia. She doesn't even send me a Christmas present.'

'Well, then who's that old lady you live with?'

'That's my great-aunt.'

'She can't be so great if she taught you to spy on your neighbours. That's sick. I bet you saw them *naked*.'

'Who told you that?'

'I'm on Braden Hawerchuk's soccer team. They *all* know. And now everyone's going to know in the whole school.'

I looked back down at my moss mound. Not long before I had read about *barrows*, ancient artificial hills where kings and queens were buried with golden goblets and torcs and swords. At that moment I wanted nothing more than to lie under a giant moss pile of my own and be forgotten for the rest of time. I kept my head down and away from the pooka-boy – not wanting to 'give him the satisfaction,' as my great-aunt would have put it. But it did not matter what I did. Everyone was going to know about the Hawerchuk world.

'Ha! You're *crying!*' he said, and ran off to report the news to the people he so badly wanted to be his friends.

Over the next few days, the story had evolved to the extent that classmates were asking me if my grandmother had taught me how to be gay. I did not know what to tell them. The school year was about to end, and I hoped that the months ahead would be enough time for everyone who had heard the story to turn their attention to other things.

It was a long, dry, lonely summer. The parched cedar leaves dropped lazily onto the back balcony whenever there was even a slight breeze, but it no longer felt good to sweep them. Uncle did it instead. Hubert went back to Taiwan, as he always did over the vacation, and the few other demi-friends I had never returned my calls. Todd Longo from down the street came once, but as soon as he realized I had no video games – only soldiers, Meccano, and puzzles – he left early and never came by again. I took out every Calvin and Hobbes book at the library one after the other, and as many illustration-heavy history books as I could find. The grass on the lawns dried up. Malarial red worms of mosquito larvae twisted at the bottom of the co-op birdbath. We did not have air conditioning, and the heat lay heavy over every room. As always, we did not go away on vacation. The next September, Hubert ended up in another class, which by some unwritten social rule meant that we had to find new friends in our own classrooms. Those who had known about the Hawerchuk world had forgotten the details – even the inaccurate ones – but something of the timbre or shade of that memory seemed to follow me into the new room, keeping me a strange and rather unwelcome presence in each of the social circles I tried to laugh at the jokes of. Though I suppose it might have all been in my head.

I do not know how to end this story except to tell you that time passed.

Bob Saget went back to working blue rooms.

William Egan Colby died of atherosclerosis in his canoe.

Some of the people who called me gay in elementary school are now evangelical Christians with several children.

Some of the people who called me gay in elementary school are now writing on the internet that there should be 'zero tolerance for microaggressions.'

Michael Hawerchuk, who killed my plant, appeared in a short CBC article about a research laboratory at the University of Winnipeg engaged in important AIDS research. He was interviewed in his capacity as a graduate student assisting with the project. He spoke with compassion about the stigma that continues to impede positive health outcomes for sufferers of the disease.

I do not know what happened to his parents or his brothers. I can only imagine that in many respects the characteristics I attributed to them were wrong. But I still believe his father was an asshole.

I have not seen Hubert Liu since elementary school. In his Facebook profile picture he looks happy. I hope he is happy.

I learned that the baggy flannel trend taken up by the teenagers I feared so much had arguably been started by Kurt Cobain, one of the softest and gentlest men in the whole nineties alternative scene, and only because it was all he could afford as a teenager in Aberdeen, Washington.

'God is gay,' he had spray-painted on a police car in town, and he had meant this in a positive sense. 'Homosexual sex rules,' he had written elsewhere. When asked by reporters from *Rolling Stone* what they thought of Kurt Cobain, two of his former classmates in Aberdeen had used the word *faggot*.

Cobain had attempted to learn about the origins of his family name by phoning people in the phonebook with the similar-sounding surname of 'Coburn.' One Coburn woman he spoke to explained that the Coburns were originally from County Cork, in Ireland. Cobain had visited Cork previously on tour and claimed to have felt an almost magical sense of connection to the place.

The Cobains were not in fact from County Cork. They were Protestants from County Tyrone. Their ancestors were French Huguenots, originally named De Gobienne, who came to Ireland in the seventeenth century – much like the ancestors of Samuel Beckett, who were originally named Becquet.

An MP for East Belfast, an Orangeman named Edward De Cobain, was imprisoned in 1893 for sex acts with men.

One day, in the book section of a Value Village where I often bought my clothes, I discovered the novel that Mrs. Hawerchuk had been reading. It was Michael Ondaatje's *In the Skin of a Lion*.

8.

I remained under the leaves of the willow with my hand on the bark, the great nested whorls of the bark meeting the small nested whorls of my fingerprints – comparing notes perhaps, notes about what it is to be a whorl. The bark was the white-like grey of ash and patterned in pleats like the frozen clothes of a Pompeii casualty plaster cast. My fingerprints picking up fine velvet particles from the bark. The green leaves above me long and thin like fingers scissoring open and closed, leaves moved by the souls of tailors, tailors trying and failing to snip at the pleats of the frozen clothes, to do as they had done in life. It was hot as a sauna and the nominal shade of the opening and closing fingers offered no relief. Away from me the soaked red sweater lay heavy and flat on the bench, steaming like the grass and the wood of the bench itself, steam coming up slantwise in the breeze. I went over to the sweater, no pretense of moving slowly now. I was too agitated. My walk to the willow had failed to still me. The sweater was old, had doubtless passed through many hands to get here. The words *Club Monaco* were peeling from the front like flakes from a fresco in an abandoned church. It was wet to the touch, but warm, an unpleasant pairing. It smelled like earth and rain. Size medium. Gender neutral. Care instructions boldly flaunted by whoever had left it outside. Dirt residues on the sleeves. Was this all? I felt like a dog playing fetch with itself. Fetch the willow. Fetch the sweater. Fetch the stranger and the money you had pledged to exchange the frame for. Fetch home. Good boy. My agitation grew. The stranger was never coming, and even if they did, my brain would be broken and the rented four-room bungalow would never be less of a tomb. I picked up the sweater and wrung it out. In addition to earth and rain, I swear I could almost smell sweat and laundry detergent. I would have put my face up close to the fabric to be sure, but CIA Jim would see me. He would take a picture and use it to prevent me from getting another job after I quit working for the accessory people or was let go by them. The accessory people! I knew the bottom would fall out of limited-run luxury streetwear any day now, that the rich parents of the little boys who paid me would convince them to cut their losses rather than shore up their business anymore. Perhaps as their final expensive product I could convince them to sell the red sweater I had found, special limited-edition warm wet sweater, for a short time only, run of one. And then I would leave and try to find another job and CIA Jim would send the image of me with a green ass sniffing the sweaty collar of the warm wet sweater to every call centre, warehouse, restaurant, bookstore, and pool hall I asked to employ me. And if I continued to resist the temptation and did not sniff it, the image could be faked. Or they could find and expose my burner social media accounts about Marxism and shooting the police. Or invent some. Or they could simply allow this suffering inland post-industrial town with 16 per cent unemployment to continue shrinking in on itself like a dead lizard drying on a desert stone. So I would go to another town, and another, and all would be shrinking and collapsing except for the ones I could not afford. I wanted to say that I too was shrinking, but it seemed better to say that I was in suspended animation. For now. For as long as this ridiculous bubble lasted. Perhaps it was all in my head, like the feeling I'd had when I walked into a new classroom the fall of the year of the Hawerchuk world. Or perhaps it was not, perhaps it was all real. I could not know. They had never called me back about group therapy. And as I thought of the call that never came, I was drawn by an almost Pavlovian tic to look at my phone and I saw that it was dead.

Almost in the same moment, the breeze stopped, and by degrees and according to the irresistible ensuing logic, the opening and closing of the fingers of the willow leaves stopped, and the ruffling of the blades of the grass stopped, and the slantwise angle of the rising steam stopped, it was rising straight up now, and the small birds that had been chipping above me in the trees in great numbers, well, that had nothing to do with there being a breeze either way, but I tell you they stopped too. I heard almost nothing. Perhaps from two or three streets away the barely perceptible whoosh of a car I could not and would never see. Perhaps the barely perceptible whoosh of the world. Perhaps neither of those things but simply the blood cycling through my ears, audible only now in the silence. And then in the middle of the silence I heard from far away and behind me the call of a red-winged blackbird. Whether the same one I heard earlier that day seemed impossible to know. But in any case, after I heard the bird call, the breeze, so subtly, began to lap at my face again, and the small birds once again chipped, and the steam moved slantwise off the rustling grass blades, rose slantwise also from the sweater-shaped outline of damp on the now-empty bench. I looked around. The stranger was still not here. No one was here. I could see no cars and could no longer hear anything remotely like one. The stranger was never coming. But I did not feel ready to leave. I placed the sweater back on the bench as I had found it, flattened the creases I'd made in the act of wringing it out. I saw on my hands some watery dirt from the sweater, saw a couple of flakes from the words *Club Monaco*. I wiped them on the thighs of my white pants. No, I was not going to leave. I was going to walk with the frame in my hand and the green on my ass to the part of the park that was far away and behind me. I was going to creep over the roots and stones and fallen trees of the woods so silently, almost as silently as the world had been in the moment before I had heard the bird call. I would find in a tree branch or among the leaves of a bush the singing red-winged blackbird. I would have no binoculars and I would not take a picture with my phone because it was dead. With my eyes and hands perfectly steady and my silence as absolute as nothing, I would slowly raise the frame to my line of sight. I would hold it forever with the singing red-winged blackbird at its centre.

Yes, I thought, as I walked in a state of what a nineteenth-century observer would have called 'enthusiasm.' This would be a sublime, a holy, a perfect act! I would continue the chain of signs, the hand-over-hand movement of strands in the inner darkness that the kids playing ring toss had begun the other day by finding or stealing the frame and leaving it hanging around a fire hydrant in a lower-middle-class neighbourhood. A red fire hydrant, by the way. Red-winged blackbirds are often found near water. Like willows. The willow I had seen by the wet red sweater. All of it somehow connected. And I would find the bird and view it through the frame and perhaps for a moment the strands and fibres would make a clear picture and people would come to the park for something other than running or walking their dogs and the limited-run luxury streetwear industry would justly implode and the workers without work in the suffering inland post-industrial towns would occupy the empty factories and make things people needed and distribute them in free communistic exchange without recourse to the value-form. Or perhaps my greatest hopes would not be realized but at least, at least, the picture I wove from the strands of the day would be clear. It would be better than computers, than images woven from weightless phosphorous strands behind glass.

9.

'26 September. No entries for two months. With some exceptions, a good period thanks to Ottla. For the past few days collapse again. On one of the first days made a kind of discovery in the woods.'
— Kafka, *Diaries*, 1922

To reach the woods I must cross the baseball diamond, skirt the public toilets, the climbing frame. I could pass or not pass as I pleased the garbage bins, the benches, the individual bushes and rocks and trees, the places where the ground rose up or dipped down. CIA Jim could watch me or not. As I reached the baseball diamond, I heard in my mind a remark George Carlin made in one of his specials, a remark I had contemplated often, despite having no personal connection to the sport. 'Baseball is a nineteenth-century pastoral game,' he said. 'It's a game where the whole point is to be safe and go home. To be safe at home!' The crowd laughed at this, perhaps with scorn for the effeteness of the old pastoralism. But I heard real tenderness in Carlin's voice, a nostalgic fondness. He wasn't just making fun. A nineteenth-century pastoral game, he said. Like cricket, which hit John Keats in the eye with one of its balls, compelling him to take the drugs that would make him see the figures on a Greek vase, the fibres of his brain, the chain of associations that had taken him a certain ways and I myself a certain ways – and now, God willing, to the bird in the frame and the clear picture and the realization of all my hopes. But in thinking of the first half of Carlin's remark I had neglected the second – no less important and connected also to this associative chain, but in another way. It was not a link but somehow the ground or need or reason for the chain.

Safe at home, he said. This was the crux of many things for me. So often when I had felt safe I had not felt at home, and when I had felt at home I had not felt safe. The only time I had felt both was within the walls of the co-op apartment with my great-aunt and -uncle as a child. They had made a world in there, their snail shell of Aberdeen in 1972 trapped in amber, a world that made sense to me and me only. Outside those walls, I only ever felt one or the other, safe only or at home only. Or neither. Merely by being on the sidewalk I was suddenly in a place called, ridiculously, 'New Westminster,' and this bare nominative fact was unsafe and unhomely, even if I did not yet quite know why. Later, as a teenager, when we argued all the time – not over anything important, just the inevitable things a sixteen-year-old and a seventy-year-old will argue about – it was one or the other within the walls just like everywhere else. When I say I did not feel safe I do not mean physically unsafe, or at least not with my guardians. I mean I was in a place I could not be sure of. Sometimes you can be sure of things while knowing they are not home, and sometimes you can feel at home in places you will never be sure of. Sometimes the one thing transmutes into the other and back again. And one more thing: when I said I never felt both safe and at home outside the walls of our apartment there was one exception. I had felt safe at home in the park with my aunt and uncle when I was four years old and heard a bird that sang to me.

Despite all my other extravagant hopes for this coming moment in the woods – the abolition of the value-form, the elimination of unemployment, the implosion of limited-run luxury streetwear – I did not dare say that when I made my clear picture of the singing bird I would be safe at home again. And yet, from wherever it is I am now, I can say that, without saying so – not even in my mind! – I dearly wished it. This was what I wished as I crossed the fences of the baseball diamond, that strange, latticed outline of a giant gem, an old-time studio microphone. This was what I wished as I approached the place at the edge of the forest where the trees parted and a rough trail ran over half-buried rocks well into the dappled half-darkness of the trees. This was what I wished as I heard again somewhere, but no longer behind me or far away, another call of the red-winged blackbird.

I aimed myself at the deepest part of the forest with the silent resolve of a questing knight or a guided missile. The differences between the two are relatively superficial. What are they both at core if not a rudimentary navigation system cased in expensive metal, an engine to goad a sharp point home? One has chivalric codes and the Church; the other has software patches and Raytheon. And both likely to explode indiscriminately in fire and violence, whatever ideological fail-safes let their handlers sleep sound at night. The only place where the metaphor failed was me. My ancestors had all been peasants.

When I stepped into the woods the air changed. It was still Ontario hot and heavy, but captive now between the tree trunks, and more still, and so even hotter, even heavier. It was through such witchcraft of atmosphere that I knew I was far from home. Or far from safety. Either or neither. Stepping into the trees on the hottest days of a West Coast summer, in the spice-box microclime of an evergreen darkness, the temperature would drop, hard. But here the forest offered no relief. The heat came swamp-like up from the ground rather than down from the sunrays. I had walked into a web of wet air. On the ground just at my feet I saw a long branch from a birch or an alder tree, a thin branch the darkened colour of something soaked. I would even say it had been sweating. It was obscene and prurient and I loved it. I picked it up, snapped off the twigs sticking out from it here and there, felt its bark slipping off and sticking to my hands like a transfer. It smelled like an exhumation. With the sweating branch in my right arm and the frame around my left I walked deeper into the stink of the forest.

There was no trail here, just a hard-packed groove worn down by – who? I hoped if I went further I could know. When the ground in the woods is braced by the buried scaffolding of living roots, tamped down by footsteps, kept damp and clayish by the ambient humidity, it turns into something like pure dark chocolate or cocoa powder. I knew because I used to dig in the dirt as a child, to hack through living roots with my great-aunt's trowel. They were red on the outside, these roots, once I scraped all the soil away. Auburn red, and tougher than wires to cut through, and the insides were white and bled milk. I must have stunted the growth of hundreds of trees that way. I imagined an arbourist the next century – if there is a next century, and if there are arbourists, and if there are trees – cutting down cedars at the ragged back lot of what had once been a co-op apartment complex in 'New Westminster,' a working-class suburb of a metropolis on the West Coast of 'Canada,' an aberrant imperial residue that no longer existed. The arbourist would look closely at the rings, count them with care, note a couple of poor growing years somewhere in the last decade of the twentieth century, and have no way of knowing their cause was an odd little boy who had madly prospected for dinosaurs, hacking and ripping his world in search of enchantments.

I walked through gnats, webs, no-see-ums. On balance, most of my problems were no-see-ums now. Inner seas and magics and mystifications. I was looking for a positive magic in the woods but there is a negative magic too. The bird that had opened its beak and broken me apart outside of the bowling alley was a practitioner. Negative magic is a vehicle of mediation between the material world and we who have allowed ourselves to float away from it. If it could, it would destroy all that flees the cold grey truth. It is the world speaking to us in the only language we can hear and calling us back. The no-see-ums pinged against the lenses of my glasses, bounced off my teeth, got sucked a little bit of the way up my nose. The webs settled on my head like a tippet of tulle. Those strange and incredible words. Hadn't that been what Emily Dickinson had said? No, not said. Written, really. I knew that. Enough professors had scolded me about the difference. But I always thought of her as speaking to me. And she heard a fly buzz when she died. No, not her. The 'poetic speaker.' They had scolded me about that too. Their greatest wish had been that I would view the objects of my study as objects and not as living things that spoke to me. I had been in love with Emily Dickinson, I knew that now. I had wanted her to be alive. But she had died a thousand times in her poems and then one time, finally, in the world, a little before six in the evening. Perhaps it was her deaths in life, her fearlessness (or fear, they seemed so similar) in going to that grey land again and again, that had seduced me so much. The negative magic must have broken her over and over but she never stopped going. Deaths in life. I for my part felt I was living a life-in-death. That had been Coleridge, life-in-death. In a poem the same metre as Emily's. Was it strange I called her Emily? Probably. 'Because I could not stop for death / upon a painted ocean.' Hymn metre. Ballad metre. The Romantics' medieval affectation. It was they and their heirs who made the knight in the forest the shining icon, the mythic hero, far more than the real people of the Middle Ages had. Bloody Scott, my nemesis. And Tennyson, who was interesting until Hallam died. The only English men that whole stupid century who could match Emily in my mind were Father Hopkins, the gay Jesuit, and John Clare, the labourer of the Northamptonshire countryside, who ended his days in an asylum writing a poem of loneliness that, when published in the paper shortly after his death, would be transcribed in a diary by the twenty-year-old Hopkins, not yet Father. Byron could meet these three as a spirit, as a human being, but not as a poet – except once, in the poem 'Darkness.' Keats could nearly meet them as a poet but not as a human or a spirit. So I thought.

The no-see-ums kept buzzing. In the crook of an exposed tree root I saw cat shit, a little train of stretched black pods. I knew it caused some communicable disease. Auntie told me. The hantavirus? I wasn't sure. I fought the urge to poke it with my stick. No other signs of the cat anywhere, or of any other wingless vertebrate life. Only the chips of small brown birds, so much a part of the ambient sound of the forest that I almost could not hear them. Inaudible as cars and invisible as sand-coloured buildings. But no signs did not necessarily mean no life. It could be around me everywhere in hiding, listening and waiting for me to go away. Or it could have been all but driven from the premises decades ago. Except for the cat, who was a special case. More like us than the others. In a way the cat who comes to expect food and comfort from a human family relates to the humans much as we would relate to an unpredictable tool we do not understand. Like software, electricity, internal combustion engines. Well, Uncle had understood some of those. But to the matter at hand. The cat relates to the family as if to a complex tool. They do not mewl to each other, you understand. Only to us. I imagined the whole interconnected superorganism of Nature herselves watching hopefully with her multibrain the first humans, coaxing them to do her bidding with wind and water as the cat coaxes the family by mewling and yowling underfoot. And I saw how at a certain point a threshold was crossed, and the hope disappeared, and Nature began to fear her all-too-complex tool. What were our science-fiction fables about the Singularity, about killer robots, about vengeful networks, if not our own secret knowledge that we had done the same, been unfaithful labourers for the planetary multibrain? The tool revolting against its user. But as I thought these things, I worried I had brought John Calvin in, that uninvited guest in this report, and retold a story of total depravity, a story I did not officially believe. It seemed a risk whenever I told a story about anything. So much of what I thought of as my broken brain was related to story form, metonymy, *this* standing for *that* until I could not remember where I began, whether home or safety or neither. But to purge my mind of false idols seemed Calvinist too. And even purging myself of Calvinism seemed Calvinist. The frame dug into my shoulder.

I swapped hands – frame on my right arm, stick in my left. After centuries of medieval Catholic legends about knights in the woods, and before the Romantics and their heirs had spun their retellings that were really about something else, neither Catholicism nor Protestantism but rather modernity tenderly and smugly denying that it had arrived and that myth was over – denying itself by pretending to worship mythic heroes – there had been one truly Protestant work of literature about knights. I mean Spenser's *Faerie Queene*. Spenser who had bayed for mass murder in Ireland, the use of famine as a weapon of war. It seemed significant. I did not yet know how. But I felt that all the willing sons of Calvin had been wicked men, and I turned the thought upon itself and examined it for Calvinism, and my brain was broken, and whenever it was not it was because its gaps and cracks had been closed and cauterized by a layer of ice.

It was all so confused. I stopped where I was, the leaves of the trees sagging above me like newsprint in a hothouse. It was time to take inventory. I had been avoiding this, but now it was coming to a head.

10.

My parents, I mean my biological parents, had lived on a housing scheme in Mastrick, in the poorer northern end of Aberdeen. Scotland, not Washington. None of that North Sea oil-boom money had come to them. They had worked low-paying jobs. Then the jobs went away, and they used heroin. Then they stopped using heroin for a couple of years. I was born. Before I was two years old they both relapsed. Through some family calculus I still do not fully understand, it was determined that my childless great-aunt and -uncle, who had long wanted children and had been living in Canada since 1972, would be my guardians. A truck driver and a shop assistant. Perhaps this scenario will not be believed. Perhaps tables will be consulted, statutes on international family law. The ability of my underclass extended family to have managed such a thing will be questioned. This is acceptable to me – it comes with the territory. But it happened. They made it happen. Perhaps someone owed someone else a favour. I believe the family felt Canada would give me the 'best chance,' as Auntie explained to me when I asked her once why. She had not elaborated at the time, but I think their idea was that by growing up in North America I would escape the accent and mannerisms and social milieu of the housing scheme, which in Scotland would have narrowed the horizons of my life. One of us, at least, would 'get on.' And so I went, and instead of becoming a permanent member of the Scottish underclass I became something else – a permanent member of the confused men of the earth.

They did not mean this to happen, and in fact they would not have wanted it to, and in fact my guardians with their store of remembered poems and stories and songs and insistence on speaking Doric at home were doing all they could for it not to happen, but the truth is that my coming here and achieving their hopes by becoming an 'educated' person meant a kind of self-obliteration. How could they have known? Yet it was the basic state of play, and the longer I stayed in this country the more I lost. I was aware always of a parallel self who had not come here, and as a very small child I talked to him in what remained of my Doric as though he were alive. Later I decided he had died, and I mourned him, but later still he was alive again to me, or she, for in fact sometimes she was a woman, and I speculated about what he or she had gotten up to, no longer with the assurance that it had been a magical life as I thought when very small, but still with the conviction I could be both sure and proud of it. Because so much of living here was tied to uncertainty and shame. There was a dialectic of shame, a jig-doll dance.

The first shame was that I did not fit in, that despite decades here my guardians, incorrigibly, did not fit in, and certainly not with the homeowning families like the Hawerchuks. It was lack of money as well as how we talked and thought. We might have managed better if only one or the other circumstance applied to us. 'Why don't we ever go back?' I asked them once, at seven or eight. Because we never did. Not even on vacation. They had looked embarrassed, each searching the other's face for what to say. 'We can't afford it,' Auntie said finally. 'And it might be hard on Uncle.' This was true enough. The shop paid Auntie minimum wage, and Uncle did not even drive long-distance, though he would have made more money if he had. He used to, as a company driver for one of the larger national firms. But to my understanding it had gotten to him somehow. Travelling a long way through this country, I mean. It had done things to his body and his mind, so that even on his short hauls, no longer for the national firm but for a truck rental company that paid him to deliver vehicles to customers, he was still not wholly well, and could not do it full-time. I never knew for certain but I think he was drinking in secret. But there was more to why we never went back. I saw later that they had not wanted me to see my birth parents, in whatever state they were in, and that this was tied up with their own dialectic of shame, the individual steps of which I cannot know. And there was something else too, something Uncle said near the very end, but I am not yet ready to tell you that.

The second shame came at the point when, at the end of my efforts to fit in, I became conscious of the loss it had wrought in me, and was ashamed of the first shame – mine, but also my guardians', and most of all the family back home who had hoped I would 'get on.' This was when the parallel self died. As a teenager my shame at the shame deepened, and I became enraged. They had removed me from my people, I felt, from good working-class Scots who spoke the Doric, for a striver's dream that wasn't even realizable let alone desirable – we sure as hell hadn't 'got on' – and here nothing made sense, and though I could understand perfectly how my guardians spoke, and speak it a little with them, it sounded strange in my mouth, and out in the street I sounded like a Canadian. It was cruel of me to be this way, and unfair. They had not wanted these things to happen, and earlier when I was trying so hard to fit in they had always gently pushed back, told me to remember who I was, to not be 'up masel,' and so I was blaming them for something I had been most responsible for. This was when our fights started, and when within the walls I stopped being able to feel safe and feel at home at the same time.

By the time of the third shame I was out in the world, or rather this country, and I was neither safe nor at home, and I had seen things, I saw that this country was meant to fold people into itself and obliterate them, that its whole basis was obliteration, that its sole premise was the theft of land from Indigenous people and their replacement with settlers who would suck the land dry, and they were still doing it, no matter what noble acts they might say they were doing officially, it was just as Louis Riel had described in his letter to the *Irish World*, and I saw too that in sending me to this country in particular my extended family had sent me to a compromised and evil place that should never have existed, and that my little private shames and worries about obliteration were nothing compared to the great shame, the great obliteration; all who had come here to settle were to partake in the greater obliteration that this country enacted merely by existing, and it was at this time that my parallel self came back and I wondered what kind of life he or she had lived, but this was a coping mechanism and in some sense pathetic, you have only one life, but in my case my life was half-obliterated and obliterating and tainted and a shame.

And there was a fourth shame, shame that in the shadow of the enormous obliteration and shame of this country I had been focused on my little private ones, shame at my own vanity, my narcissistic wish for a spotless soul when in truth this was nothing, and when you have reached this stage in the dialectic of shame where you have practically bent yourself in half you are liable to become exhausted by shame itself, which is good, because to do what must be done with your one life I think you must go beyond shame, and at the time when I was in the park I think I had, or nearly so, although you must also go beyond many other things besides, which may not even take very long, the times or events or conditions may vault you over all of them at once, but at the time when I was in the park I had not yet gone beyond all of those.

I had wanted this inventory to include Calvinism, but the truth is I find it very hard to talk about directly. I never received any formal instruction in it, so in my life it is as invisible yet substantive as the wind. My guardians were secular socialists, but they had not been able to escape the imprint of a Calvinism that took a very strange form with them, and I suspect with many other secular working-class Scottish people. On paper, as system, Calvinism is insane, a bad joke. Total depravity, they say, and no salvation by works – it does not matter how many good deeds you do, you are still shit in God's eyes – and predestination, they say, so those who are a part of the elect and will go to heaven are a small minority and they were chosen already and nothing will change it, which naturally leads to absurdities – James Hogg, the shepherd from the Scottish Borders, wrote a dark satire about a man who determines that because he is a part of the elect he can kill people without divine repercussion. Insofar as America has a Calvinist aspect, it is this interpretation they went with. But the Calvinistic stamp on the minds of the urban working-class Scottish people seemed different. These people had received notions of predestination, the elect, total depravity, and assumed they were shit in a world of shit, that people with money and nice manners were better than they were. *Those* people were the elect, while they themselves were the damned. And because they lived in a predestined world of total depravity they could do nothing about it. It made them pinched, fearful, self-loathing, inward. Anything they did would only make a bad thing worse. But on the other hand, they maintained the secret possibility that *they* were the elect, the chosen, and they veered wildly between these two opposite poles, and the poles sometimes achieved a brutal synthesis: you are terrible, you are special, you are especially terrible. Now, as secular socialists, my guardians had ostensibly rejected these ideas as means by which the ruling class kept working people down. But the imprint could not be wiped clean away. They were fearful, inward, thought everyone else was better than them. But on the other hand they sometimes thought the opposite. Even watching the Hawerchuks was a part of this: in one sense the gathering of evidence that our neighbours were better than us somehow, and because we were damned already it didn't matter if we sinned in watching them, and in another sense our clear prerogative as people who were much better than them and destined for glory. You flicker constantly between the idea that you are a part of the damned and a part of the elect and there is no peace and quiet within you.

The confusion grew for me because the country to which we had come to live, Canada, was not in a foundational sense Calvinist at all. Canada, I came to believe, was a Methodist country. The Methodists were a product of the eighteenth and nineteenth centuries rather than the sixteenth and seventeenth centuries that produced Calvinism, and in the strictest mathematical sense were their polar opposite. Their credo: all can be saved, all must be saved, all may know themselves saved, all may be saved to the uttermost. On paper it seems kind, benevolent, but in practice it is just as insane as Calvinism. It is this sentimental lunge to save everybody that has fuelled all of this country's repressive institutions, its frenetic bayonet-armed liberalism. When the Methodists ran Toronto – the 'Methodist Rome' – you could not even get a drink. They pushed the Jewish, Catholic, Black, and Chinese immigrants into ghettos. They fomented a riot against the Greeks. Toronto didn't have a mayor who wasn't in the Orange Order until 1954. And yet at the same time these spiteful Methodists poured the honey of their philanthropic enterprises into the wounds made by their own supercilious lashes: soup kitchens, charities, temperance movements. But all conditional, all linked to proselytizing and 'moral improvement.' It goes without saying that this belief system was compatible with colonialism, with the missionaries, with the residential schools, with racially segregated tuberculosis hospitals, with the child welfare system that effectively continued the work of the residential schools under another name. Egerton Ryerson, who had conceived of residential schools in the first place, was a Methodist minister. And the Methodist spirit – suffocating, scolding, rule-following, proud in its humanitarian self-regard – is the governing spirit of the country's institutions even now. The clue is in the word *safety*. All must be saved. You see now why I could not feel safe at home here, where *safety* is understood in this way. It is the first word out of the mouths of the police as they close in on strikes and protests. It is the retroactive justification for the founding of the RCMP – that they only wanted to keep Indigenous people 'safe' as they removed them from their lands. It is the pretext by which the police show up when Black and Indigenous people call 911 for help with relatives in crisis, and it is the excuse the police make when they shoot them instead of helping them. The safety state, even more repressive on some deep spiritual and psychic level than America, America which kills and surveils but botches the job by telling its people to love freedom as well. Yes, the American love of freedom is hypocritical and false, a child's sophistry. In its official form it has only ever meant freedom for the rich whites. But the Canadian love of order and safety has made me believe that the multiracial toiling American masses will someday soon far surpass Canadians in their radical political consciousness, if they have not already. Canada will meanwhile languish in worse sophistry, worse hypocrisy, meting out violence in the name of safety with one hand and penning eloquent, academically vetted apologies in fine Methodistical humanitarian language with the other. Those bloody Methodists. Canada is the culmination of the Anglo-American liberal ideal in a way that will never be realized in the United States because the Americans will instead surpass it, have no need for it. For all the right-wing American jokes that Canada is 'socialist,' Canada has never been that. It is a liberal-Methodistical state, keeping just enough people on this side of non-immiseration to prevent a fight for real socialism, real radicalism, and hushing anybody who tries to with its smothering and suffocating and rules. So that the immiserated American working people, with so much to fight against and with no respect for the rules, might even reach not just socialism but communism first.

All this to say that the inward-looking self-hatred I had learned from my guardians did not resemble the smug rule-following of Canadian Methodism. I felt the tension in my bones, living here. What had one of Irvine Welsh's characters said? 'In Scotland we've been exporting every straight cunt tae Canada fir generations. Result? They're boring fuckers, and we're a drug-addled underclass.' This seemed true. I had come in a belated way to a place that my erstwhile 'countrymen' in days gone by had already come to and ruined, but coming there later as a product of the 'drug-addled underclass' who had stayed, I did not feel at home, did not recognize what I understood to be Scottish attitudes in the Canadian people around me. I did not know what to do about it. But I knew that my guardians had inherited something in its way more radical in its theology than the American or Canadian theologies, which perhaps made it easier after all for them to have passed through it and become secular socialists in the first place. Their gutter Calvinism had driven them so far into their own minds in snail-shell wisdom that they let go of themselves, let go of the world. The result seemed closer to Buddhism, Judaism, Shia Islam, or the melancholy reflections of certain lapsed Catholics (Irishmen who abandon their religion, said Lenny Bruce, are Jewish) than to anything Protestant. Or at least the people whose views of the world I had most appreciated as I became a young adult were often informed by Buddhism, Judaism, Shia Islam, lapsed Catholicism. But perhaps it was vanity to say we had much in common with those obviously superior traditions, a pseudo-Calvinist desire to make myself belong to yet another special group of the elect. I could not say. Here in the heat under the trees I remained unsure if any of my thoughts were true diamonds or false zircons or those crystals of the inner ear that give you vertigo if they wander too far from where they are supposed to be.

Because I had gone so deep into the woods I was out of view of the concrete buildings with small sepia windows. No servants of the Methodistical state could see me. Unseen, they were free to imagine me instead, if they did imagine me. I imagined them imagining me as I stood in the trees, the hundreds of people inside, began to hear their singular and collective voice, all the servants of the Methodistical state joining together in unison like an audio version of the frontispiece of Hobbes's *Leviathan*:

It is a slander to say that we bore him ill-will. At times we did, of course. True unmitigated enmity and loathing. But it is a slander to say so. At other times – in fact most of the time – we bore him no will at all, of any kind. On balance we simply hoped that he would die.

I breathed out slowly in the broken light under the broadleaves. The whole ground and brush around me seemed to crinkle with potential energy, like crumpled paper just about to relax into flatness again. They may have felt they were masters of life and death, those Methodists, and I could grant them death, but surely they had not gained full dominion over life. Surely this green secret must remain so. Surely Nature's strange and dangerous tools had not yet made that final and fatal jump in the hands still so shakily holding them. Surely, I said to myself again, surely. A word I could say over and over to soothe myself, like *perhaps*, like the 'as … as … as' constructions I swung in front of myself like a censer in the chapel in the inner darkness. My own unique bird calls, watery sounds, the *shhh* of the sea and the hiss of streams. And as I thought these things, I heard again at last the sound that had drawn me so far through the trees in the first place.

11.

In that moment my thoughts of the wider world and the past fell away. The world contracted to the small sphere of free space around me in the trees, the long continuous present of the search for the red-winged bird. My senses seemed to touch the world directly without the need of vetting by my brain. A rare thing.

There were greens in my eye line of all possible shades. I thought I could keep my new-found presence alive if I gave an account of each one, starting with the light green of the new leaves on the twigs sprouting in a random and tentative way from the lower trunks of the tall older trees. The green of the tail plumes of quetzals in Mexico, I thought, or the skin of a lime not yet ripe. The new skin of brightness, the tail plumes of sunlight, the banner of all indefinite and tenuous things – for new leaves pass on soon to the next stage, limes ripen and fall to the earth, and the winged princes of Mexico with their splendid ceremonial tails fly away. Though through no fault of nature's, this green also tended somehow to fakeness in my mind, to the electric lime and neon greens of candy packaging and energy drinks, the radium cousins to the near-white ghost green of things that glow in the dark. Which was cousin itself, I supposed, to seafoam, which no plant I knew of bore, let alone the foam of the sea. True foam of the sea was a white shot with yellow-brown sodium, churned ancient ivory, or at least it was so when it foamed at the crest of the waves coming in from any sea I had ever seen.

But in beginning to think of the sea, I was moving away from the greens I could see in the place under the trees. And I had considered only one, the bright new green, when I said I would enumerate them all. I had said that the past and my thoughts of the wider world fell away, that my senses were open and touching the near world of free space around me, and in the moment I said this it was true. But I fell out of the airy sphere of the pure near world and back to the murk of the wide one so quickly – the wide world in the guise of the sea, though I waited and listened and tried to extend the pure presence for as long as I could and think about nothing but green. These states of pure presence were as indefinite and tenuous as the new bright green of the young leaves. I was riding a bicycle with no pedals and I was bound to fall.

I remembered what they said at the Zen Centre the second and final time I had gone there to try to meditate. My hands. 'Think of your hands,' they told me, 'think of your hands making the shape of the cosmic mudra.' Soto Zen, I should say. The Zen for peasants, homely and simple, less focused on doctrine and the intellect and gaining enlightenment through koans, more focused on sitting. I could respect that. I think that wherever it is I am now, I am if nothing else engaged in a type of sitting, just sitting, that perhaps for a brain as broken as mine this long and ink-stained outgoing breath is the closest to sitting I could ever come. My ancestors were peasants. I have said that before. I gripped the frame tightly in front of me and thought of my hands. I do not trust my hands, I said that before as well. That was a good one. No, stop, I thought of my hands, not the phrase *my hands*. My hands as they were and how they felt. I was back, I was flying through air. And my thoughts – not gone, but flying too through the air in my head, not staying: a tarantula. A puppet. A knife in a drawer. And I listened to the wind that was rattling the leaves like static or signal jams over the absence of the bird call I had heard minutes earlier and expected again to hear. And around me was green. Closest at hand was the green of the grass and the leaves of small flowers and weeds. We say 'weeds.' An unhelpful designation. Human-centric. We should not say it. But I am slipping again from the presence, sweat on the seat of the bicycle, slipping back down into the murk of Aristotelian and post-Aristotelian miscategory. The fog of words at war with one another across the pages of ancient and modern books. The gore of dead terms.

My hands, my hands. I broke out again from the murk like a gas bubble in brackish swamp water. Back to presence and green. Closest at hand was some subclass of clover, so beautiful, a four-pointed pattern like something at the edge of an illuminated manuscript, the webwork of a bored monk's dream. I am telling you more about the shape of the clover than its colour, the colour it shared with the quote-unquote weeds and the grass. It is difficult to say anything about the colour of healthy grass, perhaps because it is everywhere. That the grass and the flowers and the quote-unquote weeds blended together so well in solidarity and camouflage seemed related somehow to this difficulty. The green of healthy grass was an ancient thing to see. Like sand, like blue sky, like the light and dark honeys of steppe and savannah. I made a sharp distinction in my mind between this wild grass green and the deeper, darker green of expensive lawns. Those lawns were not grass. They were close-bladed, plump, like a cake for some reason. I do not know why but expensive lawns made me think of a cake. More fake in its way even than seafoam, a colour that if not present in the green around me here under the trees or the foam of the actual sea must surely be somewhere in nature – perhaps on the back of a tropical bird or the spots of a fish in a coral reef. Well, the less said about the coral reefs the better. But the minds of the people who had chosen to care about plump and dark green cakes of lawns, the whole vision of the world it implied, did not seem unrelated to the sickness that was making the reefs go away. How could they not be? It had not escaped my notice, as at least nominally a very unimportant member of the 'fashion industry,' that the 'colour of the year' for this year, as selected by a company whose service appeared to be the selecting of colours and nothing else, was 'living coral,' the colour of a reef in pink health. These people could make a decoration of anything they had seen to it would die.

I paused for a moment and looked up through a small window in the overhead leaves. The window through the leaves looked out onto a cloud that was itself parting like a window onto the limitless-seeming blue beyond. Had there always been clouds up there this day? I do not think so. Earlier I think I may have said it was cloudless. I cannot be sure. But in any case the cloud seemed new. Thinner vapours crawled across the blue patch, thin like clots of dust under a bed. Under my bed certainly. I said 'limitless' but I knew that was not true. 'Limitless-seeming.' Because the island of blue (or rather the pond, the lake, the inland sea of blue) was an illusion, a shared hallucination of the earth-bound, and beyond the fugazi stage magic of light refracting through our planet's modest cough of vapour lay the true celestial limitlessness of darkness and night. The very advent of a cloud on this boiling Ontario summer day was itself some minister or herald of night, some small sign of the progression of the day, the subtle change in temperature. Yes, night would be coming soon enough. I had no idea how long I had been here or the time, but I nevertheless knew it was coming. Night and its ministers reminded me of another shade of green, my favourite perhaps, if there is a point to having favourites. I mean the occult dark green of holly leaves and ivy leaves, represented in this small clearing by the vines rushing from a cleft in a nearby linden tree like dark blood flowing from a wound too deep to close. Velvet, poison, death, I thought when I thought of this green, and for this it would have my endless love. So different from the dark green cake of the expensive lawns. This green was yet darker, a permanent shadow, a living funeral. Ivies and creepers and vines could kill trees, I knew somehow, kill trees and erode the masonry of old stone walls. I remembered another creeper that killed: the autograph tree of Trinidad, which smothered and suffo-cated its neighbours, and was also known as a Scotch lawyer. One of those eighteenth-century English jabs that probably had some truth to it. The lean Scotch lawyer, poisonous flower of the Scottish Enlighten-ment, hungry and flint-mean and burying his enemies in shrewd little suits. Scotch tape, that was another one. Because it is cheap, you see. And I myself defied no stereotypes in this direction: I rented a minuscule house and my clothes were second-hand and my greatest expenses were tithes to the Party of Socialist Workers. I was keeping them in banners and leaflets and facilities rental fees for discussion groups I never attended on account of the deeper cheapness in my soul, the cheapness that kept me from the great and small expenses of the heart, the capital risks of the heart in going out into the world to meet people. These expenditures drained me as the idiot Lowland bourgeoisie and landed gentry had drained the coffers of Scotland in the 1690s with their stupid idea to colonize Panama. Darien. A place Keats would write about later in his poem on Chapman's Homer. But to the matter at hand, which is no longer the many shades of green, my bicycle wheels are upside down and spinning in the ditch and I must talk about the cheapness of the soul.

I read once about a man in New York named George Bell who died alone in a disastrous hoarder's apartment, with no heirs, no friends who had seen him in years, and no close family. He had been a working-class man, a furniture mover. When I read that his parents had immigrated to New York from Scotland I understood everything. He too had kept himself inside, in the snail's shell, with the Calvinism of the Scottish poor, flickering between grim acceptance of his damnation and joy at his special election. Bell's few friends were those he spoke to in long monologues on the telephone or in parked cars (I imagined both staring ahead in the car and not looking at one another) as though the cheapness of the soul permitted emotional largesse under special conditions only and for just one person at a time. What had Kierkegaard said? Kierkegaard, from another cold, northern, Protestant land? 'The crowd is untruth,' he had said. 'Only one receives the prize.' He had addressed his writings to 'the Single Individual.' And George Bell, the big man who moved furniture, had moved through the world with his own home-spun version of the same philosophy. The cheapness of the soul. The snail-shell wisdom. It had killed him, I was sure of that, and if I were not careful it would kill me too. My best, no, my only chance was to hold on, to dig deeper, to go so far inside I broke out again and fell into the world, but changed, and for the better. Auntie and Uncle had done that.

I mean it! They truly had. Yes, we had spied on the Hawerchuks, and yes, anguish had often lain between us, but yes, this other thing was true too. No one is all the way one or another thing in the world, no matter what Calvin said. They loved me, truly, and I loved them, even though to be with them was a reminder of something terrible that had happened, or a cascading set of terrible things, and even though I resented that I was in this place, and that their hopes were tied however inadvertently to my obliteration, so that in their company as I got older I was often in the company of pain, and I was no angel, I inflicted pain myself – you know my uncle always called me 'son'? Well, once in an argument that was ostensibly about Russia but was really about everything, everything that had gone unsaid between us since my arrival in their care (and let me say too that the opposite is always true, always, you may think you are arguing only about matters of the heart and of fathers and sons but you are really also arguing about the history of nations and the common ruin of the contending classes), I said to him, 'I'm not your son,' and I have regretted it ever since. But they put up with it. They put up with me. Putting up with things seemed part of how they broke out into the world and changed. They were patient people. They reminded me when I was angry at all I had lost that they had done nothing but remind me of who I was, that they had told me the poems and songs and stories, that they had spoken to me in Doric, had even written it down as my 'language spoken at home' on the form they filled out for my kindergarten teacher. And they were good to me, my great-aunt and -uncle, even though they were old to be parents, very old, nearing sixty when they became my guardians. I missed them, that funny little white-haired woman and man, missed watching them march to the newsagents (as they called it) in their matching tan raincoats that must have been thirty years old, Auntie with a flowery headscarf and Uncle with a flat tweed cap, missed how they always came back with good news about Mr. Grewal's children at university, and on the days when 'our ship came in' came back with their pockets bulging with licorice or 'boiled sweets' for me, or a style or music magazine when I got older. They had been trained to cast a pinched little glare at the world but they had turned it into a genuine interest. They said hello to people no one else said hello to, and I believe they meant it (this perhaps was the real core of their grudge against Mr. Hawerchuk). They knocked on doors for the left-wing parties in municipal elections. They were part of a social group that Mr. Grewal's sister-in-law had started to welcome new immigrants to the neighbourhood. And so the mystery to me is how I came away with their convictions, if not more so ('Lenin, son,' said Uncle to me in my teen years in the course of one of our many arguments about Russian history, 'a great man to be sure. But what about all of us who are not great? What about those poor sailors at Kronstadt?'), but also came away with the cheapness of the soul that in themselves they had over-thrown? How had it leaked back in? I wondered if it had remained in my guardians as a kind of ghost. That behind their love of the world and the true warmth they had for other people were nips at their heels from the hounds of hell. So that they had to be kind to prove they were predestined to be. Perhaps. They are still mysteries to me, even more in death than they were alive. But if they had managed to break out even a little from the coils of the shell – even if their actions were still governed by its deep logic, even if they saw nautilus spirals and Fibonacci sequences before their eyes when they died – there must be some hope for me yet. So I thought, without being sure if it was true, but thinking nevertheless that I must think so, and that if I did not I could not go on.

The window through the leaves remained as it was, but the window of cloud around the island or rather the inland sea of blue had torn apart on invisible currents of air. Explosions and falling and frames upon frames and windows upon windows – for the picture frame within which I must place from a distance the singing bird was its own wooden window. If there was a window, was there a house? And if that were so, was I looking out from the inside, or inside from out? I said before that my secret wish was to be safe at home but it was so secret that I could not even say it to myself in my mind. Officially I knew there was no house. I had a frame but no painting and a window but no house. What had Rilke said in the great and terrible poem 'Autumn Day,' the poem I had read at nineteen or twenty and known with an exquisite rumble of pain was spelling the contours of my whole life?

Who now has no house, builds no more,
Who is now alone, will long remain so,
Will stay awake, read, write long letters,
And will wander restlessly here and there,
Along the avenues, when the leaves drift.

I had no house and would never. When I was younger and had fantasies of being a mendicant professor of history or philosophy, travelling from small town to small town on short-term contracts while holding within me the 'hard, gemlike flame' of visions and whispers and saintly devotion to Time and the Word, relic and melancholy and the *lachrimae antiquae* on lute, the lines at the finish of the great and terrible poem to a day in autumn had seemed like seduction and beauty and wonder – a wounded life, yes, but one still worth living. More so, I imagined, than the ordinary lives of the unrestless housed who never wondered or wrote letters. How sad to me now that this romantic vision of my small life, at best a consolation prize, a booby prize, a salve applied to a wound unclosing, was at one time my entire goal. Had seemed like purpose, adventure, an improvement of my state. Sad precarious life that for my enemies the nice middle-class people would be an unthinkable fate, terrible, one to rage against. Why had my hopes for myself been so narrow? It is simple. I had grown up poor, I was mad, I had started university almost exactly the same time as the 2008 financial crash. I had come to expect nothing and to make nothing my virtue. This, I realized, was the match that lit the fuse of the cheapness bomb inside of me, the Scottish working-class cheapness bomb. But I saw now that the one who was alone and would stay alone in the poem was no hero of romance and mystery, no figure of black-clad seduction or high sainthood, but rather a matter of fact, a piece of the world as much as the dry leaves blowing on the street were a piece of the world, a phenomenon you could set the watch of the year to. I would remain without a house, writing letters late into the night, for the same reason the summer collapsed into ice blasts and brown dying, for the same reason Orion rose up again in a sky of plush and spangled infinitudes. Kids playing ring toss. The big kids. I was what I was as a cosmic certainty, no cause for alarm or joy. And in seeing this in that moment under the window through the leaves I felt free. I had peace and quiet. I had no house and no reason to worry about it. I knew of course that this way of being alive, so separate, would mean pain for me again as it so often did, and I knew that my brain was broken. But by knowing that it would happen again and again – and that so too would the gifts of sight that came with being separate, the clarity of having no house, no walls around me, to stop me from seeing – I did feel free. And the brokenness even, did it not come from seeing so much? Would a smooth story let me see what I saw? A smooth story was a house with few windows pulled along like a trailer on the road of and-then-and-thens, you could go nowhere else and see little. So I thought then under the trees, feeling for the first time that day that after all I had thought of I finally had something solid to hold on to, to work with and to use. And then I blinked and it was gone, that feeling, that knowledge, whatever it was I had just articulated. Of course. Acceptance that my brain was broken could not unbreak it. And this thought, of all thoughts, made me angry. I cannot say why. Perhaps in secret I hoped that by tricking myself into an epiphany of clarity and acceptance and feeling free I would no longer need to accept anything I did not want to accept. Like giving an apology in the hope I would then be told, 'No need to apologize.' But I had accepted that my brain was broken and my brain had not said, 'Oh, no need.' It had just broken again.

And so when I heard again finally after all that time another call from the red-winged blackbird I busied myself with real intensity in looking for it because I was desperate to break the impasse I had reached inside. I would look for the bird with true care through the frame of my houseless window and no longer be plagued by these thoughts. So I looked.

It was somewhere to my right, maybe six metres up in a tree. I knew it could fly away at any time. I moved slowly, bent low to the ground, used the long wet stick to hold back the flexible branches as I passed. And above me at last, more like seven metres than six, in a tree of a species I do not know the name of, with leaves of the common and wild-grass green, the cloverleaf green, was a bird with a patch on its shoulder of ringmaster crimson and gold. It sang. Do-wreeeee-do. And I held up the frame to the bird as it sang and I watched through the frame and it opened its beak and it sang and it sang and it sang. It was a clear picture, all right. I looked at my hands on the thick wooden frame and then down at the long wet stick resting on one of my shoes and I saw how my white pants were green on the knees and brown at the ankles and I felt like the stupidest man who had ever been alive.

12.

The bird was still singing. I was stupid and a madman, I was squatting in the woods in damp, stained clothes like a hermit, like a wild man, like a green man of the Middle Ages, a foliate head with branches sprouting from my mouth, a pagan avatar of springtime. But I did not blame the bird for these things. How could I? There was no 'bird,' not in any sense in which the bird understood things. There was no bird and there was no stick. I angled my foot, let the stick roll to the ground. It was no longer a stick. It was world, matter, again. It was chemical reactions and bug food. But the frame – I was stuck with the frame, it was the window of my house that did not exist. I hung it around my neck, as though the borders of my invisible and fake house were coterminous with the beginnings and ends of my body. This hurt me – but I wanted it to, a little. I stood up and walked back as I'd come, to the coffin-sized green door in the forest, its borders garlanded with leaves. No, not a door, any more than the window I had claimed to see earlier was a window. Merely empty space I saw as a door because, like so many others, I had spent so much time in built space that even in nature I saw its afterimages. Doors, windows, columns, seats, tables all coming into being from nothing. These things visible but not real rather than invisible *and* not real, if such a thing can be said. But without waiting to resolve the metaphysics, I passed under the door shape in the leaves anyway and out into the open space of the park. The forms and shapes I had passed on my way to the forest were present as before: the toilets, the benches, the baseball diamond. Only they weren't those things now. They too were in some sense visible but not real.

The game of baseball had never been played. There were no games. There were arbitrary geometric dances across temporary lines in the sand. Nothing on earth was truly the name we called it by. Nothing. So I felt in that moment, and with each second that passed, the workings of a certain familiar mind virus grew stronger inside of me. It often came to me after I reached the heights of an enthusiasm and my enthusiasm crested and I was left panting and ragged like a defeated army on a plain. *Enthusiasm*, that nineteenth-century word. The virus was a strange hyper-correction to enthusiasm, a dousing in the coldest and deepest waters of the inner sea the former flames of my broken belief. The mind virus of skepticism of all things in the world to the point of drowning. It troubled me, this virus, because it was shot through with half-truths, near-truths. I could not dispose of it with satisfaction as one more thing in the world simply wrong. It was one leg of a dialectic. With its partner by its side I could control my slow falling: this, that, this, that, this, that. End result, I could walk in a straight line. But with this one leg on its own I could do nothing but fall. Exquisitely, and with a perverse pleasure, through miles of water and with the currents beneath the surface billowing and toying at my clothes, but falling regardless, and running out of air, coming at last to a place of true bottom where nothing could withstand the pressure, no concept, no notion, nothing, all ideas breaking apart under that brooding and skeptical immensity the inner sea. All were shown to be fakes, figments, fragments. Made up. The obvious ones broke first. Canada I already knew was made up, conceived in blood and darkness like a hideous deep-sea fish, but not nearly so hardy, Canada split apart as one of the most laughable forgeries ever conceived in the world, it did not surprise me, I welcomed it, I laughed. Ah, but I also saw the breaking of the petty localisms that seemed more true – the West Coast was made up, the ocean and the estuary made up, and all the towns I had lived in. And Ontario was very, very, very made up. And Scotland was made up, and Scottishness, and Scottish people. Of course they were. Made and remade from every direction – Sir Walter Scott's sickly Romantic vision a lubricant for the dispossession of the people, a condescending bourgeois Lowland myth as real Highlanders were cleared off the land; MacDiarmid's dialect poems in 'Lallans' a pastiche, something to show that it wasn't just the Irish who could have a revival. Ireland made up too, as much as it pained me to think about. The rising of the moon, the moon rising, the moon itself and its light blown apart and scattered like the men who had brought their pikes to the old spot at the river quite well-known to you and me. And so of course the 'snail-shell wisdom' was nothing, was no stronger under all this weight than a real snail shell in a real garden. All began to fall away. The 'I,' the 'me,' the 'brain,' they too were nothing. Yes, in the course of my daily life I might have a flash of this feeling of all falling away. But it took the mind virus to feel it truly, to see it, to follow it all the way to its fundaments at the bottom of the inner sea. And the inner sea was made up, and every metaphor I had ever used, every simile – those 'like … like … like' constructions I swung in front of myself wherever I went like a censer of smoking incense, I know I said this before about 'as … as … as,' a censer, sacred protection against – what? Something made up. So concerned I had been to probe and investigate myself that I had not managed to step away from the 'I,' from 'step,' from 'manage.' And the ideal-material distinction made up, binaries made up, one, zero, something, nothing, nothing itself was nothing.

I had lost the thread of myself. Where was I? I was in a green and interrupted space. But every word I added to my account of this place was spoiling it more. I should burn the threads. I should be moving my finger like Cratylus. He was the only thing still true.

I had first heard the name Cratylus in Billy Bart's class, at nineteen, at a time in my life when I felt intimations almost of the sort I feel now, junior versions, I have mentioned them before. My problems of perspective and slowness, the road to the mountains that were not worth my time. Billy Bart was a professor you do not get nowadays – a down-home American with a Canadian academic pedigree, the years of his degrees in Canada lining up almost exactly with the worst years of the Vietnam War. Metal hummingbirds in the jungle retching orange fire, the imperialist bastards getting their asses handed to them by an army of villagers and schoolchildren, villagers tempered like steel in their cadres, schoolchildren building secret roads by night. Billy Bart would have seen all that coming and said, 'Hell no.' Or at least I assumed he had studied here to avoid or otherwise protest the war. I hoped he had. He was not like the polished young American professors you might meet briefly at our school, their grudging first appointment before they published their way out of Canada and back into the rankings in the *US News and World Report*. Billy had a mock-irascible, almost rustic energy in the classroom, gesturing and declaiming in his blazer over a black T-shirt in a deep and husky voice, a mug of coffee always near at hand that he joked about having whisky in. He was an Ohioan who told us he had once been a decent high school baseball player. He called Parmenides a 'space cadet,' dismissed the Stoics and Epicureans as 'expensive weekend seminar philosophy.' And almost as an aside during a lesson on the presocratics he mentioned someone named Cratylus, a radical interpreter of Heraclitus's theories of the flux and non-similitude of all things. So radical that he deemed language itself incapable of expressing anything true, and when spoken to merely gestured with his finger. Billy Bart didn't say exactly how, or for that matter which finger. But the story of this man who had come to doubt language too much even to use it had spoken better to my intimations of the slow and pointless road than almost anything else at the time. When I told this to Pia she had thought I was crazy. 'Cratylus was the best phil-osopher,' I said once when we were hanging out in her dorm room, and she looked him up on Wikipedia and then turned to me in her office chair and frowned in the way she always did when I said something she thought was 'insane.' It's an odd thing. In hindsight I think we liked speak-ing to each other this way, but at the time I would have told anyone else that Pia was frustrating, infuriating, impossible, and she would have said the same about me. I realize now that we had been circling each other warily, two idealistic virgins with high standards, to see if each might be for the other their first girlfriend, first boyfriend, and that we had both for whatever reason decided we were not compatible, not similar enough. I am sure we would have been and were, but of course because we were so similar neither of us would have been able to see that. And of course neither of us did. Our hands were pressed symmetrically one facing the other on either side of our two inner seas of ice. Pia was still working her way out of the nominal if disavowed Islam of her parents, who had not even given her a name typical of Muslim girls; I was still working my way out of my guardians' nominal if disavowed Calvinism. We were both so serious and so inexperienced, at once ahead of and behind all our peers. But what am I talking about. I said that my metaphors were not real, the inner sea, the ice. And if that were so, then certainly neither was Calvinism, or Ohio, or baseball, or virgins, or the university. I said that only Cratylus was true. As before under the trees when I could sustain real presence for only a moment, now out under the sky I could hardly stick to my story, to any story, for more than an instant. And the mind virus was not even a 'story,' it was a force, an equal and opposite reaction to the enthusiasm I had felt before. Of course it could not be sustained. I had escaped beguilement by the shadows of the flames on the cave wall, climbed up and out of the cave, and out into another cave, another flame, another shadow, another wall. Caves upon caves upon caves. The dialectic was bucking and kicking in my hands like a live thing, thesis and antithesis and thesis and antithesis with no synthesis, a sick live thing, sick and full of life. I thought of something I read in *Gravity's Rainbow*: 'If there is something comforting – religious, if you want – about paranoia, there is still also anti-paranoia, where nothing is connected to anything, a condition not many of us can bear for long.' Nor could I bear for long the mind virus of total skepticism, or the thing that came before it, or the thing after. Was this what I meant when I said that my brain was broken? It seemed possible. I had felt the joints of things eroding all around me. 'All that is solid melts into air,' Marx had said. Yes, he was right. And he a materialist. But he knew how this worked, knew that the fake and unreal and invisible inner sea kept claiming the phenomena, warping them like wrecks, like driftwood, like thousands of tons of plastic floating in a snail-shaped gyre. Working material into immaterial. The waves banging crates of jetsam around until they leaked dreams.

What was the constant, what was the painted background on the wall of each cave? It was trees, a pond, a baseball diamond, benches, toilets – or if you preferred it was the occult and ever-retreating forms we mistook for those things, the leavings and dross and ectoplasm. It was the park itself, I had not left the park, the stranger was never coming and I had seen the bird singing in the frame and nothing had changed except the contents of my brain and even then not much and I had never left the park, it had become the final cave, the one most like the world as it really was while still not being that, the world I could feel washing me into its painful and beautiful shape, feel but as yet not truly see aright, because I was still inside the park, the final cave, and would not see unless I left the park. I thought it was high time I did it. So I walked, finally, to the gate nearest the woods – for this was a park of the old style with gates, black nineteenth-century wrought-iron batwings to cartoon heaven. Or hell. I got about two feet away from the opening and stopped. Still no cars on the streets. The branches of the blue hydrangeas on the lawn of the red-gabled Victorian house across the street circled and dipped rhythmically without stopping. The windows were too darkened by daylight to look in. I could only guess. I knew many of the houses in Dice-town had been made into offices for dentists, lawyers, real estate agents, therapists. A tooth could be leaving a jaw in there, the down-curved tusks of the roots slipping from the socket at last like a sigh. Assets and capital could be shunting around in the switching yards on the fake and invisible rails of the law. Buildings could be turning into money and back again. A therapist could be prising a brain from its housing and dusting it with compressed air. Same time next week. I assumed it was something like that, therapy. My employers, suffice to say, had not provided me a health insurance plan.

No matter. It was time to leave and then this would all be over. The park, the final cave. I could forget the stranger, my brain, the frame. I would put it back onto the fire hydrant. No matter.

I watched the branches circle and dip. I could not leave.

13.

When I say I could not leave I mean I could not leave. I could not do it any more than I could fly, or change colours, or shit an asteroid that spoke to me. It was not within the scope of things that I could do. The scope of things that I could do was narrowed to my stupid uncalculated movements within the eighty-five acres, to my perceptions, and to my reflections and recollections as prompted by those perceptions. My perceptions had something to do with beauty and something to do with my inability to leave, and my reflections and recollections had something to do with the relation between my perception of beauty and my inability – not only to leave, but also more generally. But in the first place my perceptions were of light.

The light had shifted since I thought of it last. What had been streams of gold coursing through the globe-like nodes of wet in the grass was now the dull glint of pewter on an ornament tacked to a sun visor. A visible recalibration of the world, as in an old British comedy when the fool runs outside and everything transitions from video to film. Only not so abrupt as that. It had taken its time. Speaking of. The light told me it was about seven forty-five in the evening, still bright in summer, but a brightness imminently reaching given limits. Soon it would smoulder into rose-gold in the creases between clouds and sky. I was confused. I had come to the park midday, perhaps one at the latest, and could not account for the lost time. I had sat under a tree and moved around while sitting. I had looked at the frame and at a snail. I had listened to bird calls. I had walked this way and that, looked at a red sweater, looked at the bark of a willow tree, walked in the woods. Above all I had been thinking, all else was brief lucid actions through an encumbering fog of thinking. Heavy actions, strained as in sleepwalk. And yet there was no mistake. It was the sky of late evening in summer. I had been here almost seven hours. Or I had been somewhere else without knowing and the hours had passed without me.

A long murmuration of birds drew out from a space between two of the sand-coloured cubes at the park's edge. The workers were leaving, I thought, but the logic of what I saw and what I thought did not cohere with clarity. They fluttered like Victorian funeral crepe, jerked like rubber bats on elasticated strings. The true name of the birds was by no means on my lips, even though they were black birds. Starlings, I thought, sparrows, swallows. They might as well be stars, spars, swells. I realized I was thinking Melville words, sea words, and did not fight that. I would let them take me far away from here in my mind. The stars of Orion's belt framed by the spars of the long-distance whaler, the sides of the frame rocking with the swells. Sea swells she sells, by the sea's door. Swells. The sea as a blood blister, pulse tracer – an open wound that will never seal. The pond in the park another such place. But I was not ready to think about the pond, that staring rheumy eye locked forever in a contest with the eye of God. I was avoiding the pond. I would think only about sea words – beautiful words – and how I could not leave. The workers could or could not leave, I had not seen one. If the workers in the cubes of sand were all CIA Jims then it was wrong to say they were 'workers,' they were not workers in the sense I had meant it. They were antiworkers, as matter has antimatter. They had been so as long as their project had been in motion. The Office of Strategic Services, their predecessor, had written manuals on this subject, counselling saboteurs to work slowly, act stupid. And the CIA Jims would delight in knowing I had felt anti-paranoia. They sowed it themselves, as they did paranoia guided to the wrong ends. But I did not know if the dwellers in the cubes were Jims or not. There could have been hundreds of people inside. The fluttering funeral crepe of the birds had not yet broken. They still poured out from the hidden place that birthed them, birds beating their wings with such speed and rhythm that they seemed to be single pennants twirling around the shafts of darts. Whose darts, who threw these fluttering objects out into the sky to remind me of sea words? Was it the same one who had made it so I could not leave? I did not know.

It had been over two years since I had seen the sea, and as a consequence it had become a quiet obsession, a recurring landscape in my longer dreams. It would not have been impossible for me to go back, or to have finally seen the Atlantic from some beach or port town in Nova Scotia, a three-hour flight away. But I never did – some grand-scale version of not being able to leave, the park perhaps not the final cave at all but rather Ontario itself the final one, and because the scale was grander I had less daily cause to think about it. So instead of going to the sea I saw it in my mind, heard and smelled and tasted it, this absent unclosing wound upon the world. To be standing in the sea on whichever coast one stood was to be touching them all, to be one node in the world-sea, to be witness to the tears of the world, its breaking with the phases of the moon. I saw that leaden line, so heavy, a metal infill in the bowl of the coast, poured when molten but frozen now in place, and rippled like it was beaten out with a hammer. I heard that panting Neptune's breath, fluid in the lungs, a massive rattle, crash upon crash. I tasted the sea in my mouth, slaked my vampire thirst for the salt of the wound on my lips, smelled the sea air in my nostrils, the low-tide funk of pickled weeds. I remembered the touched places along-side or near the sea, the wooden docks with orange buoys tied to their barnacled stilts, the boats with waves of rust on their sides like strange climate graphs or population diagrams, the tree-grown cliff faces butting right up against the water. And more than anything else I remembered arbutus trees.

They do not grow in the estuarylands or shorelands of the flood plain at home but can be found on the islands a few hours south by ferry ride. My aunt and uncle never travelled even that far, so I had to find the arbutus trees on my own. They are lovers of temperate coasts and salt air and mists, red-barked with matte-green leaves, evergreen, neither coniferous nor deciduous, growing all the way down the coast to the San Francisco Bay and scattered points more southerly beyond – Santa Barbara even, and pockets at the mountain of Palomar. Madrona, it has been called, madroño, bearberry. Dis-tā'-tsi, it has been called, kou-wät'-chu. It is a metamorphosist, its bark cross-hatched and crocodilian at its outermost layer, a swamp thing, until the rough edges fall away and only a red paper remains, the pages of red books, books soaked in red wine or blood. Then the paper itself peels away and the flesh underneath is of smooth beige arms or tusks or whalebones, and the matte-green leaves like holly or ivy jangle in crisp arrhythmia under sea wind and sun. When I think of the skin of these red books of trees peeling and blowing away in the winds coming off the island-mazed causeways of the Salish Sea, green islands and blue water glowing in August as if blown with dust of gold or diamonds, and I think of how far away it all is and how impossible, I ache as though folded over a dull but unbreakable knife. Red books blowing in the wind. Salt and seaweed on the wailing or whispering or sighing air.

The gulls on the air, I almost forgot to mention the gulls of that coast and the fullness of their voices, deeper and longer in calling than the squeaks of the Great Lakes' tiny imitators. I woke up in hospital once as a boy after having my appendix out, junk-sick from morphine but not knowing that, and floating in my bed and surprised by all things and especially to be alive, and hearing from a half-open window that long and searching cry. A cloudy day, I remember, I could see from my bed. And so often in my memory the gulls of the coast I grew up on flew and cried on days of mist and rain. I heard their wails without seeing them through white or grey walls. I had lived so much of my life stirred to my depths by distant and invisible things.

And so here in the park, as the last three or four birds came out from behind the sand-coloured cubes and melted away in the far distance and I still could not leave, it seemed that all the world, nearly, was distant and invisible to me. It was not long of course before I entertained the thought that I could not leave precisely *because* I had felt most alive as I pondered and sought the distant and invisible, had grown used to it and come to crave it, like a gambler addicted to losing, and so within these eighty-five acres I could ponder and seek the whole world, I could love and know the world only as a thing lost, an absent thing. But of course. It is only natural for those who believe the things I do. My red books blowing in the wind, the secret world, the world to come, burning within me as Durruti had said – 'We carry a new world here, in our hearts. That world is growing this minute.' Like Gnosticism almost. That Durruti remark had been my high school yearbook quote. But after thinking this I naturally also thought that of course this fog of mystical defeat was precisely what the Methodistical state and the CIA Jims would want me to feel, it had been what all Europe had wanted the Highlander MacPherson of the Gàidhealtachd to feel, in his hazy and misty elegiacal Ossian poems of defeat, it was what all powers wanted their scattered and disunified enemies to feel, yes? And yet how could I move through the world without some elegiac distance, some painful and searching remove? I thought of Byung-Chul Han. What had he written about beauty? 'Beauty is a hideout.' It comes in a veil, like Nature in Spenser's *Faerie Queene*. And beauty, this whisper from another world I could never truly see, had, yes, been a sustenance to me. The sea, of course, I had been speaking of beauty for as long as I had been speaking of the sea and the arbutus trees. The calls of birds, the red-winged blackbirds and the gulls. The mountains too, yes, the black silhouette of a range against a sky thirty minutes before the finish of a sunset, a silhouette like the ragged edge of paper torn in half. Even concrete, in a way. And yes, when I spoke of beauty at the start of my vigil here in the park I had shied away from it, distrusted it. The blanket of cold grey beauty billowing out and enfolding the true picture of the world. Obscurities of beauty, I said, desperate and stubborn, I said. It was not enough for me to accept that beauty be a hideout, it seemed. A part of me was compelled to make it somehow sinful, untrue, an error. I recognized finally that this too was the gutter Calvinism of the Scottish poor, that script I had tried to escape, telling me that one of the few forms of solace I had in this world was false, sinful, untrue, error. For it had been a solace to me. It had kept me alive. And so at last I did not think, nor do I now, that the ever-receding hideout of beauty I had turned my face toward as a flower to a distant sun, this rough-hewn beauty of crying birds and flaying trees and broken mountains and devouring seas, this beauty that murdered me and kept me alive – I did not and do not think this beauty was a sin, not truly, I had been wrong to say so. I said it without thinking. It was not false consciousness, this beauty, it was not fooling me into the reaction, it was not 'sapping my revolutionary energies.' On the contrary, I thought, it had given me something to fight for, to want for a communist world to come. If I followed the logic of the kind of beauty I believed in truly I must be ready to fight for all peoples, alongside all peoples, against the world as it was. No, not the whole world. The capitalist world, the imperialist world. I had used that phrase earlier, 'the world as it really was,' and said that it came in waves and that the waves were washing me into something both more beautiful and more true, but I had then immediately doubted myself, I had thought I was obscuring the truth by insisting it be beautiful.

And now here as the funeral procession of the swallows or sparrows or starlings was gone and the workers, perhaps, were leaving, I saw that, no, beauty was not truth, nor truth beauty, and by no means all one needs to know, never ever, but that beauty *was* one of the true things in the world, the world as it really was, as were horror and exploitation and death, birds and seas and arbutus trees, workers and antiworkers, there were many true things, even true things in seeming contradiction, and this was why we must set our wooden dolls of dialectic at play, and the world as it really was could wash me into a true shape that was beautiful or a true shape that was horrible or a true shape that was strictly speaking neither, and these true shapes would surely be just one true shape of many, for me and for everyone, we are in motion, we are bucking and jigging, the doll with hands to the sides is as true as its opposite and incomplete without it – this, that, this, that – and this dance itself was at least partway beautiful as much as it was not, though for the moment it was less beautiful or unbeautiful than painful, the dance, because my brain was broken and I could not leave. 'The world is all that is the case,' Wittgenstein had said, and he said moreover that 'the problem of life' disappeared for one not through a solution but simply as a thing that disappeared, and I wondered if, in the case of my broken brain, this would be true. That one day I would simply have no option for it to be anything *but* not broken, just as at this moment in the park I had no option but not to leave, just as time and events and circumstances may vault people at once over all they have yet to overcome before they may do what they must. It seemed possible, more than possible. But for the moment I could not leave, and for the moment my brain was broken, and for the moment I lived as an internal exile far from the sea that sustained me.

14.

As before when I knew the light was changing so too now I knew that night was well on its way. I had given up trying to square what I was seeing with my own eyes and feeling on my skin with the sense I had in my mind that not nearly enough time had passed for me to be seeing and feeling the true advent of sunset and not long after it night. Whatever my memories did or did not tell me, the sky at the western fringes of my visible world – over the tops of the trees and the roofs and ornate frontage of the Victorian yellow-brick or red-gabled houses now serving as offices – this sky on the western fringes was now not blue only but mixed with a pink of liquid fineness, as if a watercolourist had spread across the page a pale rose so diluted with water it only just registered to the eye. But I knew that this pinkness would darken and fill the sky, and that behind this plush band and around it a quartzite light would flash and refract off the surfaces around me in the park, and especially off the sand-coloured buildings, the light making true again for a moment the origins of the concrete in so much sand and stone, making for the moment the buildings geology again, not structure but living rock, and flashing too off the sepia glass of the windows and making me believe again they were melted sand, newly blown, molten living castles of sand in the light of the sky's red ending. Sandcastles. Red endings. The images in my mind that I expected to see soon before me in reality reminded me of the last known written words of Rosa Luxemburg, in 1919, a hundred years before this day of my vigil in the park and a hundred years after Keats was hit in the eye with a cricket ball, this magic number nineteen, the quiet true scansion of history as far as I was concerned.

'Your order is built on sand,' she had written at the close of her essay on the day that the Freikorps came. And it was true, this had always been true, but the endless hunger of these enemies had meant that they would melt the sand, bond it, make glass, make concrete, blow it in our eyes, do all that can be done with an empire of sand to lock it in place, even if it meant the ruination of the world. The sun's red ending. Did sunset and the coming of night mean that I would leave? The faded green sign at the nineteenth-century gate had read, 'PARK CLOSED FROM DUSK TO DAWN.' Perhaps I was bound to these rules too. But I knew that this park had its second life in darkness irrespective of all signs. Would I stay in the park until nightfall? Or later? Alone with the lights of the now-empty office buildings and the lead-cold weight of the air? I could, perhaps. I thought of the place that I lived in – the four-room bungalow with my books of dead words, my plants that would die without my constant attention – and I felt it a carapace around the soft and still-living parts of me. I lived in a dust-ridden husk. I had filled my tiny mastaba with indifferent grave goods. So that if I stayed away from my house, and sleep, and the unwashed comforter I'd brought with me from my guardians' linen closet on the terrible day when I had to clear away their things from the co-op apartment, my guardians now dead, I would defy, postpone my death. By falling into the jaws of the greater death of a summer night in a park. Perhaps someone would finally come. Several someones. Local teenagers looking to drink, who would beat me senseless from fear I was a sexual aberrant out to harm them. 'There goes Norman,' as the Undertones had sung, Catholic boys from Derry, the meaning of the song about the nighttime prowler biting more keenly if you knew that 'Norman' in Northern Ireland was a name given mostly to Protestant boys. No. So overdramatic of me to think this. No one would come. But far away across the little streets I might hear shouts from the main road, shouts of the young in line for the handful of lousy nightclubs in town. 'Straight bars,' I had heard someone say once, and liked that. Stranger shouts too, from the side streets, the house parties flowing out onto the living grass, the hot breathing green in the darkness.

Or perhaps I would hear nothing. Summer silence, or silence underscored by passenger planes passing over. Or the chilly onrush of a transmigrating soul. From an airplane, or an out-of-body experience, the town I lived in then would look in the night like a throw rug of shimmering sequins in black velvet, a thousand votive candles in a cemetery. Ecstasy and grief, indistinguishable at a distance.

I had been a teenager in a park in the darkness once, you know. This was no mean feat. It had taken me months to persuade my old, old guardians that I would be 'safe' out at night with my friends, that 'nothing would happen to me.' I had also needed to cultivate the right friends. That strange crew. The word *queer* was not yet in common parlance as a self-descriptor among young people then, nor did we have words yet in our circle for what it meant to be trans. But later in life I would look back at the people who had made up this group and recognize that nearly all of them were queer, and that some were trans. I liked them because they were clever and funny and kind to me. They taught me how to smoke and drink. My guardians did not know about this part. But on the occasions they had cause to meet my friends they would remark that they were 'decent boys and girls,' 'polite,' 'artistic,' 'gentle.' They approved because they concluded that my 'decent,' 'artistic' friends would not commit the outrages they recalled in Aberdeen, in Mastrick, from the boys in gangs with hair like Marc Bolan. And so my friends and I smoked and drank in the parks, and hooted and hollered, and peed in the road. And the air on those warm nights in summer was cold and tactile, like metal against skin, sensuous, electrical. We would lie on the grass playing fields we so scrupulously avoided in daytime and listen as a 'larger than life' 'raconteur' girl in vintage cowboy boots told us about the time she had genuinely seen a ghost. Of course I had a crush on her. A ghost in an old house she had lived in once. The grass under me was soft, damp, plush, and alive with heat. I did not disclose my feelings. I was stricken by them. Her voice in the darkness. Other voices in the darkness asking questions, trying to get the story straight. And under us the warmth of the earth and over us the cool of the air. I knew I would never tell her even though at any possible opportunity, maybe walking with her somewhere after school, another part of me insisted, violently, *do it, say something*, and my heart would almost vibrate out of my body and my hands would slick. I knew I would never in the same way I knew in the park that I could not leave. And the secret unspoken reason was of course that this feeling too was a hideout and a distant and invisible thing and existed most fully in my mind – and beyond my mind, my body itself, my veins, so that I was truly stricken, not eating or sleeping – and it could not exist in the same way after I disclosed it to her, this feeling, even if she felt the same way. Such a strange thing. I would not be able to feel things for others in ways less intense than these until I was out of high school. But all this to say that those nights telling ghost stories on the grass had been magic, occult, luxurious, and that this was a truth known to all world folklore and mythos, Nyx and Hecate and all pantheons of lightless working and moving and shaping in secret of the new. So perhaps even if I could not leave all night, these magics would bring me consolation.

But yet another coil was coming in this long spiral in my mind, another kick at the board under the folklorist's ass. Or my ass. I believe I had allowed the terms and the nature of the scene with the wooden puppets to shift. Another coil was coming because magic exists on a knife's edge with terror, terror on a knife's edge with death. Night might come and I might go mad, or die. It had not escaped me that although I had spent hours here I was not hungry. Perhaps I would starve without realizing, as nights and days flashed by me and I remained unable to leave. I looked up again at the sky. The images I had expected, the red ending, were coming now to pass. The faint water-rose of the sky earlier had darkened and thickened and swelled, the sky was half red now. What was it my guardians used to say? 'Red sky at night, sailor's delight.' Or 'Shepherd's delight,' they said that too, they even mixed it up by accident sometimes: 'Red sky at night, shepherd's delight. Red sky at morn, sailors be warned.' I do not know if any of this is true. Meteorologically, I mean. For my part, sunsets could often send me as a child to a place of indescribable sadness. I cannot explain. I have no indication that the 'sundowning' known to afflict the very old has similar purchase with the very young. But when a day would end through the glass door to the balcony of the co-op apartment, molten gold or pewter light infiltrating the needles of the pine trees outside in the courtyard, and the sun began to sink behind the mountains and the trees like a wounded god falling from the sky, I mourned and felt afraid and imagined my own death. Yes, that is it. In my mind I had linked sunsets to death. And I feared death as a child, feared it even in abstract metaphysical ways I should not have done. I believed at the time in the Christian heaven, not so much because my guardians taught me to but rather because it was simply in the air, right down to the TV commercials for Philadelphia Cream Cheese or the radio ads for Chock full o'Nuts or the fates of characters in cartoons. But the concept of a heaven that lasted 'forever' – indeed, 'forever' itself – filled me with deep terror. I was driven to panic states by the contemplation of the infinite. Worst of all by the Gustave Doré engraving of the Dantean heaven, the endless tunnel of angels, seen by accident in a library book just as I had read by accident the last words of Keats. And the setting sun, the end of the finite day, paradoxically always brought the infinite to mind. It brought it to mind now, albeit with less terror. I have been alive too long for all that. And yet it occurs to me now that I never disclosed my age, I only hinted at it by mentioning various things that had happened to me. You may have forgotten those passing mentions and concluded from my mode of address that I am old, very old. But no, I am not that old. I was born in 1988, and it is 2019 now. It is merely that my guardians were old, old even when I was a little boy. I never knew them at the age that I am now. And yet I am old enough not to feel instinctual terror at the thought of the infinite, not like I did before. Not terror. But as the sky's blue bled away and the atmospheric skin of the world was now purpling like a bruise and as darkness, I knew, would be coming, I felt not terror, but a heightened awareness that this long vigil in the park with the frame and the absent stranger Onyx would be entering a new and unpredictable phase. Not terror, but the raised ears and dilated eyes of the animal in the underbrush knowing that terror might come.

15.

The sky continued to darken and as it did so another thing happened in perfect and diametric opposition to it. Other lights got brighter. First a star – or more probably the planet Venus – and then another star, and another, each faint still in the navy-blue near-night, forbidden here beneath the dazzle of city lights to reach the gemlike purity I understood they might in country fields and distant places I had never been. The city lights themselves now made their appearance, windows once smoke-black now amber and see-through, Victorian houses repurposed as offices now emptied of workers and perfectly open to view: coat stands, desks, and monitors, many nondescript white waiting rooms with pictures of the sea. An insult, I always felt, in landlocked towns. The street lights now planted their cloudy yellow cones of light on their appointed intervals of sidewalk. Only the sepia-toned windows of the quartzite cubes remained opaque. There could have been hundreds of people inside. There could have been the devil, eating sinners in a vision of medieval hell. There could have been naked contorting bodies in a Boschian orgy scene. There could have been nothing, nothing at all, no rooms or floors or walls, nothing, like the inside of a pyramid already robbed, or perhaps like a real pyramid empty except for a couple of shafts pointing up to the sky for no clear purpose. Aligning, perhaps, with powerful stars. I hated these buildings, I feared them, I could not stop looking. But around them more and more lights were coming on. I thought I should surely see the lights of cars now, although I had not yet. I thought I should surely see, through the windows of the yellow-brick Victorian houses farther down the street that I knew to be homes and lived in, the silhouettes of people moving around, watching television, eating food. I saw the lights in those houses but as yet saw no silhouettes of people.

I had mentioned before the possibility of planes passing over. They would appear to me at this stage in the night – yes, now it was night, truly night – as a cluster of lights, a Southern Cross in motion, red, yellow, perhaps a blue-green, some blinking, some steady. It was technically possible. I had seen them up there before. But I had seen only one all this day, now night – and that had been early, before my phone died. I had not seen another plane any more than I had seen a car. And the shouts from distant streets I had not heard, despite predictions, nor had a group of teenagers come, or even a couple. I was walking now in the open field of grass I had looked upon at the start of my vigil and compared to the sea. I heard the blades of the grass rustling in a slight breeze. I could no longer see the blades well. I doubted they were steaming anymore. I would have been frightened if I saw they were still steaming after all this time. But I could not see well enough to know. I had the frame in my hand. Its details in the darkness were obscure to me. It could have been covered in snails and I would not have known. Or only in stages would I have known, from the light reflecting from the coils of their buttermilk shells in smooth pale yellows. The rising of the moon. The moon itself I expected or rather hoped to see. I did not know if this was a night when the moon was set to appear or not. Nor did I know its expected position in the sky on this night, or whether that place would be obscured by trees or buildings from my vantage point in the park. I did not even know – and this frankly embarrassed me – whether the moon should be visible immediately in the night (it was after all sometimes visible in the day) or whether it had to rise, like the sun, into prominence. The song of course. The rising of the moon. I assumed it meant something. Meteorologically, I mean. I knew it meant something – no, more than something, everything – to me, in another way.

For the song, 'The Rising of the Moon,' the song calling on the men from the mud-walled cabins to gather by the old bend in the river with their pikes, was a song of the United Irishmen and their revolt. Pikes against muskets, a uniformless army of the people against the red jackets of the British army. A defeat and a bloodbath, the leaders in exile or dead, the flight of the wild geese to France, to America, the unlucky ones to Australia's prisons. If only they had won, if only the armies of Revolutionary France had landed in numbers to help them, if only the wind that kept General Hoche and Wolfe Tone from landing in Bantry Bay in 1796 had not blown, if only the Royal Navy had been sent to the bottom of the sea – we would be living in a different world. For the United Irishmen were united in a very moving sense, Catholics and Protestants together, fighting for a free and independent Ireland with no religious discrimination, fighting to, in Wolfe Tone's words, 'substitute the common name of Irishman in place of the denominations of Catholic, Protestant and Dissenter.' A tortuous history inhering in that three-item list. At the time only members of the Anglican Church of Ireland could ascend to the heights of Anglo-Irish society, and 'Dissenters' here meant non-Anglican Protestants, most notably the Presbyterians who had come over from Scotland in the Plantation of Ulster more than a century earlier. They were largely excluded from political power as Catholics were, and were animated at the end of the eighteenth century by the same revolutionary foment that had already gripped America and France. 'Americans in their hearts,' reported a concerned British observer, Lord Harcourt, the Viceroy of Ireland at the time. He died in a well, by the way. He was saving his favourite dog. It was only after the defeat of the Rising that the British brought Presbyterians and other nonconforming Protestants into the fold of the 'acceptable' faiths, exploiting sectarian division as they always have everywhere. They would coax the Dissenters over the course of the nineteenth century to see themselves as British, not Irish, laying in the process the foundation for the violence of the century to come. But in 1798 the rising of Wolfe Tone and Napper Tandy had offered the hope of an Ireland free from Britain, all of its inhabitants Irish no matter what faith, all bearing the common name.

This victory would have reverberated beyond Ireland. There were in addition to the United Irishmen the United Scotsmen, inspired by their Irish brothers and like them seized by the radical promise of the French Revolution. They too wanted independence from the hated Britain and a state founded on the egalitarian republicanism stirring all hopeful people in the world at this time, not only in France but also in Haiti – the miracle of Toussaint ¿nd Dessalines – and soon enough in Latin America with Hidalgo's Grito de Dolores. The most famous of the United Scotsmen was Thomas Muir, whose life was incredible, not least because it had improbably taken him among many other places in the world to the very sea that I in my youth had gazed upon and from which I had drawn sustenance. Muir the radical was exiled for his politics to Botany Bay, as so many others were in the great repressive century of Britain's hubris. And yet he escaped, on a ship called the *Otter*, which took him across the Pacific Ocean to an island the British and Spanish in reluctant compromise had named 'Quadra's and Vancouver's Island.' And to a great inlet on that island, properly called Mowichat but named by the British 'Nootka Sound.' This last name was granted by Captain James Cook in the classic benighted misprision of the British, who brought the ship into the sound with the help of a Nuu-chah-nulth guide. The Nuu-chah-nulth people were already used to the presence of sailing ships, particularly those from Spain and for some reason Boston, and in describing the lay of the sound, or in giving sailing directions to Cook, the guide used the word *nootka*, meaning 'circle around.' In their nomenclative obsession, a thing they shared with most Christians (remember Adam and Eve giving everything a name in Eden), the British disregarded the possibility that the guide was giving them practical instructions or a description of topography, concluding instead he was stating the name of the bay. The British, remembering Adam and Eve, believed that to name a thing was to own it in some way, and so they hungrily and without bothering to ask confirmation decided that the inlet was Nootka Sound and that the Nuu-chah-nulth were the Nootka.

But this all happened several years before the voyage of the *Otter* and the improbable arrival of Muir. I almost think I can see what he saw as the land came out of the Pacific – the sharp rocks all the way down to the water, black rocks and dark grey and light grey, the evergreens grabbing hold by their roots like knotty hands paused forever mid-grasp of stones to throw into the sea, hands untroubled by the sharpness, they want to hurl the rocks far out back into the line of the horizon to see if they might skip, but they cannot, they are paused forever, and the tops of the firs seaward so blown by salt winds and riots of mist that they grow like bonsai trees, a thing of which Muir almost certainly knew nothing; from the deck of the *Otter* he would simply have seen trees almost all trunk and branch, their greenery in miniature, clustering at the edge of the land, and the wet black rocks at the coastal breakers running like endless fountains, white foam rushing from the cracks. And he may have seen – it is possible, just barely possible, their presence has occasionally been attested to as far north as the inlet of Mowichat where one must circle around – the flaking red paper of the bark of the arbutus trees. The red books coming apart under the matte-green asterisks of the leaves. *Note:* say the asterisks, *note: note: note:* What are they noting? To what do they request our attention? What has been forgotten, what has been left out of the flaying red books in a text that everyone or no one or only a few someones can read?

A Spanish ship, *Sutil*, was also anchored in the sound. Muir learned from its commanding officer, José Tovar, that there was a British ship nearby, the *Providence*. It had been at port in the prison colony in Australia not long before Muir had escaped, and those on the ship would know who he was. Muir had to act quickly. Here, as before and after, Spain and the Spanish language offered the ambiguous prospect of liberation for a Scottish person. It had happened before, in 1719 – a hundred years before Keats was struck in the eye by a cricket ball, two hundred years before the last letter of Rosa Luxemburg, and three hundred years before my vigil in the park with the frame. Spain had assessed the chessboard of the competing European nations and decided at this time to aid the

Jacobite Highlanders risen in the rebellion of 1719, landing troops on the Isle of Lewis for a campaign that would end in the mountains of the northeast Highlands under the bombs of the English Coehorn mortars. And now, in the summer of 1796, John Keats incidentally an infant less than a year old, Muir the radical with his knowledge of Spanish learned in school convinced the Spanish José Tovar to violate the rules of his realm, allow him to board the *Sutil* and travel with him southward to Mexico, out of reach of the British ships. Tovar's generosity was likewise extended by the governor of Monterey, California, Diego de Borica. But authorities further up the Spanish colonial ladder were suspicious of Muir, and the Viceroy of New Spain ordered him sent to Havana. He was to remain in the prison until a ship could conduct him to Spain as a possible enemy spy. Here Muir was somehow able to get word to a French diplomat that he had escaped Australia, but he was put on board a ship to Spain before the government of Revolutionary France could intervene further on his behalf. And on its approach to Cádiz this Spanish ship was intercepted by who else but ships of the British Royal Navy, that enemy of all progress in the world, and in the ensuing battle Muir was wounded horribly by the ships of Britain, the left side of his face ruined by shrapnel, his cheekbone lost and his eye destroyed, wounded so badly that the Spanish took him for dead, or at least had a pretext to say so to the British, and he went ashore with the injured sailors rather than into a British or Spanish prison. Finally after much diplomacy he was allowed to leave Spain and join the community of revolutionary exiles in France, where he would live only a year and a half longer, still trying to organize from abroad the rising of the United Scotsmen, dying as a result of his wounds.

Among the exiles Muir met in Paris was Napper Tandy of the United Irishmen, the Napper Tandy named in the song 'The Wearing of the Green,' the song that has the same melody as 'The Rising of the Moon.' The melody of both songs shared also by a song called 'The Orange and the Green.' The biggest mix-up that you have ever seen. My father he was Orange and my mother she was Green. And me being strictly neutral

I bashed everyone in sight. A song of the twentieth century, a song of the scars and schisms of sectarianism, a sectarianism the British fostered in the century and a half after the defeat of the United Irishmen and that exploded finally into the Troubles, a conflict that would never have happened if Napper Tandy and Wolfe Tone had won the day with the men whose pikes had gathered by the river at the rising of the moon. And if they had prevailed, and if Muir had prevailed, and if all the songs with different words and the same melody had been sung – But I will say no more for now about songs with different words and the same melody. I will wait until the appropriate time. The rising of the moon.

And I wonder as I recount these things in my mind whether the convalescent Muir, the left side of his face covered with cloth dressings, recovering in some room in the dense and ancient seaport of Cádiz, would look in a mirror, or in the water of a washbasin, at the blood-soaked dressings falling in tatters from his face, and think of the flaking red paper of the arbutus trees.

16.

The moon not of song but of space had not risen, or if it had risen it was hidden away from me behind the trees of the park and the buildings around it. If my view of the moon were obstructed by the quartzite cubes it would be an instance of quote-unquote symbolism too ham-fisted to be believed. I chose not to believe it. Perhaps it was true regardless and I would have better luck observing the moon down by the river at the other end of town. Moon river, I thought, and did not think anything else about those two words together. The song meant nothing to me. An American song. But the river itself was worth lingering over. It was named of course after another one. In England. A repulsive gesture. Wellington. Boyne. French exits. Irish goodbyes. And this low and shallow river with its green-brown slow-moving water flowed not to the ocean but rather to an inland sea, one of those great lakes that could take up at times an entire horizon with their distant silver-grey flat lines, nothing in the distance to indicate that in fact these lakes were bounded on all sides by land, nothing but rumours only, rumours that from some very high building one could see Rochester, one could see Buffalo, and yet something in the way they sat on a landscape, their puny tides, the smallness too of their gulls, a certain near-invisible but legible ambience, told me that, no, this was not the sea, not really. More than anything, I think it was its flatness and stillness in comparison to the real sea. I wondered if it was still proper to call the place where this town's preposterous river ran into the inland freshwater sea an estuary. I could not imagine what it must look like, could not imagine it to share the special alchemy of a place where salt meets fresh.

I missed estuaries. I missed the dry, hollow stalks that stuck out at the edges of the water like baskets everybody had forgotten to weave, and I missed the sandpipers that landed on the stalks for a second, whipped their heads from side to side like jump-cuts, and flew away. I missed the mixed aromas of low tides and chlorophyll. In summer I saw minnows or bullheads of some kind in the shadier reaches, shadowy bodies vibrating like nervous systems encased in nothing. I saw, in the place that I most have in mind when I think of these places, a single large spreading tree – an oak, I think – alone in the centre of the yellow grass, the faded, antique yellow of grass at the end of summer. The yellow grass moving in the wind with the spontaneous heave-ho of gathered revolutionary masses under the oak's green jewels of leaves, masses striving in unison for the finest things in the world. The tree was so far from the established paths that it felt almost sinful to walk to it. I almost never did. I looked instead. But it was the winter estuary, and winter in this place in particular, that I loved and missed most. In the winter the grass on the sandspits and streambanks was a rich, almost auburn brown – not dead so much as spent from an excess of life, taxed to its limits by the summerwork of greening, sated by its celebratory late-summer orgy of yellow. Each stalk and twig and blade in the estuary as brittle as an ancient bone. This was the time of mists curdling in the hollows, in the wet between patches of woods, the carding of raw wool in the teeth of the trees. Phantom transpositions and mysteries, wind in the dead reeds. Wind humming in the neck of a brown broken beer bottle half-buried in mud, hissing between the mouldy slats of a vinyl chair a few feet away from it. Corrosion pervasive up and down the bent aluminum legs of the chair.

Before I had been speaking of estuaries in general and the winter estuary in particular I was speaking about the river in this town, which I had said was worth lingering over, and in fact all rivers are, the concept of a river itself is worth this; this vigil in the park has also been a pilgrimage and as I have travelled in this small space I have picked up fellow travellers, more and more images and figures to describe what has happened to me and what might happen, fibres and snail shells and blankets of cold grey beauty and seas of ice and explosions and falling and skins and flayed red books and chains and Hawerchuks and jig dolls and windows and houses and the moon and George Carlin safe at home and Muir's broken face and broken brains, and each has come and gone and so in addition to these fellow pilgrims in their onrush I make friends with onrush itself, with the river itself, the river in this town and rivers more generally, I had not yet said all I meant to about any of these things and will say more later, I can feel it, what exactly I cannot yet say, only that I can feel it coming, but before I do I want to say that the estuary in winter was a consolation to me in a season that in other ways had been a difficulty, and I want to tell you about those difficulties.

Yes, in the winter I had difficulties. When I moved back home after my one year on campus and started commuting to my undergraduate school I would wake up at seven-something to a purple world, a plum-skin world, more precisely the kind of plum skin that breaks out into a hive of almost-white at one end. This white hive was the sun at the corner of the morning under a cloud. They would be cold, these plums, I remember, from the fridge, as cold as the mornings doubling their colour out the window. I would have time to eat breakfast, or to shower, or to exercise by lifting the fifteen-pound weights I kept under my bed, or to read a book, or look at the internet, or write a couple of lines of poetry, or record my dream, but not more than one of these things before I had to take a bus, a train, and another bus to campus. I could never wake up any earlier. So I regained my consciousness each morning already staring down the fact of loss, missed opportunity, failure. It would be with me the whole day. Yes, the skin of ice was around me then, certainly. But not so tightly that I could not feel the loss, missed opportunity, failure. I felt it all the more if I had dreamed and failed to make a record of it. I knew I was losing my life in purple semi-darkness, giving away pieces of it in exchange for a credential, a credential I could barter for just enough money to keep alive and keep giving away pieces of my life. I saw no end. Did I have 'creative outlets'? I did, if curatorship is creation (and it is perhaps no accident that a theory of curatorship-as-creation was in vogue at that time). I had my YouTube playlists of languorous and echoing music – Sex Church, the Chills, the Jesus and Mary Chain, Dum Dum Girls – and I had my compilation videos, taken from films not made in North America, of long, still shots that looked like paintings. This was of course before YouTube had come down hard on copyright violations, but also before it was possible for your videos to make any money. So that when one of my echoing, languorous music playlists gathered seven thousand views I got nothing more than a sense of satisfaction from this, albeit a not inconsiderable sense of satisfaction. Ultimately because it made me feel less alone. I had a Tumblr too, a books, quotations, and photography Tumblr – aphorisms from Nin and Kafka, washed-out colour photos of Scandinavian marshlands in snowless coastal winter, grainy images of Russian dachas on the verge of falling apart (I had been a Russophile since high school and my earliest communist leanings). And finally, near the end of this time, I started to write poems on my own, aphoristic ones, little fragments never longer than eight, nine, or ten lines. It was all I could do, I thought. I was twenty and twenty-one and twenty-two and I felt completely weary of life. Could you blame me? I lived with two very old people in a two-bedroom apartment, an arrangement that even they were getting tired of. None of us had known that within a short time after my leaving for Ontario they would both become very sick.

I was 'weary of life' before my life had even begun, before even the wearying forces had compounded themselves for everybody. I was already weary on the late-aughts internet, the early-teens internet, the unprofessional internet, and I was weary off it. I wondered again about Onyx, my brother, my sister, my sibling in time, my counterpart, like the little wooden boy and girl who bow to each other on the hour before slipping back into the guts of the cuckoo. Had Onyx made playlists, collected photos of landscapes they would never visit? I wondered. The name itself, onykx22, and its retention along with a Hotmail address for all these years, suggested perhaps – perhaps only, it would be unwise to make generalizations – a certain continued lack of the particular kind of self-awareness that had come to me somewhere along the line, the fall into 'irony,' the pursuit of a perceived anhedonic and discerning 'cool.' Onyx had fallen perhaps down completely other aesthetic and cultural rabbit holes than I had; maybe they had loved anime and gaming, and memes and trolling, and gone on 4chan or Reddit instead of 2011-aesthetic Tumblr, and had debates about the finer points of libertarian minarchism and monarchism rather than Marxism-Leninism and anarcho-syndicalism. But I did not know, how could I know. Perhaps their retention or even whole-cloth recent invention of the Onyx address was itself an 'ironic' gesture. I do not know. This question and possibility bored me. For the 'irony' that was supposed to suffuse the more cutting-edge cultural forms of the late aughts and early teens, and was supposed to be in some kind of anguished tension with 'sincerity,' and furthermore was supposed to be in dialogue with slightly earlier forms from the nineties (the 'detachment' of the so-called Generation X) – this all was just a weaker version of the one half of the dialectic I mentioned earlier, the conviction that all was fake. Weaker, much weaker, because the 'irony' and the worries of that time were airless, placeless, contextless, without history. And so the equal and opposite reaction of the other half of this lesser dialectic, 'sincerity' and worries about sincerity, was likewise feeble, stunted, incapable of casting great light.

I thought of the books that had been such talismans for the clever young people of that time, and how so many of those books' attempts to capture real or imagined history – or people shaped by history, or life outside the elite Anglo-American bubble of comfort their authors were never brave enough to shed the epistemic certainties of – so often rang false, fearful. It was only the subaltern Others who were granted the 'authentic strength of their convictions,' in a way that the neurotic and ill-informed bien pensants of the comfortable imperial core so often do to those 'out there,' as though only the comfortable have the luxury of doubt, a gesture they no doubt consider generous even as it denies the people 'out there' full cognitive function, a complex inner life. In my experience people without education who felt the weight of history upon them were full of doubt, full of uncertainty, open certainly to irony, to cynicism, to bitter jokes. I mean of course my guardians and their neighbours in the housing co-operative whose lives were more or less similar to theirs. And I knew that their children – that I myself – if we were granted the good fortune by the apparatuses of the welfare state, the loan- and scholarship-granting bodies, to attend universities and become educated people, we too would often develop for a time a kind of irony as a mechanism of self-protection, when really what was happening to us was the seismic and terrifying movement of history sorting us from one platform to another in a great sifting machine, with all of the confusion and anguish that must come from this. A psychologist would observe these things and say, I don't know, dysthymia, generalized anxiety disorder, adverse childhood experiences, PTSD, all true enough in their way as names for the outward manifestations of these things, but without the full accounting that comes from history, the deeper 'why.' But on the surface and for a few brief moments the sine waves of the shocked and uncertain children of those without money or educa-tion, alone and at sea in the universities, might cross paths with the sine waves of the bored and disaffected children of genteel comfort, those who could freely and truly act like all of this meant nothing, and their irony and ours might appear to be the same, and because the children of money and comfort always, always set the agenda, we loan and schol-arship people were trained in our way to desire what they desired, to think good what they thought good. But our irony was not their irony, our disaffection not their disaffection, and I knew in time that I could not stay there, that the footfalls of the dialectic must always keep falling, *this, that, this, that,* and they would, and they are, but I was alone and in the university at a time when many young people were alone and quietly afraid and nothing had yet urged them en masse toward real union, the markets had crashed but as yet there was no prospect of real union, we were stuck for longer than we should have been on the feeble and airless imitation dialectic and not the real one, red books blowing in the wind, a convergence of currents joining in an estuary of lonely stupidity, dry grass blowing and clacking together and breaking, all the lonely molecules together in the massive sea but not touching, and the clever novels and songs and films of the time as conduits had seemed to celebrate this fact, and scorn it, and celebrate it, finally to crown it, the feeble Anglo-American dialectic of sincerity and irony, back and forth, equal and opposite, a stagnant sea, a dying sea. Anyone who had truly been paying attention would have known how short a lifespan this cut-off and isolated and inland sea of molecules together and not touching would have.

17.

In thinking of these things, those winters ten years ago, I had forgotten to think of other things, ones related to what I had begun to think of earlier and had not finished thinking of. I had forgotten the river. I had forgotten the problem of Onyx, whom I had also forgotten to refer to by their proper title, onykx22@hotmail.com, which was in any case a mouthful. I had forgotten the night. I had forgotten the frame. But in thinking about forgetting, and in remembering again the name of Onyx, I did also think again of an idea I had meant to express. For if Onyx had not, for whatever complex set of sociological, psychological, historical reasons, adopted the pose of self-conscious 'ironic' 'detached' 'cool,' I rightly or wrongly assumed they had instead lived earnestly within the opposite half of the weak dialectic, the world of the 'awesome,' the 'epic.' Each half as narrow and desiccated as the other. But the word *awesome* reminded me of yet another artifact of the first half of the decade I was now, along with all other people alive, seeing out the end of. I remembered the title of an article in a small online magazine of criticism, the kind that may or may not still exist now, a magazine full of dense articles by clever young people and junior professors. The title was something like 'The Awesome: The Metamodern Sublime,' and it had an image of a Transformer-like giant robot of the kind that Onyx might enjoy looking at and thinking about, if Onyx fit the profile I had perhaps completely inaccurately and unfairly imagined for them. It was everywhere for a very brief moment, this 'metamodern.' It represented perhaps the last time that the comfortable Anglo-American core, bathing in its ridiculous

Lethean wash of lonely sea at the 'end of history,' had attempted to push its head to the surface and look around and proclaim what kind of age it was living in, the last time it would do this before history, which had of course never ended at all, swam into the sea from its own rivers and its own estuaries and found it, and bit. And fittingly this 'metamodern' concept, this last concept from the time after and before history, had nearly and without meaning to hit upon something true, albeit framed all the wrong way. For this concept of the metamodern proclaimed that 'we' (who? 'subjects' they would say probably) 'now' 'vacillated' between habits of mind associated with the postmodern (irony, distance, freeplay) and habits of mind associated with the modern (self-expression, new movements, anguish). And when I encountered this idea of minds vacillating between sincerity and cynicism, earnestness and irony, the traumatized self and the complex bricolage self at play in borrowed finery, I recognized yet again just another version of the dialectic I have discussed already, less feeble this time, cleverer, but only by so much, and still blinkered by the comfort of the core, and emptied of history in the sense I understood it, for the more 'vacillations' in tone and commitment I had observed in nineteenth-century authors, eighteenth-, seventeenth-, sixteenth-, medieval, ancient, the more I recognized that the silly and comfortable people of the pampered core had accidentally rediscovered a thing that at all times and places all thinking people have done, they have moved from one foot to the other in the dialectical slow falling of a walk through the brain, they have weighed and measured, and the nature of this walking and weighing and measuring has been shaped by history – the monk has prayed fervently and made an obscene drawing in the margins of the illuminated manuscript, the lady in the elegant dress at the gathering has let a statement hang in the air like a slow-spinning sword of Damocles, each turn of the blade and the sword handle revealing the glittering phrase in further and yet further lights of various meaning, she has done it in Babylon, Luxor, Ur of the Chaldees, she has done it in the cities of the Yucatán in the shadow of the observatories and the cities of the Horn of Africa with triangular sails of dhows on the turquoise sea behind her as numberless as gulls. Yes, any proposition in a social world opened the way within the mind considering it for the other dialectical foot to fall, for the new synthesis, and if the mind considering had bracketed off such footfalls because the buzzing pain of cognitive dissonance was too great, then the footfalls would come at the base of the wall, on the side of safety, they would come regardless, they could not be avoided. Zeno's arrow. Even Onyx, who in my mind I had imagined as my cultural opposite, someone who would see how I dressed and the things I liked during the difficult winter years and say 'hipster,' someone living in the cheerful unselfconscious world of Redditors excited about technology, who 'fucking loved science,' even Onyx too was, whether they wanted to or not, stepping, stepping, stepping, slowly falling, weighing and measuring, they too had doubts, they too had at times moments of awareness practically outside their own body. The pampered thinkers of the core had, in their rush to codify and name their own age, their advertiser's lust for the new, the definitive break, the one weird tip, had forgotten the continuities of things, the long genealogies, the markings of history. They had forgotten so much. And it seemed to me that the prevailing condition of life in our time was forgetting, probably to some degree or another a prevailing condition of life before and elsewhere, but not the same way, not so much *a* prevailing condition as *the* prevailing one.

How many times, being in the world in this way, had I forgotten what I had been doing and begun again – perhaps differently than I had begun before, or perhaps in exactly the same ways, or perhaps in ways that bore degrees of similarity to the beginnings of before, and continued onward likewise either differently, or in the same ways, or both, without knowing, but beginning again and continuing onward as if through a desert, a rain shower, the golden light of sunset after a rain shower, the navy or smoke-obsidian velvet of night after sunset, the charcoal-dark silhouette of the unilluminated portion of a moon otherwise crescent just visible against it, but perhaps not even in that order, and with no knowledge of the shades and gradations and connective tissues that join these things in a normal world, make them one long continuous river of everything unfolding, no knowledge of that, so that instead of a river I knew strange discrete rooms of rivers, rooms of flowing water, infinity pools, rooms upon rooms of infinity pools that I entered and experienced and forgot again, forms upon forms of beginning and continuing, forgetting and beginning in place of anything like an end?

I felt like a slot machine. The levers pulled and the wheels turned and the rebus of cherries and lemons and coins was each time remade. I began again in forgetfulness and with the feeling of the world and forms around me as new. No, not new. Not the new in its shock or exhilaration, and the world and forms did not imprint themselves upon my brain with the special seal of the new. Rather, old forms assembled in new ways, or rather, old forms assembled in old ways that in my forgetfulness I deemed new, but only the new of the old, not the truly new. I thought of the cherry blossoms back home. Many times you could walk down whole streets planted with nothing other than cherry trees – white blossoms, or pink blossoms, or both, pink or white clouds reaching up to the telephone wires hanging slack over the streets or crowding over the roofs. To walk these streets in the weeks of mid-March was to walk through a perfect dream image of Japan, a dream Japan, transposed onto another place as if one colour transparency were laid upon another. But this world was no sooner begun than I would go back inside, think about other things, sleep, wake up, and go out again into another world completely different and just begun, the new world of blossoms blowing from the trees in a constant pink-white snow falling almost horizontal on the wind, and this was as much a revelation to me in the street that I forgot the day before, the dream image of perfect Japan, and saw instead the surreal and melancholy pink-white snow only, as if it were almost the first thing I had seen in my life. I would go inside again and read and think. I would drink tea or beer. Sunset would come later than before and I would turn my light on later than before. I would sleep and forget. Whole days might go by in forgetting to think about cherry trees or perhaps only one day. When I next walked on the street I would see a world that in its newness obliterated all memory of the world before. Or perhaps I have it the wrong way round. Perhaps forgetfulness came first. Already even as I write about forgetfulness I forget. When I began, did I mean to say one thing, or the other? Perhaps I meant to say a version of both. But the world I saw, in any case, felt new, and I forgot the world before. This world was in its own way a great, an incredible, revelation. Now the petals were mostly on the ground, on the tops of mailboxes, on the roofs of cars. Because of my forgetfulness I could not say that the previous world of the pink-white snow had caused this new world of petals on the ground. I had forgotten that world. And the world of the transparency of the dream Japan was gone as well, the transparency itself off the page and put away in a drawer, leaving nothing of itself behind. I bathed in the waters of today's world only. The petals lined the sidewalks like an opulent votive carpet in a festival; every car was a wedding car. This too was a new and incredible world. And yet the creep of some new doubt or lack of ease arose in me the more I walked down streets where some great ceremony appeared to have happened without me. I was late, I was lost, I was missing. At the edges of the carpets of the petals I saw the tea-brown rot that all would come to. I remembered that I had forgotten, that I had done so again and again. And I remembered – as though the transparency, thought missing, turned up again in the bottom of a seldom-opened drawer – the dream Japan, and I knew that in the Japan that was not the dream of a distant and ignorant amnesiac such as myself, the cherry blossom was the object of centuries of poetry, of festival, of painting, and that the theme of so much of this reflection on the cherry blossom had been loss, the ephemeral, the incredible and self-destroying rupture that will change the world and then erase itself, and that I had begun again in forgetting.

I had forgotten again and again in the evenings when I lay on my bed or the small couch I had found at the Saint Vincent de Paul shop and read books with rhythmic prose, books I felt a kinship with and wanted to read, books of the interior world, the evening world, the world of knowing from the lick of the sun on the skin or the gold-green of the needles on the trees that summer was coming, a change in the world that for me had meant always a moment – a moment only – of every thought and feeling slowly filling up and opening, spreading, touching almost all that I wanted to, again like a flower, filling and colouring very nearly to that brim of me, that point in me, that state in which I truly felt I could do and feel and say all that winter and darkness had kept from me, a fullness as in music, but as every note, even the note that sustains for minutes and minutes in the vibrating air of an empty concert hall, must die, and every flower fall, and every full thing come to its point of collapse, so too must the feeling of a night in May as I listened to Hiroshi Yoshimura's 'Wet Land' and a hummingbird phase-shifted in and out of my vision, its movements the same as a cursor on a screen, moving so imperceptibly quickly from one point to another, resting there for a moment like a pause in a sentence, and shifting again. Books of that feeling. But on the evenings when I chased that feeling through the pages of a rhythmic book at the end of a day that had worn at me, I would start, without wanting it, to sleep. I would read the sentence again. Perhaps I would manage to read another sentence after. Perhaps another. And I would sleep. And I would wake up. And the line I had read last would look like a stranger to whom I knew I nevertheless owed some special obligation, as if from another life. And I would read it, and sleep. And now I would dream, a very compressed dream, fullness in a small space like an immensity written in tiny text on a scrap of paper. Like Robert Walser's Pencil Zone. A full story, a completely realized landscape. But I would wake up immediately and forget. I would hold a vapour of a picture of a souvenir from my dream – a comb made from tortoiseshell, a room with no windows in green-painted steel, the mouth of a whale in the deep sea – and I would forget. I would look again at strange lines, read and reread and sleep and wake up. A time would come when I would forget to try to read, would merely sleep and dream and wake up and repeat, perhaps remembering for a second I was holding a book before sleeping again. And then I would forget to wake up for almost forty minutes, and when I woke up it would be dark and my mouth would be dry and I would have forgotten where I was and who I was. So that even in moments of calm and repose with my rhythmic kindred books, forgetfulness would find me again and always, I was a marked man for forgetfulness, a bounty, a small fish with no school in the deep sea.

Thinking about forgetting I forgot the park, I forgot the frame. I forgot I had been wearing white pants and sitting on the grass. I forgot the house I rented with its one storey and four rooms. I forgot it was night. The present and its sensations and imperatives slid from me like snowmelt without a sound. I was in reverie, I was inside, I was on the invisible brass causeway in the darkness between the park and wherever it is I am now. They had always existed at the same time, the parallel worlds. To bridge them in the darkness of the space between I had to forget so much. The invisible brass causeway was a structure actuated by forgetfulness, dreamed from a blueprint of forgetfulness that burned away after use with a cold flame like creosote, a forgetting of a special kind. Not the forgetting of sleep or the forgetting of the days of the blossom, the forgetting that came to me from outside and hunted me. A new forgetting I had to learn inside, to remember how to do, forgetting all that plagued me from the inner sea and the land outside, forgetting the skin of ice and my broken brain, forgetting like the bird who flies because it has forgotten how not to. I had to forget how not to be alive. It was one of the hardest things I had ever done. I did not know how long I would manage to do it, to keep the invisible bridge of brass trembling between worlds in the darkness. But I knew that as long as I felt the sliding in place of one word after another in inevitability, sliding as if in a wooden game, I would be walking the bridge and not falling, forgetting and mothering into being the commerce of two worlds. I knew now one thing I could say without doubts – I was not only thinking wherever it is I am now, and not quite speaking, but writing. I was feeling the slide into place of word after wooden word. I do not say 'wooden' simply to reintroduce my metaphor. I knew they were wooden words, that I spoke the language of a man made of wood with a stick out his back, bucking and kicking on a flexible board while a folklorist sang, badly. I wrote in the language of a wooden man bucking and kicking to the tune of the materialist determinants of history. Fennario. The rodeo. Me being strictly neutral. The rising of the moon. The captain's name was Ned and he died for a maid. Someday I would even forget language itself, would be a wordless manikin, would be, in effect, a mutilated part of a tree. I did not remember being a living tree. It was not that I had forgotten. I simply did not remember. I could hardly begin to imagine what it had felt like. I thought it would feel like drawing a circle. Slowly. Many thousands of autonomous auxiliary processes no more known to me than my endocrine system as a man (so I say) is known to me, or the mites in my eyebrows, but all nevertheless true and working, all coming together so that I in my peace and my silence could draw another circle over the span of a year. Perhaps as far as the autonomous processes were concerned my drawing a circle was merely a banal mathematical inevitability, an eccentric by-product of the mighty and important things they did. Perhaps. But all of this could be wrong. I did not remember. I was no longer a tree but a wooden man. I say man. Force of habit. The truth is I really don't care. A wooden man with an endocrine system and no memory of being a tree. But a longing, so strange, for that time. I could have been water or wind or a stone before that. In fact I was sure of it. I felt more like water or wind or a stone or a tree than a wooden man. And yet here I was. The stick out my back was held tight in the folklorist's sweaty hand. And in thinking of this I had forgotten to forget. I fell through the absence that had once been an invisible bridge of brass.

18.

Having forgotten to forget and having returned now somehow to the steadily increasing darkness of the park and its yet-unrisen or perhaps risen but obscured moon, which if unrisen was also necessarily not present on the river in town but if risen might be, anyway having come back here I remembered that in a quiet way and in addition to whatever else I had been thinking of this last while I kept returning to the image or memory of rivers, the remembered rivers and estuaries I had seen before in my life and the actual river running at this moment through the town, and also more abstractly the image of the river or the estuary as an image of thinking, rooms of rivers I had said, or equally abstractly the image of the river as the causeway of history, history swimming into the lonely sea from its own estuaries and its own rivers I had said, and the river as the pilgrim of pilgrims, the onrush pilgrim, and I remembered as well that I said I would say more about rivers, what exactly I could not say, only that I had felt it coming, and now I supposed that whatever was coming was here and I was saying it, and that because I had no better idea I would start with the river that was closest to the location of my body at the time. The river was elsewhere in the town and I could not see it. I could not see its banks, which had something of an artifice about them here in the centre of town, shored up as they were by reinforcing walls of concrete slabs. Nor could I hear its flow under the bridge or along the banks, but I could not hear this even if I beat a path through the birch trees and bushes down by the banks and closed my eyes and focused only on the sound – and as a matter of fact I had done this, in the past, alone or with friends, friends gone now, we had come to the water on those long summer days in the life of a graduate student in a small town, days when no one has to teach and no one wants to write and it is too early to start drinking, summer middays where we turned into overgrown suburban children, all of us, even the strangest and most self-serious and most grave, even me, though I was only a little those things, well, no, I was very strange, but in some respects and in comparison to some others I was only a little self-serious, only a little grave, anyway together on those days we would go down to the water, certainly not to swim or even get wet, we knew better, we assumed we were downstream from factories, from sewage plants, from god knows what else, and the waters of this river so rarely ran clear, only in the shallows closest to the banks could we see down to the bottom, and here with my stumbling aimless friends I would close my eyes and try to hear the flow of the river and I would not hear it, I would hear only the crack of dry grasses and reeds as my friends walked around, the water moved too slowly to be heard, too slowly and without division or obstruction, it slipped along without a sound. It was quieter therefore than many smaller streams I had known, not only the little crystal tether in the ditch with its burlap sacks of concrete, by the bus stop, you remember, the stream beneath the branch on which a red-winged blackbird sang, I cannot remember if I said anything about the sound of the stream itself, I doubt I did, but it had a sound just as the bird did, and like the bird it was a trilling sound, the crystal tether broke against the little stones at the bottom of the ditch, broke and remade and broke again, a magic tether of living crystal on the stones, anyway not only this stream but others I had heard, many loud and little ones in the parks of my childhood, wilder and more unkempt in the main than this manicured old-style park with its batwing gates, parks where among the nettles and the stones and the twisted roots a brook might run and smash against the rocks and be just deep enough in places for me to set toy boats at play, and watch the boats and guide them and think the hollow in the stream was the whole world and be carried along by it without moving. I relate these things and a phrase comes to mind, a phrase I have not yet used although perhaps you would expect me to, but I had not yet squared away in my mind my feelings about this phrase and have not yet even here wherever it is I am now, although at this time I may make an attempt, with no thought of its success or failure, anyway the phrase I am thinking of is 'stream of consciousness,' you have probably heard of it, you have probably heard it applied to books of a certain style or styles. What styles? I no longer know. I know that near the end of high school I began to shape an idea of myself as an 'artistic' person, without yet knowing how or in what ways, as did many of my friends from the group of friends I mentioned previously, and that during this time I sought out books that had been described using this term 'stream of consciousness,' I do not know why beyond the obvious fact that I had come to be aware of myself as a mind engaged in the act of thinking and I could not 'get over it,' it was too frightening to ignore or too much of a problem to put away, and I suppose that even now I have been unable to ignore it or put it away, but at the time and with the limited contents of the high school library and my unenlightening sojourns through the internet or the hearsay passed on to us in our group by knowing older brothers and sisters who liked to read, by twenty-one-year-old delivery drivers at the restaurants where we washed dishes, the books I was able to find with this term 'stream of consciousness' applied to them were the books of the American stoner canon, I mean William S. Burroughs and Hunter S. Thompson and Jack Kerouac, and I read all of *Naked Lunch* but it felt like a punishment, and I read *Hell's Angels* and *Fear and Loathing in Las Vegas* and *Fear and Loathing on the Campaign Trail '72* and I thought they were pretty good but I left unsatisfied, funnily enough I think I was not old enough to get much out of them despite their popularity among the young, and I could not get more than twelve pages into *On the Road*, I could not stand it, and anyway each of these three authors had very little to do with one another, I thought, in terms of style, and especially in terms of their representation of consciousness as a stream, and so I tended afterward to think the term was of no use to me as I looked here and there for books that would give me strength as I faced the fact too frightening to ignore and too much of a problem to put away, I mean the fact that I was a mind thinking. In one case only the term 'stream of consciousness' directed me, like a mislabelled sign, toward something I had hoped to find, namely the books of Virginia Woolf – though it is ironic that she was the first great novelist I found in my time of self-tutelage, for she is another one like Keats, one who has haunted me and sustained me and looked at people like me with an enemy's eyes. 'An illiterate, underbred book it seems to me: the book of a self-taught working man, & we all know how distressing they are, how egotistic, insistent, raw, striking, & ultimately nauseating,' she wrote in her diary while reading *Ulysses*, and for all my later baubles of education, even my master's degree, I too am a self-taught working man – everything that has been dearest to me has been won by a long and blundering process without knowing the direction or the rules, rules that those who are not self-taught acquire almost in utero and that save them years and years of their lives. We self-taught are at the mercy of the *Encyclopedia Britannica*s, the *National Geographic*s, the *Reader's Digest*s, so that often the ones we meet first and who sustain us are the ones who would have hated us one way or another. And so I found Keats before John Clare, I found Woolf before Joyce, and on my first encounters with Joyce I was standoffish, I misread the situation, I did not immediately see why he was the way he was, even though he grew up pauperized by his father's addictions and living under the loathsome British flag and so was in some sense kin to me. We self-taught so often misread the situation or, worse, we begin to see with our enemies' eyes. So that while it was ironic I found Woolf first it was also practically inevitable. When I was a boy one of my prized possessions was an illustrated history of the world – all of it, all the history or so I thought, and more or less from the beginning. I was at its mercy. On a page about the interwar years was a small colour illustration, based on what had surely been a black-and-white photograph, of a woman named Virginia

Woolf. The caption indicated that she was a 'literary Modernist' whose novels exhibited a 'stream of consciousness style.' I had read this history book so many times as a child that, later, coming on the heels of my efforts to read *Naked Lunch*, Hunter S. Thompson, and *On the Road*, nearly ready to give up on the 'stream of consciousness' altogether, as I was browsing the carousels at the front lounge area of another library, not the one at school but the small local public library this time, I found *The Virginia Woolf Reader* and remembered vaguely that she was also associated somehow with the 'stream of consciousness.' I brought the book home and read it, and saw that she was doing something else, something more and better that at the time I did not have words for. One story in particular affected me more than anything else. It was called 'The Mark on the Wall.' In it the narrator notices a spot on the wall of the room she is in and wonders what it might be, but in the course of her wondering she begins to think about almost everything but the mark, it falls to the cognitive wayside in a tumult of asides, digressions, clarifications, distractions, exclamations, until at last an unnamed male figure curses the war ravaging the world at the time of writing (the so-called Great one) and remarks that, all the same, he doesn't see why there should be a snail on the wall. Yes, the narrator assures us at last, it was a snail. It struck me at the time and it strikes me now. Because in one sense, yes, of course, it hardly matters what the mark on the wall really was, it was merely an engine for the story's true contents, its asides, digressions, clarifications, distractions, excla-mations. But in another sense, no, it is incredibly strange for a snail to be inside a house and climbing up a wall, no matter how damp or cold it might be, how dire the shortages of the damned war. She could have made it a fly or an ant or a beetle. As she did so famously in 'The Death of a Moth' she could have made it a moth. But she made it a snail. As I related to you earlier John Keats's theory of the snail-shell wisdom, and as I described to you earlier the actual snail that came out of the wet grass and scaled like a priest the steps of the frame like a ziggurat, it had not escaped me that I was seeing and thinking about the same creature that had climbed up the wall and initiated the tumult of asides, digressions, clarifications, distractions, exclamations in Woolf's story. Of course it did not escape me. I have been thinking about it the whole time and was merely waiting for the right moment to tell you, and I am telling you now. It was a snail. But the tumult I described, the digressions and all the rest – was it right to call it a stream? I did not think so, or at least not a single stream, and certainly not a quiet and unobstructed river like the one that flowed through the town that I lived in. If I were forced to use the metaphor of moving water to describe the movement of ideas in the story of the mark on the wall I would say it was a whole stream system, my 'rooms of rivers' earlier came close but now I think I can do better and say it was an entire water cycle, a water table, aquifers, groundwater, glaciers, all of it, the splitting and breaking away of little white lines of foam and froth as one might see in a waterfall tumbling over shelf after shelf of sharp rocks, I said earlier that a weeping willow looked like a waterfall in a classical Chinese landscape painting and I will say now that the waterfall in my mind looks like a weeping willow, I have brought the whole gang back together, anyway the movement of thought was not a single stream and the water could be frozen or gas or locked underground or moving en masse like a sea, all seemed possible both in this story by Virginia Woolf and in everything else she had done – *The Waves!* It is no accident she called it *The Waves* – and indeed in thought itself as it really was, or mine anyway and I presume yours, though I may be wrong. After all my brain is broken, and after all I am a self-taught working man, and though I too have my asides, digressions, clarifications, distractions, exclamations learned from Woolf, mine are in some sense not hers, in the final analysis I must be, am, can only be distressing, egotistic, insistent, raw, striking, and ultimately nauseating, and I am not sorry. But if consciousness – on the page if not in the mind, though perhaps also in the mind – is more than stream, is stream system and water cycle, then why had this phrase 'stream of consciousness' taken hold in the first place? Later, long after I read the story about the snail, I would learn that the term 'stream of consciousness' had originated not in literary criticism at all, but rather in the philosophy of mind. There is an 1890 usage by William James that probably introduced it to the literary people but even he was not the first. The oldest printed attestation I know of comes from an American doctor named Daniel Oliver in 1840, but he is not the most interesting of the early users. That honour goes to one Alexander Bain, who used it fifteen years later in a book called *The Senses and the Intellect*. Now, even before I knew anything else about this man I had a strong suspicion I would be dealing with one of my countrymen. So many of them were called Alexander in the nineteenth century. And Bain? Surely an anglicization of McBain, a name common enough in Scotland including as a clan in the vicinity of Inverness whose members fought in both the 1715 and 1745 Jacobite risings on the losing side. And yes, I was right, and in fact more right than I expected, I was right in an almost eerie way. But first let me tell you what he said, in one of the earliest written attestations of the phrase 'stream of consciousness':

> The concurrence of sensations in one common stream of consciousness (on the same cerebral highway) enables those of different senses to be associated as readily as the sensations of the same sense.

It is clear he is not using the term with reference to literature or even strictly to thought. He speaks of 'sensations.' I suppose sensations come in a stream. As a matter of fact I do not find sensations all on their own very interesting. I find them interesting when linked to thoughts, or emotions, or memories. What this says about me I cannot guess. Perhaps those speaking of streams of consciousness have always just meant sensation, perception, only, not thought, and so perhaps I am making a mistake to conflate them as I have done all this time, and as I have conflated thinking and writing, and writing and speaking. But to me these things have hardly ever seemed separate. One other thing I wanted to say. Bain said 'the cerebral highway.' I too in attempting to think of the function of my brain before it was broken – if it was broken, and if there was a before – had used the image of the highway or the road, I cannot remember which, and specifically the yellow lines down the middle, and then and then, and I had said it was the brain of the data banks, the twentieth-century computer brain, and before it was the nineteenth-century brain of fibres as imagined by people living through the dominance of industrialized textile production, and that the twentieth-century data-bank brain inhered in the industrialized textile production, Monsieur Jacquard and his loom, Ada Lovelace and her algorithm, and this Alexander Bain I was astonished to learn was inseparable from these matters also, all of them, every matter. Alexander Bain, like Monsieur Jacquard, was the son of a weaver. Like those who Woolf found distressing, egotistic, insistent, raw, striking, and ultimately nauseating, he was a self-taught working man. At the age of eleven he left school to become a weaver himself, perhaps not imagining the heights to which he would ascend in later life as a philosopher of the mind, although perhaps imagining them, for it seems that in addition to working as a weaver he continued his education through two free institutions available to working people in his city: the Mechanics' Institutes and the Aberdeen Public Library. Oh yes, I meant to say. Alexander Bain was born in Aberdeen. Of course he was. And can you guess when he was born? Approximately? Perhaps you can but anyway I will tell you. He was born on June 11, 1818. A day of some significance. Because eleven days after this eleventh day of June, 1818, on the twenty-second, John Keats and Charles Brown would set out from London on their trip to Scotland – stopping first in Liverpool to say goodbye, forever in fact, to George and Georgiana, of whom I said before I had something to say but which I will continue to defer – and continuing afterward to Ireland and then Scotland, as I have said already. This day June 11 of significance also because it is today – or rather it was today, it was the 'today' it was on the day I went to the park with the frame. I had not said that yet. I had said that it was summer but not that it was the eleventh of June. But it was, so that this day in the park was the 201st birthday of one of the first people to write the words 'stream of consciousness.' Perhaps it meant nothing. I said already that I do not think my consciousness is a stream. But perhaps what I think is immaterial and I am being told, incessantly, something important in a language I do not understand. And perhaps the span of my own life and its pattern on the calendars of my years will likewise spell an illegible phrase for someone else, someone later, after whenever it is now.

19.

My digressions had taken me far from where I started. The fingers of white foam breaking on the rocks had spread like a fractal out of control, so that I had nearly forgotten the place I had meant to end up when I began to describe the river not visible to me here but flowing nevertheless elsewhere in the town. I had meant to say something more of that river itself. I said already that it had a preposterous and offensive name, the name of a river in England, just as this town had the name of an English town and even the town's neighbourhoods had names, often, that corresponded to the names of their originals in England. It was absurd. And in fact the river had another name in addition to its preposterous and offensive one, a name that I was sure would outlast the name given to the river by the settlers and would in time return to its proper place. This was the name of Deshkan Ziibi, which had been given to the river by the Ojibwe people. The name means 'antlered or horned river' and in viewing this river from a high vantage point one may see a series of bends like the series of prongs on a set of antlers. How could the absurd and preposterous name of another river thousands of miles away in what had once been the imperial capital, the capital of the most sodden and miserable empire of all time, bear even a fraction of that descriptive power over this particular river in this particular place? It seemed to me an emblem of all things wrong in the world that the one name had supplanted the other. And after all and in its own way the name of the original river bearing this name thousands of miles away, 'Thames,' had likewise been the record of an empire arriving and attempting to erase and rename the landscape, only in this instance failing or at least not completely succeeding. For although the name of the city in England through which this river ran was a Latin name, a Roman name, albeit based perhaps on a name used by the people who had been there before – the city itself was founded by the Romans, you understand, but even the places that are not yet cities have names – the name of the river that ran through the city was not Latin. In fact it is one of the few words we have left from the language of the Celtic Britons who lived in what is now called England, though not yet called that because the arrival of the Angles was yet to happen. We know from the cognates in the surviving Brittonic language of Welsh, as well as in the languages that share the same proto-Indo-European mother – Russian, Lithuanian, proto-Slavic, Sanskrit – that the original name of this river through the Roman-founded city, the river Tamesas, most likely meant 'darkness.' Was it a dark river? Is it now? Conrad's Marlowe on the yacht with his friends on that river reminds them that this too had once been one of the 'dark places of the earth.' He meant it in the context of empire, of Caesar, of the desire of the empire to frighten itself with metaphysical sojourns in fact quite ridiculous, though it is difficult to say if Conrad himself truly knew they were ridiculous or if a part of him, even a greater part of him, believed the darkness was a real darkness and not a made-up darkness. Certainly it seemed to me that the Celtic Britons most likely called it a dark river with reference to the colour of the water only – rivers all over the world are so named for that reason in a hundred languages, and the land on which the Celtic Britons lived had perils that must be heeded and dangers and fears, but I doubt they meant 'dark river' in the sinister sense implied by Conrad, or if they did mean it in a sinister sense it was not his sinister sense. But at any rate the name of this river, this last live ember of an extinguished language, persisted through the coming of the Romans, the Angles, the Saxons, the Normans, the Danes, persisted even through the warp of new spellings and pronun-ciations, the inexorable forgetting of the original meaning. This had happened to many rivers in the world, and especially to those on the continent upon which my body was located at the time I sat in the park.

How many people had forgotten or never known that the Mississippi, like the Deshkan Ziibi running through this town, had been named so by the Ojibwe, and that the spelling and pronunciation appearing now on most maps warped and Europeanized the Ojibwe pronunciation, Misi-ziibi, and that this name meant 'Great River'? Or that 'Yukon' was a Europeanization of the Gwich'in name Yųg Han, 'White Water River,' and that this is just one of many names given it by Indigenous peoples, it is Kuigpak, 'Big River,' to the Yup'ik, Kuukpak, 'Big River' also, to the Inupiaq, and it has yet other names, phonetically somewhat similar to the Gwich'in, for the Deg Xinag, Holikachuk, Koyukon, Hän, and Southern Tutchone peoples. So that this Tamesas, last remnant of the language of the Celtic Britons of England, was superimposed over the Deshkan Ziibi in a way that strikes me as an especially bitter irony, the empire of the hybrid Anglo-Saxon and Norman language and culture taking a word for a dark river from the lost Brittonic language, a name warped in time as the Europeans warped Misi-ziibi, warped Yųg Han, and placing or rather misplacing it so brutally as they had done everywhere. But in saying this and observing these things I say and observe also that the comparison goes only so far. The genetic studies of the British Isles tell us that the people speaking this hybrid Anglo-Saxon and Norman language of English were nevertheless still largely the descendants of the people who had named the dark-watered river Tamesas, there had been no cataclysmic destruction of the people and replacement with new ones despite the arrival of Romans, of Angles, of Saxons, of Normans, of Danes, the people there already had received from these conquerors new languages, new cultures, new political orders and hierarchies, but their conquerors had not eliminated them from the earth. Meaning that those who attempted to diminish the cataclysm of these American continents by pointing to the waves of historical conquest in ancient or medieval Europe were drawing a most false equivalence, they were making a most inapt comparison of the unlike. What happened in the Americas – the genocide of peoples and their replacement by settlers – was something unprecedented and new in its terrible scale. Some climate scientists even suggest that the Little Ice Age – the cool period after the Medieval Warm Period but before our own, perhaps final, climatological age – was the result of the killing of millions of human beings on the American continents by the Europeans. And so these rivers with their names, whether the names given by Indigenous peoples and warped in European tongues or the names of places or people from Europe, names bearing their own record of movement and conquest but not on the same scale, not like this, these rivers flowed from the springs and the mountaintops and out into the lakes or the estuaries at the borders of the seas like so many open veins, the veins of the two continents, veins that early on had been the entryways of the European disease, Hudson on the 'Hudson,' Fraser on the 'Fraser,' Mackenzie on the 'Mackenzie,' Francisco de Orellana on the 'Amazon,' Coronado on the 'Rio Grande,' these conduits each carrying their own poison capsules in the form of caravels, of barques, of North West Company canoes. I call them open veins and in doing so I am thinking of the name of a book in Spanish, *Las Venas Abiertas de America Latina, The Open Veins of Latin America*, a book by the Uruguayan leftist Eduardo Galeano, full name Eduardo Germán María Hughes Galeano, an interesting name, since we are speaking already of names, since we have in fact been speaking of names the whole time in the park just as we have been speaking of frames, skins, explosions, brains, fibres, rivers, all the pilgrims, the onrush of pilgrims, my pilgrims or rather my images and figures or if you like my metaphors or if you like my names, for metaphors are a kind of radical naming, 'the figure of transport' as sixteenth-century rhetoric books called it, meaning that metaphors take something and put it somewhere else, and I say the same is true for names. This was what all the warped or usurping names of these rivers were doing, with a special brutality, they were taking something and trying to put it somewhere else as a weapon of war, and this is not true of every name but any name could so be usurped or so be warped or so be used. And this author Galeano's full name too bears a record of transport, for one of these names is not like the others – so much so that when he used it as his pseudonym when writing for a socialist magazine as a young man he chose to render it phonetically for Spanish ears as 'Gius.' He was 'Hughes' because he had a Welsh great-grandfather, and in fact many Welsh people immigrated to South America in the nineteenth century, and in particular to Patagonia, where the hope was that they could preserve the language that at the time their children were punished for speaking in school, including by means of a humiliating necklace called a 'Welsh Not' – but in hoping to preserve their language they were coming to settle in a place where the Argentinian army had wrought a genocide of the Mapuche with the most expensive weaponry of the nineteenth century, where farther south in Tierra del Fuego the ranchers had paid bounty money to anyone who could prove they had killed people of the Selk'nam, so that again we see in these things differences of incredible degree and kind, when the Europeans came to these continents they had stopped at nothing, no barbarity was beyond them, and to see this and say it had become the mission of Eduardo Germán María Hughes Galeano, who saw the place in which he lived as a body with open veins, the image I myself had used in thinking of the rivers with warped or usurping names.

I said I would say more about the River Thames itself but instead I spoke of its name and of the names of other rivers and of naming itself, and this has been my curse or my vocation, whichever, to fall into the spirals of the names and the metaphors, the onrush of pilgrims, and not to speak of the things themselves, so that before, at the start, when I was worried about my obscurities of beauty concealing the truth I was part right, even if I felt I had made peace with beauty later as a true thing in the world, because I see my problem is beyond just beauty now, it is about true things obscuring other true things, the obscurity is true as the beauty is, they are true things we can say obscuring the true things we cannot say, and to trace the process of obscurity upon obscurity is to trace true history, but there is a special irony to my naming fixation because I have not even told you my own full name and so in some sense have not even allowed you to guess at what I cannot tell you even if I wanted to – and that is a whole world – by talking to you about my full name instead. I have been hiding even the hiding that is a name and thus hiding a part of history, and so at last I will pare back one layer of hiding and tell you that my full name is Hugh Dalgarno, and that as I was telling you about Hughes Galeano it was becoming harder not to say it, because from sheer kinship of phonology it kept coming to mind. I am aware my surname is unusual. Depending on the background and experiences of the people I meet, it has been variously mistaken for Italian, Spanish, Portuguese, or even Sephardic. I do not blame them. It ends in a vowel. At the age of seven or eight the aforementioned Todd Longo attempted to recruit me into his 'Mafia Club,' along with four or five genuinely Italian boys and a Filipino boy named Chris Sotto. Chris and I were extremely confused but by the end of the school year had nearly convinced ourselves we were Italian. The activities of the Mafia Club were restricted to looking at Pokémon cards and fashioning 'guns' out of wood. But the truth is that my name, Dalgarno, is found almost uniquely in the northeast of Scotland and the city of Aberdeen in particular. It is the transmutation through English, or rather Scots, of a Gaelic place name that appears to have meant either 'garden land' or 'cultivated place.' You may be further interested to know that my aunt and uncle had a different surname than me, which made everything strange, for I bore the surname of my father, a man who my maternal great-aunt and great-uncle said had broken their hearts, and yet they never changed it, almost as if to do so would disturb a perfectly intact tomb protected by a curse, and so I proceeded in absurdity as Hugh Dalgarno, legal ward of Jimmy and Elsie MacPherson, and did not know what to say about it when people asked. Having things we cannot say or can only with difficulty say is general to all humanity but in my case is so often related to these two people and myself and our history together. 'Elsie,' by the way, was not short for anything. It was the name on her birth certificate. 'Jimmy' was short for 'James.' 'MacPherson' is Gaelic and means 'son of the parson.' It has not escaped me that 'James Macpherson' was the name of the poet from the Gàidhealtachd in the eighteenth century who in swindling the Anglophones as his small measure of revenge for what they had done to his language chose to flatter their sensibilities with hazy and mystical Ossian poems of defeat. Nor has it escaped me that in the seventeenth century a famous outlaw called Jamie or James MacPherson was hanged on the gallows tree in the Aberdeenshire burg of Banff for the crime of 'being an Egyptian,' meaning a Traveller, and that there was a song purportedly written in part by this man, or by someone recording his last words, in which he looks out at the crowd that has come to watch him die and he breaks his beloved fiddle so that no one else may play it when he is gone, and in a verse he certainly could not have written himself it is disclosed that a messenger is coming over the bridge with a reprieve, but the local worthies, on seeing this messenger, play one of their usual tricks, they put the clock ahead by fifteen minutes to the time MacPherson's sentence is to be carried out, and they carry it out, and in effect they murder him with time. The name of this song is 'MacPherson's Rant.' I am sure these things had not escaped my uncle's parents, who while not long in the schools had nevertheless memorized by heart all the poems and songs of the rural places their families had come from. If there is something at all to nominative determinism, to destiny as inscribed in a person's name, there must be something to this, but for now it falls among the things I cannot say. Only one thing about nominative determinism I can say now, which is that I have had a long-standing fascination with the languages my name was erroneously considered to be the product of, and especially with Spanish, all the more so when I became a leftist and learned the revolutionary histories of both Spain and Latin America. It is another way to dream a parallel life, as I have discussed before, which is why it is easier to say. And it relates to something Keats said that annoyed me. Keats went to Scotland partly as a literary pilgrimage to sites associated with Robert Burns, and his remarks about Burns are both the proprietary feelings of the 'fan' and the patronizing dismissals of a young writer who has used an older model as a stepstool in his mind. So that when Keats, the young pirate, comes to Burns's cottage, by then a tourist site, he is dismayed to find the keeper 'a mahogany-faced old jackass who knew Burns,' adding that he 'ought to be kicked for having spoken to him.' This is a theme. Keats wants Burns without Scotland and Scottish people, and especially without poor ones. He laments that Burns 'talked with Bitches' and 'drank with Blackguards,' and finally he declaims on 'the fate of Burns – poor unfortunate fellow, his disposition was Southern.' I do not think that by 'Southern' he meant 'English.' I think he meant the Mediterranean sunshine that beckoned not only Keats but Shelley and Byron, and where, as fate would have it, all three would die. Yes, it annoyed me. Once again Keats wants to step on his poor broken stepstool and climb over him, and to have him without his context, his environment, the working people and farmers of Scotland. And yet in a certain sense I too with my absurd name of Dalgarno and my concomitant thirst for the Spanish language and the history of Spain and Latin America, I too in my way wondered if I did not also in some sense have a 'Southern' disposition. But the old virus, the deep knowledge that all is fake, it tugs at my sleeve as I consider this, it tells me there is no such thing as a Southern disposition, as there is no south, and no north, there is the undeniable phenomenon of the magnetized needle always returning to its place, but what you call it is no concern of the needle's, or the magnet's, and the waters of the rivers flow silently or clatter over the fractured stairways of the rocks – poor broken stepstools – and the charnel houses of the rapids, and the twigs and leaves, sensitive leaves, delicate leaves, on the surface of the rushing waters turn around the corner and are never seen again. If consciousness is a stream it is a stream in one sense only, it is a stream in the sense that you cannot see the same waters twice, one time might be akin to the others and the banks might only slowly yield to new directions, new habits, if at all, but always truly different and singular are the wave patterns and the current, the impulses and the through lines of thought, which was the insight of Heraclitus, who I mentioned in relation to follower Cratylus who only waved his finger, it was Heraclitus who said that everything flows, and while I know I have returned in my mind to thoughts and people and places and things I mentioned earlier, I know it is no longer the same river, and even if I repeated verbatim the things that I thought in the forest, or by the red sweater, or at the very beginning, it would not be the same, my mind reproducing it would think something different this time and yours receiving it would do likewise, and it will always be this way for you and me, even if we meet again and I try again to say what I cannot say and you try again to hear it.

20.

The river – which river? – not the river in the town, and not the river in my mind, or not only that one, the river of rivers now, bigger than you or me, *the* river – has bent far, bent back on itself, looped like a ribbon thrown carelessly onto the floor. In time the flow may bypass the bend, the loop – the meander if you want to be technical about it – cutting it off and leaving it to become something else, an oxbow lake, a living testament to a dead detour. Wherever this river runs there are many such lakes, lakes in the shape of clipped fingernails littering the land at either side of the river, the meanders and course corrections of thousands of years. I think of thousands of years and I feel as if the floor – is there a floor? I said that wherever it is I am now I am sitting, and so I suppose there must be a floor or at least a ground – was falling out from underneath me and I was falling with it, falling far. Eternity or near it, time immemorial or near it – my head swims if I try to imagine these immensities. I think of the moment in Milton's *Paradise Lost*, the most modern moment, the most far-seeing moment, the moment that as far as I am concerned secured the place of this poem among the ages – none of the moments you might be expecting, certainly not Adam and Eve leaving the garden, I mean something different, earlier, the moment when Satan falls through space:

Ten thousand fathom deep, and to this hour
Down had been falling, had not by ill chance
The strong rebuff of some tumultuous cloud
Instínct with fire and nitre hurried him
As many miles aloft.

And to this hour! The chasm of time opens for us in this moment like nowhere else in the poem. And when I think of the chasm of time I think of Roberto Bolaño, and his books in which nothing will be revealed until 2666, a deep time he links always somehow with Mexico, and I think that the story of time on the continents with their absurd and inappropriate name cribbed from some Italian cartographer has yet to be told or grasped or understood by the people who repeated again and again the name of the Italian cartographer without it feeling strange in their mouths. For what is 2,000 years, that lump sum of Christendom's self-regard, in the light of the true time of this place? What, for that matter, is 150 years, a span that in this country marks nothing more than the consolidation of some British assets, it does not even mark the start of a successful war of independence for there had been none, not even a compromised and partial one at the hands of the local bourgeoisie and planters who merely wanted to out-Britain Britain in their slave-holding and dispossession and theft of lands, I mean the Americans, there had not even been a victory in this country by people like that, Britain had consolidated its assets merely and the 150 years of 'Canada' were an arrogant nothing, a drop next to a river, a grain next to a shore, a whitish curl of air from a dog's mouth on a cold morning next to a sky full of enormous and luminous clouds, but a drop, a grain, a whitish curl saying, 'I am the river, I am the shore, I am the sky full of enormous and luminous clouds,' and by forces subtle or brutal or both, demanding that everyone agree that this was so, even and especially those who had been by the river, on the shore, under the sky long before the drop, the grain, the whitish curl and the dog's mouth, and could see and remember the long course of the river, the great sweep of the shore, the numberless clouds reaching across the prairie of sky, the thousands of years and the hundreds of peoples and the movements and changes as recorded in their histories. This too was something so many settlers had failed to grasp, preferring to imagine that the continents before the arrival of the Europeans were places where nothing had ever happened. When Cortés and his murderous band arrived in the city of Tenochtitlan on the lake in the Valley of Mexico, they did not know, and it has been poorly recollected, that the Aztecs had been a great power in the region for only about a hundred years. Powers and civilizations had risen and fallen, people had travelled great distances, the Aztecs recording in their histories their flight from the place of Aztlán and their wandering for two hundred years, arriving to find the Toltec civilization in a state of post-collapse and adopting many of its features, the so-called 'uncontacted peoples' of the Amazon possibly the descendants of the Amazonian civilization whose great cities and tracts of farmland are now known from their yet-visible outlines in the rainforest, a civilization of mixed agriculture of great complexity and requiring great care, practices honed by many generations of study, the civilization possibly ended only by the introduction of diseases from Europeans the victims may not even have seen. When I think of the thousands of years of the two continents joined by their umbilical isthmus and compare them to the paltry hundreds of years of European, capitalist, Christian domination, I think of how long the peoples of the two continents maintained equilibrium, learned it and studied it, knowing from the experience of thousands of years better than to break it as the spasmodic frenzy of capitalism had broken it practically within a single human lifetime. I thought especially of the prairies, of the complex system of prairie grasses, prairie fire, the tramping of bison hooves on the ground, their grazing, the hunt that sustained the peoples of the plains and kept the balance, and how the malign magic that turned the bison into money, the prairies into the causeways of trains, into the sites of farms and ranches, especially for cattle, who eat and move all wrong for the prairie ecosystem, turned the Indigenous peoples of the plains into enemy aliens on their own lands, deliberately deprived of their food source, how all this within a short time would eradicate the prairie grasses and break the equilibrium and summon, like an avenging host, like a symbol of all the mass death wrought in that short span, a cloud of dust as huge as the continent in the decade of the 1930s, and it would gather up the topsoil of the farms and blow it all away. So that the frenzy of this small parcel of ruinous time, perhaps erroneously called modernity, was making a grave of the people and the equilibrium that had come before and also just as rapidly making its own grave. They had created an empire of dust, prematurely old, decrepit from the start, the dust of the past and future graves blowing over the tracts of land in their geometric regularity, the nasty little towns in which the biggest building was the Loyal Orange Lodge. I had spoken once to someone who had grown up in such a place, or rather outside it on a wheat farm, and he had told me that the frightening regularity of the blocks of acreages on a map he would stare at as a child had made him realize he was in his words 'living in a computer chip.' And it was true, he was, they had made a necrotic computer to run the same creaking codes over and over again in the empire of dust, and we only had so much time now to undo them before they undid the bonds of everything. The arrogance of modernity's trifling years. I remembered one of the great arrogant statements of the drop, the grain, the whitish curl, the statement of a judge who in 1991 was to determine the right of Indigenous people to their lands, and was shown the oral histories and songs of the Gitxsan and Wet'suwet'en people, the storehouse of ten thousand years of knowledge as held by those who had withstood everything, all the efforts of the empire of dust to break the chains of transmission through time, and he had been completely unmoved, it had made no impression on him, and he had written in his ruling, the stupidest ruling ever produced by the boiled brains of that whole idiot clan of the judges of the British Commonwealth, that

it would not be accurate to assume that even pre-contact existence in the territory was in the least bit idyllic. The plaintiff's ancestors had no written language, no horses or wheeled vehicles, slavery and starvation was [sic] not uncommon, wars with neighbouring peoples were common, and there is no doubt, to quote Hobbs [sic] that aboriginal life in the territory was, at best, 'nasty, brutish and short.'

I can see him writing this, this passage so emblematic of the sententious idiocy of legal writing, the unearned pomposity, and I see his red face billowing and flapping as he satisfies himself he has done an excellent job. I am sure his face was red and flapping. After all he was another of my alleged countrymen. His name was Allan McEachern. By now you must understand that this sort of thing is like shit to a pig, for me. I am a descendant of people who were once among the nosiest in the world. And so, when I learned of this Allan McEachern who had been shown the treasure of Gitxsan and Wet'suwet'en genealogies as passed down through the generations and felt nothing, I did the only thing that seemed appropriate to me. I traced his genealogy. Anyone can do it. The old censuses and marriage licences of the nineteenth century's dead are all readily available. So I learned that this Allan McEachern had grown up in Vancouver and Penticton, 'The grandson and son of pioneering BC families who instilled in him a love of "God's country," the magnificent natural setting of British Columbia, and an appreciation of his Scottish heritage.' I am sure. I read these words in his obituary, these buckshots of necrotic cliché, and I read also that 'later in life he spent his leisure time "crashing around the Bay" in his sailboats Skye I, II, and III.' Three sailboats, all named after the same Hebridean island. I dug further, learning from the marriage licence that his parents had wed in the Rocky Mountain town of Cranbrook, and that his father John's occupation at the time had been 'lumber merchant.' His mother, Blanche, was born in North Dakota to an Ontario-born father and an English-born mother. Her religion was listed as Methodist, as was the religion of the clergyman who signed their wedding papers. What can I say? Scratch any of the nasty people in this country and you will find a Methodist somewhere. John McEachern meanwhile was born on Prince Edward Island, one of the most concentratedly Scottish parts of the country, and in particular populated by the descendants of Highlanders – often Gaelic-speaking, often Catholic, and often fleeing the Clearances. John's father, Murdock, was likewise born on the island, bringing his family out to British Columbia relatively late in his life. It is not until the preceding generation that we find the immigrant McEachern, Lauchlin, who came to the island with his family in 1806 at the age of three. He was born on the Isle of Mull. Yes, the Isle of Mull – not Skye, as the names of the three sailboats suggest his descendant may have believed. The island to which, fifteen years after Lauchlin was born, Keats and Charles Brown would arrive and observe the hesitation with which the poor simple Gaels handled Brown's spectacles. Here is where time folds back onto itself. Here is where it twists like a moebius. I said that Keats and Brown, in this country where in Keats's words people 'clattered' and 'gabbled away' in Gaelic, where Burns 'talked with Bitches' and 'drank with Blackguards,' regarded themselves when among the poor peasants of Mull almost as the first 'civilized' men in the village, and the boundaries of 'civilization' are so often understood in terms of race, and certainly as the Gaelic-speaking peasants of the Highlands and Islands were forced off the crofts so that the big landlords could make more money from sheep-farming, the editorials in the Lowland papers likewise were sure to make a sharp racial distinction between the comprador Lowland bourgeoisie (pretentiously now cast on baseless grounds as a type of Anglo-Saxon) and the Gaelic speakers of the Highlands and Islands. 'Some people say,' begins a passage in an 1851 treatise extolling collective emigration as 'the removal of a diseased and damaged part of our population,' 'Some people say that it is the effect of race; and they point to the Celts of Kerry and of Barra [in the Outer Hebrides], distant some 400 miles from each other, yet precisely in the same condition of hopeless, listless, actionless, useless penury.' Later that year, in the *Scotsman*, an author appealing to 'the utilitarian march of Lowland enterprise' and 'the imperious laws of political economy' states that 'the Celt must give up the mountain to the sheep-farmer. He must be "improved out" as the Americans call it ... ' As the Americans call it indeed. These sentiments are reaffirmed with force just over a week later in the *Fifeshire Journal*: 'Ethnologically the Celtic race is an inferior one,' the author pronounces, 'destined to give way before the higher capabilities of the Anglo-Saxon.'

Appealing to 'the natural law which had already pushed the Celt from Continental Europe westward,' the author determines that 'emigration to America is the only available remedy for the miseries of the race, whether squatting listlessly in filth and rags in Ireland, or dreaming in idleness and poverty in the Highlands and Islands of Scotland.' The landlords were so enthused by this scheme to get rid of a surplus population that they even paid for their passage across the Atlantic. So that when the infant Lauchlin McEachern arrived in Prince Edward Island with his family in 1806 they may have been part of this wave of the unwanted and the dispossessed. It is likely. But in the ensuing march of the generations something terrible and remarkable happened. Little by little, capital accumulated. The ethnic and sectarian designations that had assigned the Gaels the status of an 'idle' and 'inferior' race in Europe redrew themselves in the Americas so that, even if speakers of another language, even if Catholic or adherents to the hard, strange Free Church Presbyterianism of the Isles, they were still 'white people.' And with the generations the language faded, and the religion was tamed and accommodated, and the ambition of 'Canada' became to create a class of happily deracinated Gaels, Highlanders and Irish both, good loyal British subjects despite all that nasty business back home. Sorry about that. Hence 'Father of Confederation' D'Arcy McGee, Irish Catholic but so loyal that he was killed by an Irish nationalist. And they would achieve this loyalty from the people they had broken by offering them the chance to do it to someone else. This was in fact practically the raison d'être of the empire of dust, in Canada and America both. We see therefore the twentieth-century phenomenon of the Irish cop, the Jewish landlord, the Sicilian construction contractor who refuses to hire Black workers – each with their small morsel of power to do what had been done to their ancestors. Frederick Douglass expresses it clearly in his 1881 *Life and Times*: 'The Irish who, at home, readily sympathise with the oppressed everywhere, are instantly taught when they step upon our soil to hate and despise the Negro. They are taught to believe that he eats the bread that belongs to them.' And a century later the same idea is expressed by Bernadette Devlin McAliskey, Irish Republican and socialist from Cookstown in County Tyrone, when recalling her 1969 speaking tour in the United States:

'My people' – the people who knew about oppression, discrimination, prejudice, poverty and the frustration and despair that they produce – were not Irish Americans. They were black, Puerto Ricans, Chicanos. And those who were supposed to be 'my people', the Irish Americans who knew about English misrule and the Famine and supported the civil rights movement at home, and knew that Partition and England were the cause of the problem, looked and sounded to me like Orangemen. They said exactly the same things about blacks that the loyalists said about us at home. In New York I was given the key to the city by the mayor, an honor not to be sneezed at. I gave it to the Black Panthers.

And so likewise the great-grandson of the 'indolent' Gaels of Mull, those people who (so said Keats) had never even seen a pair of glasses before and were terrified to hold them in their hands, had jumped at the chance to do it to someone else, to say that another people were indolent and unproductive, that their culture did not matter, that it was an inevitable fact of the iron laws of utilitarian political economy that they would be 'improved out.' He had jumped at the chance in part because the passage of four generations in the empire of dust had caused the authentic memories of dispossession to fade into kitsch, into an amorphous 'appreciation of his Scottish heritage' as the obituary put it, into three sailboats named after the wrong island. And in fact he was by no means unique in this respect. This country was full of vaguely Scottish people at three or more generations' remove from knowing what the hell they were talking about. They were like Jersey Italians with worse food. And so I myself in my own way had moved among these people in profound confusion. You must remember what Irvine Welsh said – 'In Scotland we've been exporting every straight cunt tae Canada fir generations.

Result? They're boring fuckers, and we're a drug-addled underclass' – and it was true, the deracinated Gaels I mentioned already of course, but also many others, not least sneaky Lowlanders eager to 'seek their fortune,' John A. Macdonald one of these of course, but so many others, that North West Company like an eighteenth-century Scottish mafia, and more, many, two whole centuries of evil Scotsmen and sour Scots-women of the Lowland bourgeois comprador class, so many colonial administrators and army officers and murderers and enslavers and absentee landlords and architects of misery and accumulators, always accumulators, and so I was now at large among the boring fuckers, who as children – despite their kitschlike vaguely Scottish names of Andrew, Fraser, Kathleen, Fiona, their last names Mac-something, Something-son – had made fun of my accent until I no longer had one and who as a point of anthropological interest had almost never become my friends – my friends were the children of other immigrants, it did not matter from where – anyway I was now at large among the boring fuckers, walking up and down streets named after the obscure Moray farm towns or Forfarshire parishes or whatever other fucking places these people had come from, recognizing the names more even than most of the boring fuckers would, boring for many reasons but in part because they did not know anything, and because I recognized the names, I moved among these streets with a sense of absolute dread, they attested to the processes I have described, they attested to the murder and displacement and forgetting doubled over upon itself in the service of this ridiculous country that if it were a living thing could not survive in the clarity of the true light of day and of fresh water but at the very bottom of the sea only, held together by pressure and lack of light. I imagine the hideous deep-sea fish (as I had called it) swimming up somehow to clearer and lighter zones with the intention at last of breeching the estuary and swimming upriver to infect the land as those whose names I had mentioned before had done – and evil Scotsmen among them, crooked North West Company mafiosi, Fraser on the 'Fraser,' Mackenzie on the 'Mackenzie' – and as Satan does in *Paradise Lost*, before he settles on the shape of the serpent to tempt Eve, the places he searches for inspiration are the estuarylands, the pool Maeotis, Orontes at Darien, the umbilicus linking together the two continents (and where by the way the idiot comprador Lowland bourgeoisie had wanted to found a colony and had instead bankrupted the entire country), the mouths of the Ganges and the Indus, and so I imagine now the hideous deep-sea fish reaching the estuary of the river – which river? *the* river – and beginning now its journey of contamination, its sunken eyes like coins of frozen wax, managing for a certain distance, a little ways in, 150 years' worth, a drop, a grain, a whitish curl of mist against thousands of years, until, what is this, the fresh clarity – for there are no factories or sewage plants on *the* river – the fresh clarity of the water flowing over the rocks, the sun on the corrugations of the ripples as if on a washboard, the clarity and light and motion almost at once caused the fish of the frozen lightless depths to dissolve, to melt, to flush away down the course of the river back out into the estuary and from there and in a state of almost complete and molecular dissolution out again into the waiting arms of the sea and its moon-stirred tides. If there is in fact a way or ways in which consciousness is like a stream, then one more way appears to me now as true. I mean that sometimes – in a rare moment of realization and peace that in my case had come perhaps four or five times only, at the end of a meditation or because the angle and penetration of the light outdoors had unhooked the appropriate latch in the broken house of my brain – our consciousness could cleanse and run clear and the truth of things could be accepted without hesitation or scrutiny and the freshness was the world's. And as was always the case this was a moment only, and memory would try to preserve what it could but without, always without, the avoidance of loss, and so if this time of the river – which had seemed a long time in my mind but perhaps had not been – was a looplike meander lunging out from the ordinary course of things to draw a circle, like a tree in its year, and if the waters of this circle had at last and only for a moment finally run fresh and light and clear, I knew that at last also forgetfulness would cut the looplike meander from the onrushing course of things, more and more forgetfulness filling in what had once been clear fresh peaceful water, so that at last alongside the river would be only a partial memory, a shining horseshoe signifying luck perhaps or its opposite, luck on balance I decided, luck that it had happened, even if now it had been cut off and would have to be attempted yet again further down the river, the river littered with silver horseshoes as if evidence of yet another of the giants' inscrutable games – the game of the partial memory of the oxbow lake.

21.

However long I had been among the rivers in my mind – and it felt like a long time, although to my mild alarm the apparent shifts in the ambient light and temperature suggested a lapse of minutes only, perhaps as few as seven or eight – it was true night now. The light that had clung to the sky's far edges was gone and the stars it is possible to see battling against the ambient electric glow of a city of just under 400,000 people were all now visible, the summer constellations. I saw the big and little dippers. I saw if I angled my head back the North Star. No airplanes though, and no cars, neither the sight nor the sound. No slamming doors, no shouts from the clubs and bars two or three streets away, no other person at all discernible in the darkness of the park. I was sitting again, the grass soft and still hot under me, yes, hot even this late, and the frame next to me on the grass with the close-packed blades just poking out on either side of its borders as though a strange textured picture, an artwork for feeling more than seeing. For in this darkness closer to the centre of the park I could feel much more now than I could see, the light of the stars was only so strong and the street lights along the sidewalks were not now near me. A great darkness had indeed come. I was not afraid exactly, although I knew I could be stirred to fear at any moment by a sound, by a shape or an imagined shape seen out of the corner of my eye or the eyes in the back of my head, the eyes we all seem to have in the darkness even as adults as we turn off a light and run up an unlit set of stairs, you probably know what I mean. You, whoever you are. It was here now in this darkness and this silence that I seemed to be experiencing completely on my own that I began to meditate more closely on this word *you* that has appeared from time to time in the course of my imaginings in the park – I have said very little about who you might be, or even whether I think you are anyone or anything at all. There is a way I could think about you that would have you not just a 'figment' or a 'creation' of my mind but something even less definite than that, some kind of epistemic or metaphysical or literary placeholder, a legal fiction, a term of art. It would be possible for me to think that way about you, but I do not want to. The reason is that it would make me lonely. Yes, I believe I have used this word already, or the word *alone*, but I did not give them my full attention, I was not ready. I believe the details I have revealed of my life must have supplied some evidence for the suitability of these words to my case. My four small rented rooms. The plants I keep mostly alive. The deaths – as a matter of fact very close together, one stroke, one cancer – of my guardians seven years ago, when I was twenty-four. The existence of an extended family, even 'real parents' perhaps still alive, in another country that since my departure in early childhood I had not returned to. My life in the suffering inland post-industrial town. My life before that. I had been strange a long time, with all the remove from the ordinary courses of life this implies. I had and had not been self-sufficient, had alternately excelled at the small arts of being alone and forgotten them all in a panic. With the exception of Hubert Liu and my group in high school and Pia, Bill, and Atefeh, I have spoken little about my having friends. I have had them of course, the ones I have mentioned already and others as well, ones who came and went from this town or ones I left behind on the West Coast, but none now, I was the only one left in the town, I had finished my master's degree and stayed, god knows why, working for years at the same bowling alley I had worked at during my compassionate leave when my guardians died, then for three weeks for the clickbait media company, then for the streetwear people who any day now I was sure would realize how little work I was doing and fire me, but most of my friends in my cohort had left as soon as they finished their degrees, a few had not left right away and stayed as I had, but in the years since they had all gone, one by one, or two by two a few times, and the ones who came through here later to work or study and who I had befriended had also left, and the ones who grew up here and who I had befriended had all left too. This was a place of leaving. I have not even mentioned any people with whom I have been intimate, but there have been some, of course there have. If you care for me to disclose them to you like an android in a science fiction or like the chapter near the end of *Ulysses* where all is explained clearly in the pedant's catechism of time and statistics and science, 'Ithaca,' home at last, all is revealed; if you perceive or wish for all to be revealed to you at this late stage in the day, now night, your nosiest speculations satisfied, I will tell you, I will tell you because at last I do not know how else to keep it all secret. If it pleases you, I have been intimate with eleven people. Perhaps that does not tell you what you wanted to learn, but perhaps it pleases me to not tell you any more. I chose who I wanted and who wanted me. Nothing serious, I had not sought out serious people, and I see now that this was a pattern, even my longest relationship, which lasted almost two years, was not serious, we never lived together, we were like two very good friends who happened to have sex. If you hear these things and are compelled to remark that perhaps after all I was simply afraid, afraid of being hurt, perhaps twisting tighter and saying 'afraid of being hurt' like that old and original hurt, the loss of my birth parents, well then I would say nothing to you in reply because I would not want to give you the satisfaction but inside myself the rightness of this judgment would burn dully and heavily like a dying star. I see now that 'you' have become my confessor, at this moment you are my confessor, you are filling a role for me that has not in my life been filled by a priest – as you know my people were lapsed Protestants, gutter Calvinists, people oppressed by Calvinism. Why this urge to confess? It is perhaps a certain kind of inevitability that I would feel it, not having grown up in a tradition that allowed me to do it. It is perhaps all the more inevitable because for a time I studied the Middle Ages, and the anguish and piety of the writers I encountered, especially women – Margery Kempe, Julian of Norwich,

Héloïse – had taken root in my mind and become real, even though I did not believe in God. I was stricken at that time by guilt over things as innocuous as speaking too loudly, improperly washing my hands. 'You are a God-fearing Catholic without God,' I was told by a classmate named Riley Beauchemin-Massarone, an Irish-Italian-French Canadian who knew what he was talking about when he talked about God-fearing Catholics. But it was in its own way a vestige of gutter Calvinism, the conviction that I was doomed and was shit, my lapsed gutter Calvinism had linked up in some way with the more personal and affective but nevertheless also self-flagellating visions of women's devotion in medieval Catholicism, it is the damnedest thing. But confession as a Catholic sacrament offers the possibility of absolution, and at that time I did not think absolution was possible for me. I was shit. What do I think now? I think that it is the wrong frame, the frame of absolution, in many if not all cases, certainly most secular cases, and especially in politics, the supplanting of concrete political aims by the hunger for absolution by those who believe themselves to need it has been a disaster, politically, a disaster and also the finest, fullest realization of the aim of the Methodistical state, nothing can be done in this country for all the wealthy educated whites tripping over themselves to gain absolution – it is not politics they are doing, it is not even a well-articulated religion. It merely slows everything down. We cannot move in this country for books and articles of scolding and absolution, of looking within, when the answers are plain to see and exist in the outer world; if half the time spent on metaphysical journeys of absolution was spent on organizing the mass – but I say these things and I admit to you that I too of course have been occupied largely with sojourns through my mind, if you have followed me all this way you will have seen that I have done almost nothing but sojourn, I have followed the phosphorescent threads through the caverns of the inner dark so long that my eyes have adapted to the cave light, my body has shrunk to fit the grottoes and the lava tubes and cramped spaces, I too am alone and apart from the mass. I am not seeking absolution down here inside myself, I am seeking the world as it really is, a paradox, to seek this inside, but as always I believe that if you go far enough inside you come out again different. Of course I would believe that. When I speak of loneliness I acknowledge that it seems to be general now, there are so many ways for a wedge to come between you and even those to whom you are closest, the wedge may not even be important, it could be trivial, the narcissism of small differences, smaller and smaller until you are alone again in the sea of molecules all in the same place but not touching. So that when I say 'you' I am speaking of someone lonely, not confessor so much as brother, sister, sibling, peer, fellow person waiting for something to change, for everything to. What was it that Lenin said? 'One step forward, two steps back.' This was how it felt, or worse, one forward and three back, as the great forms and forces battled over our heads and we tried to pull them this way and that like giant dirigibles led around on party ribbon. My red ribbon, my red party. Pulling this way and that and looking up again at the forces and collisions and seeing if anything that happened up there was because of us. Once in the greenhouses of the university in the suffering inland post-industrial town where I had written my master's thesis and then worked in a bowling alley and then for a clickbait media company and then in a strange stroke of ambiguous fortune had been approached on the street by rich-kid fashion students at the technical college who liked my thrifted outfit and had been given by them first a modelling job, which I had not been asked to do again, and then strangely a clerical job, thirty-six thousand dollars a year, incredible, I did not have to live with a roommate who hated me anymore, even though I knew that the days for limited-run luxury streetwear were numbered, this good fortune could not last and it would be back to the bowling alley, back to a room-mate if at least not one who hated me, God willing, anyway once in the greenhouses I had seen a plant with the label 'Creeping Red Thyme' and the truth of the words had struck me, creeping red time, this was time as experienced by communists, those who were honest and open to the world as it really was, most of the time at least, the creeping red time with its build to a push, to hundreds in the street, then thousands, then the navigating of the shoals of co-option and exhaustion and distraction and misinformation, the absolution-seeking bien-pensants counselling that instead of fighting we look within, instead of daring to fight even the most glaringly heinous and brutal wielders of power we instead look within, if we navigated these and other shoals we might, we might, this time ... I have never not believed it possible, you may or may not believe. I see now that when I say 'you' and think of you I am seeing you grow in my mind – you are not one anymore or even a hundred, I want you to be all of you, I want with the provincial-bumpkin enthusiasm of communist sympathizer Roberto Benigni (seriously, look it up) at the Oscars to love all of you, be with you, is that not what all of this is about, you will say perhaps that Mao once said that communism is not love, it is a hammer we use to crush the enemy, you will say perhaps on the other hand if you want to agree with me that Guevara once said that a revolutionary must be guided by feelings of love, I do not see a contradiction, I do not take back anything I have said up to this point – all of you together I want to be able to love and all of you on your own, a kind of 'oceanic feeling' as I believe Freud once expressed it, though he rather discounted it and I do not, he said it was a residue of a time in our infancies when our ego was everything and I tell you it is more than that and not just inside of you, the true full ocean rather than the individual molecules in the sea. I met a poet once who told me, 'All I want is to lie in bed and to feel nothing, to think about nothing.' She paused, took a beat. 'I know that sounds like death,' she said. But I understood her, it was the lure of the amniotic whoosh of the inner sea, a shadow of the vastness of the oceanic feeling but in a diminished sense, private, privatized. But we had to allow the boundaries of our inner seas to touch, to flow together, to form the currents and the causeways of a whole world ocean. We had to. But in the meantime I was here alone in the park with no light, and the ridged surface of the frame, the ziggurat, was clammy when I touched it, the finest condensation was forming on the steps of the grey ziggurat now that it was truly night and becoming colder. The robes of the priest swaying as he climbs the steps to look at the stars. The damp steps, water soaking the hem of the robe. The images came to me, image upon image, memories of the day, memories from before, images of things I had never seen in life but had only imagined. And in my remembering and forgetting I forgot about 'you,' all the yous, whether a near-non-existent placeholder you or personal self-address you or confessor you or brother, sister, sibling you or all-spanning world you of collective love, all of the forms of the you were now gone, and my mind in the night with nothing before my eyes to see began instead to populate itself with visions, the priest at the top of the ziggurat seeing real and unreal together and laughing in the dark wet air.

22.

What were the patterns of my wanderings this day? Infinite loops and criss-crosses within a rectangle. Frantic backtracking and second-guessing, spontaneous quests taken up in a state of euphoria for the farthest corners, the damp hidden places under trees, quests abandoned again no sooner than I had arrived at the hidden places, overcome as I saw them by fits of perfect and desolate futility. The farthest corners but no further. I did not know why. Have I mentioned what the botanist said? No. I never even introduced him. It seems late to introduce new people but it cannot be helped. Suffice to say he was one of many souls who had come and gone from here, doing a year or two of hard penance in the seminars and study rooms of the university's infamous Centre for Theory before leaving this place, this suffering inland post-industrial town where against all earlier intentions I had stayed and might even die. Oh. I had not thought of that yet. I had not thought that I would die here. I will not think about it now. The botanist I was telling you about. A farmtown Dutchboy who got the devil in him. The only man I ever saw steal Dos Equis from behind a bar on a crowded dance floor without getting caught, and in his own way a fellow ex-grandson of Calvin. He was writing a theoretical treatise on certain desert cacti long known to humankind as study aids to the science of metaphysics. He could walk you through the campus farmsteads and greenhouses and tell you whether any plant you pointed out to him would live or die.

It was on one such walk through the greenhouses that I told the botanist how I had been reading old Scottish censuses. Obsessively, to the point of fact-sickness. I shared what I had learned about my birth mother's father's mother, who like Uncle's grandmother had been a farm servant in the Northeast. I explained how her father was a crofter and an agricultural labourer, and that the family farmed five subsistence acres while also going to work on the neighbouring large estates.

'Like Tess of the d'Urbervilles,' the botanist had said, and I had agreed.

'It's funny,' he continued, as he bent down to look more closely at an agave, its leaves like a posy of blue sharks' teeth. 'They probably would have been obsessives too. They would have been desperate to wring as much as possible from that tiny patch of ground.'

When he said this I had been silent and thoughtful, knowing as he touched the leaves of the agave quite calmly and with no awareness that anything important had happened that I would never forget what he said. And I thought of it again in the park as I made my frantic or euphoric or dreadful movements back and forth inside an eighty-five-acre rectangle I could not leave. And as I thought again of my obsessive forbears I thought also of the etymology of my name, Dalgarno, 'garden land' or 'cultivated place,' and I thought, my god, which was it, the farm or the park? What if I woke up suddenly from this long dream and saw that all this time I had only been behind the plow, that it was growing late, that I must not doze anymore but rather move fast if I wanted to get the potatoes in the ground on the five acres? What if I woke up in a stiff dress of cheap muslin, my hands bleeding from the work of picking scraps that fell under the strands of the spinning mule, the strands so taut and uniform and modern, the weird white lines vibrating over my head like a network? It could all still be going on now. And as a matter of fact I knew it was. Just not, today, for me.

I was farming the diminishing returns of my brain. I was thousands of dollars in debt, I had been at university the year of the financial crash, I did not know my ass from my elbow. In another time I could have been a priest, a nun. I could have written 'shilling shockers' about murder, small bylines at the backs of the free papers. I could have been like Giambattista Vico, a tutor for shitty aristocrats, coveting the times in between lessons – the cycles of forgetting and remembering that all writers and thinkers who must make their living at some other task know so well – as moments to think up a theory of cyclical time itself. But the acreage of the mind and the word had been sold off by the big landholders to pay their gambling debts at the craps tables of world finance, and now we poor crofting tenants of the mind were rack-rented. Dice-town, Craps-town. I lived on the field of a game played by idiot giants who did not care where they stepped.

From an airplane, or an out-of-body experience, yes, but never from the eye of a bird. I had not been describing a 'bird's-eye view.' The eyes of birds were something sacred and unknowable to me – perfect shining void domes, like negative stars in the daylight, and as small to my eyes as the stars in the night might be. I had only ever seen them from very far away. What had my aunt said to me? 'If you want to catch a bird, you must put salt on his tail.' More cryptic folklore. Something about correlation and causation. My guardians had given me the night wisdom of the textile mills and the five acres and I did not know who to tell. 'Oh! to whom?' had gone the poem Shelley wrote, the poem of gathering every kind of flower under a copse in a dream, bundling them into a nosegay, returning to the place he had started: 'That I might there present it! – Oh! to whom?' This line repeated again and again by the people in *The Waves* of Virginia Woolf, people I loved and who would have hated me, the book I had read at the age of nineteen that unmade and remade me, for better or for worse taken me apart and rearranged me into the person I am now, a person forever unfit for this world. The dreamer gathering flowers for no one.

I could rule out one 'to whom.' The stranger was not going to come. Onyx, a rock broken open showing bands of obsidian and alabaster, the bands of an unknown planet in a galaxy no human would see. Did it matter that no human would see? Why should it matter? 'I hate travelling and explorers,' said Claude Lévi-Strauss, in another book I read when I was nineteen. That same summer. A matter I will likewise defer, that cataclysm of reading that destroyed me, perhaps defer for the duration of whatever it is I am doing wherever it is I am now. Writing, I believe we had established. I was, am, will be (it is not clear) writing. But why should it matter if a planet that looks like a split-open onyx exists or not, be seen by human beings or not? Nosiness writ very large, it seemed to me. I supposed humanity must be the big 'to whom,' and remembered what Tennyson wrote: 'to strive, to seek, to find, and not to yield' – was there ever a worse thing to have encouraged people to do? Well, yes, so many things. My broken brain manufactures hyperbole from the sharper pieces of itself like prison weapons. But I did not like that sentiment in the poem very much. Most of what has ever existed or will exist we cannot see or know. We must yield. And so I yielded to the probability that I would never see Onyx, never know why they had named themselves that. I could not ask them how their life on the internet had begun and whether they had ever come out the other side.

Ah, but I was sad about this. I had made my nosegay and had no one to give it to, no nose to make gay. This was sad. We must yield to certain truths. We will never see the planet of the alabaster and obsidian bands. But we may give our nosegays, yes? At some time? I was not ready to accept that I would never. And so I stood in my rectangle and it seemed that night would last long and I did not know if I would ever be able to leave.

Fennario. The rodeo. The captain's name was Ned. I had said these things some time ago and not explained them. You must have wondered if you had missed something, in your mind you must have run though all you could remember of this account looking for a clue and found nothing. Or perhaps you let the strange words wash over you without thinking about them, which is also perfectly acceptable. I probably would have done the same. I said I would defer the matter of songs with the same melodies and different words until later, but I said that elsewhere, not when I said these strange things, I did not tell you that these strange things are words from songs with the same melody. But now that I have mentioned my forbears, the peasants of the Northeast of Scotland, it is only right that I make an attempt.

There is a song that comes from the same place they did, the same to an almost geometrical exactness. I did not always know that. My aunt had sung this song from time to time when I was a child, but into adulthood I remembered only the melody and two fragments, the first line of the first verse and the last line of the third:

There once was a troop o' Irish dragoons

.

.

.

Bid a last farewell to your mammy-o

I remembered somehow that the person supposed to be bidding farewell was a woman, not a man. But I did not know where she was off to or with whom. I did not know that in fact she is quite pointedly not going anywhere.

It was not until later, here in this town, in the grip of my fact-sickness, that I came across the name of the River Ythan in a nineteenth-century book. Threads knit together. In almost no time at all I had learned of a song called 'The Bonnie Lass o' Fyvie' (Roud #545), realized it was the song I remembered, realized moreover that the places named in the song were the ones I had been seeing again and again in the old censuses, the church records of the peasants and the tenants and the farm servants who made up the rural part of my ancestry. Ythanside, Fyvie, Auchterless, Oldmeldrum, the Garioch. I felt I had been touched by a cold wind, that the windows and doors had blown open and would not close again. Word followed word with the inevitability of something foreknown to me:

There once was a troop o' Irish dragoons
Cam marching doon through Fyvie-o
And the captain's fa'en in love wi' a very bonnie lass
And her name it was ca'd pretty Peggy-o

There's many a bonnie lass in the Howe o Auchterless
There's many a bonnie lass in the Garioch
There's many a bonnie Jean in the streets of Aiberdeen
But the floower o' them aw lies in Fyvie-o

O come doon the stairs, Pretty Peggy, my dear
Come doon the stairs, Pretty Peggy-o
Come doon the stairs, comb back your yellow hair
Bid a last farewell to your mammy-o

A funny thing that, the Irish dragoons. In a live version of this song by
Ronnie Drew and the Dubliners, Ronnie said this was one of only
two Scottish songs the group knew, adding, 'It's debatable whether
it's Scots or not. Some people say that it's an Irish song.' And insofar
as the song has a narrator, an assumed 'we,' it is the Irish troopers
themselves, observing their captain's doomed courtship of the maid
Peggy in the small provincial Scottish town they happen to be passing
through. But on the other hand the song is in Scots and has a local's
knowledge of the surrounding country. It would seem either to be an
Irish song betraying intimate knowledge of a highly specific region of
Scotland or a Scottish song from the point of view of Irish people – or
both somehow, an alchemical transfer. I can see it being carried in
both directions on two different winds from its point of origin at the
contact zone of Fyvie. When another Irish group, the Clancy Brothers,
played it live at the Ulster Hall in Belfast in 1964, they introduced it
as a song about 'one poor unfortunate fella in the army who fell in
love with a girl.' What army? someone in the crowd wanted to know.
The response: 'Doesn't matter what the hell army, he was in the army!
Ah, you want sides and everything! In the bloody army, that's all.' A
bitter truth there. Belfast was a place where sides mattered. Within
two years the Ulster Volunteer Force would begin its terror campaign
against Catholic civilians, led by Gusty Spence – ex-soldier in, what
else, the British Army.

But the question remains. What army? They may have been Irish troops serving in the army of the Scottish Royalist Montrose during his stunning series of military victories in 1644–45, which included the capture of Fyvie Castle and Aberdeen from the Parliament-aligned Covenanters. Montrose was a Protestant, but a moderate one, and politically a Royalist. His Irish troops – not dragoons but infantry – were sent to him by the pro-Royalist Irish Catholic Confederation, and their commander was the Gael Alasdair Mac Colla, a Catholic born on the Hebridean island of Colonsay. Mac Colla had previously acquitted himself well on the side of Catholic rebels in Ireland, with whom he had allied after first coming there in the service of the Scottish-Irish Catholic Marquess of Antrim, a large landholder who was on almost everybody's and nobody's side at one time or another. Scottish, Irish, Scottish, Irish. It is all as tangled as the song, which in any case may not be about a thing that really happened.

We do not know how they meet, the captain and the maid, in the short time the troopers have in the little town on the southbound road to Aberdeen. Like in so many narrative folk songs, elements are flung together without much connective tissue; time races and lurches and before you know it somebody is dead. But we know that Peggy refuses the lovestruck captain's hand. 'I never did intend a soldier's lady for to be,' she tells him, adding also, 'I never did intend to gae tae a foreign land.' The captain begs the colonel to let the company stay in the town longer, to 'see if the bonnie lass will marry-o,' but he does not get his wish. The company must leave, and Peggy will not join him, and in another typical ballad move the narrative voice changes without warning; it is a 'we' now, the captain's countrymen, who tell us that by the time they arrived in the next major settlement down the road, Oldmeldrum, 'We had our captain to carry-o,' and that, by the time they got to the streets of Aberdeen, 'We had our captain to bury-o.' And the final verse takes us out of the cities, out of the towns, leaving us with rivers, fields, trees, and an epitaph:

Green grow the birks on bonnie Ythanside
And low lie the lowlands of Fyvie-o
The captain's name was Ned and he died for a maid
He died for the bonnie lass of Fyvie-o

I said before that quite possibly none of this actually happened. But if it did, my forbears the obsessives on their five acres in the Garioch and Fyvie and Oldmeldrum would have known about it. They would have known her. They must have. They were some of the nosiest people in the world. They would have looked up from their work by the side of the road, brushed the hay from their hair, seen the tall Irish captain carried on the cart, and wondered what had happened. They would have seen the brittle twist at the mouths of his men, hard cases who had seen death a hundred different ways, but not like this. They would ask the men about it, and through mutually incomprehensible dialects of the English that was strictly speaking the mother tongue of neither they would puzzle out the cause. They would think it the damnedest thing. Pretty Peggy-o. And somewhere in the brain or brains of someone Scottish or Irish or both the germ of a song would begin to unfold. And the grain of this song would be carried away and milled in another place.

So that in 1962, when a twenty-year-old Jewish shopkeeper's son from small-town Minnesota partook in the folk-music craze of the time, a craze that offered him the chance for his own poetic self-reimagining, he chose for his first album what to his knowledge was an old American song about a soldier unlucky in love, a song about a girl called Peggy who an army met on the way to a place called Fennario, and before he begins to sing he admits, 'I've been around this whole country, but I never yet found Fennario.' It is and is not the same song. It begins like this:

Well, as we marched down, as we marched down
Well, as we marched down to Fennario
Well, our captain fell in love with a lady like a dove
The name that she had was pretty Peggy-O

And it ends like this:

Well, our captain he is dead, our captain he is dead
Our captain he is dead, pretty Peggy-O
Well, our captain he is dead, died for a maid
He's buried somewhere in Louisiana-O

No, he had never yet found Fennario, and no one who searches the pages of the atlas up and down the whole American continent ever will. To put it in sufficiently paradoxical terms, it does not exist and it is in Scotland. Fyvie and the Irish troopers of Montrose, all the details and specifics, the grain of the song now milled, were folded into America, flattened into America. Fyvie-o to 'Fennario,' the Doric dialect shorn off, Peggy no longer 'a very bonny lass,' the line now 'our captain fell in love with a lady like a dove.' A new character, the lieutenant, 'a-riding down in Texas with the rodeo.' The original melody's stiff seventeenth-century march time loosening up and rambling in American hands.

This young Minnesotan played with the Clancy Brothers, who were in fact some of his early musical heroes – he called their songs 'Napoleonic in scope' – and I wonder if they ever spoke about this transformation, the song's three centuries' folding. They certainly could have, but if so I have not found evidence of it. I will note also that the young Minnesotan's surname of 'Zimmerman,' or 'carpenter,' has its Dutch analogue in the name 'Timmerman,' and that there are Timmermans, perhaps descendants of a medieval Flemish immigrant, in the Northeast Scottish farm country.

I must share one more version of the song. Because, on the opposite coast of America a few years later, a group of loose and rambling American players made Peggy-O a part of their repertoire, another Peggy-O, its lyrics suggestive of yet another American milling and folding. They are not marching, now:

As we rode out to Fennario
As we rode out to Fennario

And it is the captain now to whom Peggy is asked to bid farewell, and he is given a name:

Bid a last farewell to your William-O

A William on a horse. William-O. I do not know if this subliminally Orange imagery was intended by those who added it, however many centuries ago. I can't imagine the Grateful Dead would have picked up on it. But it colours the song for me, adds greater weight to this version's already manifest menace. For what starts as promise,

Will you marry me Pretty Peggy-O?
Will you marry me Pretty Peggy-O?
If you will marry me, I will set your cities free
And free all the people in the area-O

graduates, after her refusal, to threat:

If ever I return Pretty Peggy-O
If ever I return Pretty Peggy-O
If ever I return, all your cities I will burn
Destroy all the people in the area-O

These stanzas, the horses, and the vaguely Spanish sound of the non-place 'Fennario' paint a picture of a bloody borderland, the filibusters and the Texan murderers crossing the Rio Grande in Cormac McCarthy's *Blood Meridian*. When the Grateful Dead played this part of the song at the Palladium in 1977, someone in the crowd whistled. I do not know what can be said about that beyond the obvious things we all know. William of Orange on his horse against a smoke-painted sky. The pierce of tin flutes. The burning season, which has come to be every season. It did not have to be that way. Wolfe Tone. Napper Tandy. My flayed red books. Mine and my aunt's and my uncle's, for they too had their hopes for the world that they tried to keep alive and intact as if from a wind of knives, though they were circumspect, mostly, about what they had done to those ends, except once, late, in a cryptic way, when my aunt was no longer alive and my uncle was alive but in some sense no longer intact, he did not know when it was or where he was and he called me 'Tam,' over and over he called me 'Tam' and I did not know who that was, 'Thomas' that is usually short for. I had managed to get a compassionate leave from my graduate school to be there those last weeks, a leave that would ultimately extend to a whole year, and over and over while calling me 'Tam' he spoke of a winter journey over the Highlands by lorry the long way and a ferry boat to the Isle of Islay, a meeting with a Presbyterian minister's son from Belfast who had gone Marxist and taken the Catholic side, the delivery of a cargo to said person, who was high up in one of the left Republican organizations, said person's departure by night on an inflatable motorboat known as a Zodiac, and because my uncle never used the personal or any other pronoun to refer to the one who made this journey I was never sure if it was something he had done, or someone else, or no one, perhaps something he had wanted to do and had not been able to, perhaps merely the hallucination of a dying man's mind, but if he or my aunt or both had been involved in this in some way, I wondered, was this the real reason why they had left in 1972 and never come back? Were they by however tenuous association in the sights of the UVF, the UDA, the RUC? I could not get anything like that out of him. I certainly tried. 'Ye wouldnae believe the waves, Tam,' was all he wanted to say.

Where was I just then? I was and was not wherever it is I am now. I was and was not on the eighty-five acres of the rectangle where it was now true night and the green of the birch trees and willows and alders and lindens was night-green and the river of the town was elsewhere so that if the moon had risen and was shining in the river I could not see it.

But I saw what was meant by

Green grow the birks on bonnie Ythanside
And low lie the lowlands of Fyvie-o

and I was and was not on the five acres by the river Ythan whose name
taught me the words of these songs, I was and was not just as I was and
was not in those other places, but this five-acre place by the River Ythan
especially so.

Chill, sea salt, and estuary on the air in May, it is May that I imagined,
the long outgoing breath of the North Sea over the floodplains and low
hills, gathering every scent in its fell nosegay, bending the reeds and the
low grasses, bending too the trees. Breath or a giant's hand. No, not a
giant's hand. No more giants in this report. A thousand small hands.
Yes, a thousand small hands of the lost coming with the breath of the
sea. I had taken myself in my mind to a place of death like a fairies' child
to abide there. On the same air of May bringing sea salt and estuary
came the perfume of burning, the coal-dark incense of wood fire, bark
shuddering off the logs and alchemizing into ash, heat making water in
the air. Next on the air came the perfume of fiddlers' graves and the
music the dead play. The ache of the reels of the invisible uncounted
dead, their hands grasping like the drowning for the leaves of the trees,
gallows trees, trees shaking and reeling from the touch of the dead. The
captain's name was Ned and he died for a maid. In all those versions
they never say how – whether by his own hand or from a 'broken heart.'
That premodern ailment nobody is permitted to die from now.

23.

The pond I had been avoiding in my wandering and have been avoiding as well in my thoughts. Not entirely. I described it at the beginning. But I have been avoiding it since then. It has a relation to all of this, this small cold pool of black water, but a relation beyond words, or rather a relation at the place where the words have frayed into sounds, the sounds into images – images in a dream story, tokens and sigils, hand over hand in a chain, and so the small cold pool of black water becomes a glossy pupil, the pupil of the eye of the world, and the red-and-yellow flush in autumn like the traditional English pattern Jack of Hearts becomes by easy associative leap a 'royal flush,' which becomes 'royal flesh,' and I think of gout and of guillotines, and I know that the chains and the fraying and the sigils of the pond are connected in some way to death, and I knew it in the park just as clearly, the park where night had for some time now been well underway. I made a quick inventory there in the darkness and all seemed clear enough after its fashion: black birds ascending on the air as night fell; stars, spars, swells; sea words; the red-winged blackbird too a lover of water, red and yellow its epaulets, like the leaves, like the Jack of Hearts; the weeping willow, weeping for – whom? For me? My inability to leave. Had I drowned? Had I drowned in the pond (on purpose if anything, I was not so stupid as to allow it to happen by accident) and returned to the place where my body had stopped, returned as a mind without body, revolving around the unblinking onyx pupil pond as its moon? I almost believed it. But why then the frame, why then the hydrant, why a stranger named Ony- Oh. *Onyx.* The word I used just then for the colour of the pond.

That was why Onyx, no longer onykx22@hotmail.com, my mind had shed the numbers and the spelling and the rest, kept only what could be a sigil in the chain of death words. If this were true. But why death? Why should I jump to the conclusion of death when we have so much life-in-death? Well then, life-in-death. Afterlife. Afterbirth. Afterimages. And if the afterimages were the images I had seen in my life then of course it was parklands and the contents of books, I had done almost nothing else, or if I had I could not remember, I must not have found it important. I had two things: I had the words falling into place in their wooden tongues and I had the spreading green of living trees, their leaves, the paper of nature, on which could be written the book of each year, the story of the passing of time. So I felt at any rate in that moment when more than at any other point all day I strongly entertained the possibility that I was dead. There had been stories and books on this subject. Films. There had been 'An Occurrence at Owl Creek Bridge.' That had been a death by water, or rather over it. And it had not of course escaped my attention that the name of the creek over which the hanged man experienced his long lurid death-dream of not being hanged bore the name of a bird. And the man had escaped in his dream through a forest of whispers in unknown tongues, strange bright constellations in the sky. Orion's belt, Orion's hands, Orion's broken neck. I had not seen anyone all this time, and no cars. I tried to remember if I had seen anyone at all the whole day. Surely I must have, on the walk over, but I could not bring their faces to mind. How for that matter had this day begun for me at all? I seemed to remember waking up, making coffee, watering my plants in the four rooms of permanent dust. But I did that every day, and the memories did not have the character of a felt thing. They had the character of memories that years ago I had remembered myself remembering, so that only this second-order memory remained, a kind of life support of memory, a cutting of a plant kept green in soil but somehow no longer truly alive. It occurred to me of course that I too might be in such a space between. I could not leave and I was not hungry and the sky above me had not been troubled by the passage of an airplane, the rising of the moon, and so I seemed in some sense out of time, in some sense apart, in some sense in suspended animation like the plant in new soil still green but not taking root. Rotating around that dark unblinking eye slower and slower and closer and closer, like a steel castor set at play in a basin of perfect circumference to ride the walls in a narrowing spiral until the inevitable end in the dark. If ends are in fact inevitable.

Life-in-death. That had been Coleridge. I said that already. But there is something more I have not yet said, something I have been avoiding as scrupulously as I avoided the pond, in my thoughts and in my wanderings. It has to do with life-in-death and the inevitability or non-inevitability of ends. I am talking about quantum superposition. I am talking about quantum immortality. I am talking about the words of a dead man named David Lewis, who four months before he died gave a talk with the title 'How Many Lives Has Schrödinger's Cat?' He refers to the famous thought experiment, the cat both alive and dead from a poison that will or will not release depending on whether an atom does or does not decay, the state of the cat only resolving into one state or the other once an observer comes to look. This resolution into one of the two possible states is called quantum collapse. But David Lewis, taking a cue from the many-worlds interpretation of quantum physics, asks us to imagine what happens if there is no collapse. Many-worlds theorists say that, instead of undergoing quantum collapse, in the moment of observation the particle in superposition behaves one way in one universe and the other way in another. Lewis then suggests what he calls an 'intensity rule' governing the prediction of outcomes in a world where quantum collapse does not hold. He needs to do this for the sake of his theory, as predictions made on the *assumption* of collapse do indeed come true. The branches of possible outcomes in quantum mechanics have different 'intensities,' Lewis explains, and we must adjust our expectations on that basis. For the observer outside the box, the intensities of the branches are equal. The outside observer can equally expect a live and a dead cat when they open the chamber. But what about the cat? What can it expect? Lewis thinks that, from the cat's point of view, the branch with the most intensity will always be the one where it remains alive. To the outside observer, the cat can die of the poison. From the cat's perspective this can never happen. But of course, Lewis reminds us, it is not just thought experiments like Schrödinger's that operate via quantum mechanics. So too do chemical processes, he says, mechanical processes. Which means, ultimately, that 'all death-mechanisms are quantum mechanical.' From the perspective of your own mind, he says, 'you should expect with certainty to go on forever surviving whatever dangers you may encounter.' The caveat here is that the branch of the most intensity may nevertheless not be all that intense, particularly as encounters with death-mechanisms become unavoidable. The decision tree of superpositions, when faced with the stark choice of 'on' or 'off,' will always pick 'on,' always, and never result in true or full death, but in the meantime may result in increasingly attenuated and negligible forms of life – another Zeno's paradox, intensities splitting and splitting and splitting away but never permitting a complete end. 'Cumulative deterioration that stops just short of death,' he calls it. 'Eternal life without eternal health.' Of course I know what you may say. Of course a philosopher dying slowly of a chronic illness would find this a cogent proposition, perhaps as awful as it sounds still thinking it preferable to complete oblivion. Perhaps. But it gives me cause to wonder. And when I say that I felt in the park the intimation that I may be 'living through' so to speak a kind of 'life-in-death,' the ideas of this philosopher – dead to you and me but perhaps by his own account still alive and thinking somewhere in one of many worlds – were top of mind, and I felt I must entertain them. I saw no cars, I saw no people, I did not as yet see the rising of the moon. If all were lost in the world, then I and all others would be experiencing ourselves alone in the world and aware of absences, alive but within limits, each of us, the lonely sea of molecules taken to its most terrifying and definitive extreme. Yes, of course I entertained this. And I remembered one more thing that Lewis expressed in this paper:

To be sure, there are also life-and-death branchings such that on some branches your life is improved. Your previous losses are regained; your loved ones come back to life, or your eyes or your limbs grow back, or you regain your mental powers or your health. But in all such branchings, the improvement branches have a very low share of the total intensity. If there were collapses, the regaining of losses would be enormously improbable, and neither is it much to be expected under no-collapse quantum mechanics.

'Improbable,' he writes, not 'much to be expected,' he writes. Not 'impossible,' not 'never to be expected.' Lewis, perhaps more for his own comfort than anything else, allows some small sliver of possibility that things might turn around even for the mind a long way down into the Dantean forest of branches. What do we call it when limbs are restored, the dead come back to life? In their most extreme and unbelievable forms we call them miracles. Where do we read of miracles, or hear of them? In the scriptures of the world's religions, in the traditions of the world's spiritual teachings and belief systems, in the shadowy corridors of myth. The deepest twists of the Mezquita.

I allowed myself to indulge an idea at this time. I was out on my own now. I did not know if any physicist would follow me. The world itself, I thought. Entropy, I thought. Lewis's fading but never-extinguished light. I had taken a class once with a very old and distinguished professor, a man with a white beard and Socrates-pattern baldness, the near-opposite in demeanour of the rustic Billy Bart. A Canadianized Englishman or an Anglicized Canadian, one or the other, and probably the last person alive to speak the dialect called 'Canadian Dainty.' He told us on the first day of class that the difference between essentialism and existentialism was shown by the catechisms of the Church of Scotland, essentialist, and the Church of England, existentialist. The catechism of the Church of Scotland begins, 'What is the chief end of man?' to which the catechumen must answer, 'Man's chief end is to glorify God, and to enjoy him forever.' I have said so much already about the hard rule of Calvinism over the peasants and workers of the land in which I was born, and I will say now that if the catechism of the national Church begins with such designs upon the catechumen, then the people of such a country have no chance, next to no chance, unless they wrestle against the bonds of their catechism as if against gravity itself. But, as I have done so many times before, I digress. My professor, the old man who looked like Socrates and spoke Canadian Dainty, told us that unlike the essentialist catechism of the Church of Scotland, the beginning of the catechism of the Church of England was existentialist. The first question of this catechism is 'What is your name?' A little joke, you see.

This professor told us many other things I still remember, but one in particular germane to the matter at hand. 'Cognition,' he said to us once, 'is a very fast Darwinian competition for cortical workspace.' I imagined, both when he said this and again in the park, the racing of electric-blue thoughts down forking paths, one fork chosen, one fork not. How had he put it? 'Survival of the fittest is a misnomer. Instead we should say, "Survival of the adequately fit."' And so the electric-blue line raced down the branches of cortical possibility, and of course when I think of this I think of the branching of the many worlds, and I think of what Lewis said about death and intensity, and I think of entropy, good god I think of entropy, I think of the racing thoughts and their options and the branches of intensity and I think of them slowing, slowing, but never fully stopping, and I think again of one line of thought in my mind, something adequately fit, that takes me somewhere I think no physicist would go. I mean miracles and I mean the entropy of the world, and as the inverse of that entropy the miraculous restorations to life in the religions and traditions and systems of the world. Lazarus, the Woman of Shunem, the man who touched Elisha's bones. Satyavan the husband of Savitri. Alcestis, Osiris, Baal. All dying-and-rising gods. Bodhidharma holding his shoe. Fuke ringing his bell. The promise of Ishtar. All branches of restoration, 'a very low share of the total intensity.' And yet the world was younger then. More branches, more workspace, fewer circuits burned out in entropic failure hastened by our own hunger to set flames at play across the world, to thicken the skies with our smoke, to lengthen the shadow of the empire of dust. Higher intensities. Could one world have drifted back into our own and restored to us our dead? In the tradition of the Aztecs and the Nahua there are five worlds, called 'suns,' each destroyed in turn, and we are living in the fifth world, and after its destruction no new worlds will follow. The restorations were for before. I entertained this, yes I entertained this, I entertained the idea that the resurrections had happened in the past and could happen less and less as the world we lived in was bled of its life by the hunger machine of the empire of dust. It had a certain sense. I thought of Lewis's 'cumulative deterioration,' his point that life that continued long would be diminished life, and I thought of how the resurrection stories after the start of capitalist modernity were stories of diminished life. Coleridge's life-in-death. Mary Shelley's creature assembled from the dregs of 'the dissecting-room and the slaughter-house,' roaming the world in loneliness and expiring by choice on an ice floe in the Arctic. The zonbi, who has one half of a soul only, a concept inextricable from the devastation wrought by slavery in Haiti, the power of the masters to diminish the life of the enslaved, to use terror and to tell those who would rather commit suicide than be enslaved that if they did so they would be enslaved forever. This terror and misery overthrown by the miracle of Toussaint and Dessalines, I called it a miracle before and I believe that all such successful revolutions are miracles, the Irish War of Independence and the Bolsheviks and China and Cuba, and I think of the failure of Karl Liebknecht and Rosa Luxemburg one hundred years ago this year, the rising that if successful would have made for a different world, and I see that the entropy of the bleeding world forestalls but never completely forbids new miracles, nothing is completely off the table, all things are in some sense in the cards. But I say these things about miracles and resurrections and risings and I remember that I am supposed to be a materialist, however many ways we might take that, and can a materialist believe in miracles? I think again of the old man who looked like Socrates. He was a materialist of a particularly fervent kind. A Marxist might call him a 'vulgar materialist.' 'What is a human being?' he asked us once. He made a drawing on the board of a cylinder with a tube running through its centre. 'A human being,' he said to us, 'is just a kind of jelly doughnut.' I think of him saying that and I think of the so-called bilaterian body plan, the basic blueprint for nearly all animals, and how at its wormlike simplest in the shape of Ikaria wariootia they truly are mere tubes, a hole at one end for the mouth and a hole at the other for the anus, the coelom or body cavity surrounding the gut that connects the two. I see what he means, the professor, but I cannot say what conclusions, if any, are worth drawing from it. On another occasion he said to us, quite seriously, 'Why don't we eat the mediocre people?' No one seemed willing to respond. I believe he was waiting for one of us to say 'morality,' to say 'justice,' so he could tell us in turn that none of these fine things 'existed.' That is the vulgar part of vulgar materialism. That and the jelly doughnut. I heard rumours that the old professor who looked like Socrates could be seen in the student pub drinking pitcher after pitcher of beer by himself until he passed out, and based on his view of the world I believed these rumours. There is one more thing I must say about him. This old man who spoke Canadian Dainty and remembered the English and Scottish catechisms also had an astonishing memory for English-language poetry. He once began to recite from *The Canterbury Tales* in Middle English unprompted. And on one particular evening when the matter of death and afterlife was near at hand in the class – perhaps it was the week we read Kierkegaard – he began to recite, out of nowhere, the words 'Dead men naked.' 'Dead men naked,' he said. 'Dead men naked.' He paused. 'They shall be one / with the man in the wind and the west moon.' A stillness in the room now, the only audible thing the metallic outrush of air through the vents and ducts overhead. He looked out at us. 'Can someone with a computer look that up? "Dead men naked?"' Quickest on the draw was a boy with long blond hair and a bandana who I had not rated highly. A surfer, stoner kind of boy, who when asked by Socrates why he was taking a class on existentialism mentioned Richard Linklater's *Waking Life*, a movie that I too had seen and loved but that I had not wanted to mention in the classroom because I thought people might think less of me. I mentioned Sartre's *Nausea* instead, a book I had taken out at the library and read that past summer, the summer after high school was over and before I went away on the strength of my loans and scholarships to one of the local universities, the less famous of the local universities. That summer I had thought I was both dying of cancer and going insane. But the point is that it was terribly unfair of me to have thought this way about the boy with the long blond hair, I had no grounds to look down my nose at anyone. I did it of course because it was easier than trying. But anyway he had found the poem in question online with his laptop and Socrates asked him to read the first verse. He read, and he read well:

And death shall have no dominion.
Dead men naked they shall be one
With the man in the wind and the west moon;
When their bones are picked clean and the clean bones gone,
They shall have stars at elbow and foot;
Though they go mad they shall be sane,
Though they sink through the sea they shall rise again;
Though lovers be lost love shall not;
And death shall have no dominion.

He stopped. The poem hung in the air as if it had been brought into the room on a wind through the metal ducts above our heads and the wind had dropped and the words flowed before us like a sacred breath. Everyone was quiet. Socrates appraised the shift in the room. 'It's not true of course,' he said, 'though we might wish it to be.' More silence. 'There's a trick there too, by the way,' he continued. 'Can anyone say what it is?' Nobody knew what he was talking about. For my part I thought he meant some sleight of philosophical logic that was beyond me. But as it happened he meant something quite other than that. '"They shall be one with the man in the wind and the west moon." It stays with you. Of course all he's done there is switch up the nouns in the phrases "the man in the moon" and "the west wind."' More silence. I felt a new chamber opening in my brain. Whatever Socrates had meant in pointing this out – whether he meant that the effects of the poetry were mere gimcrack, or whether as a logician he felt a professional respect for this example of chiasmus – I knew I had discovered something about language that seemed more important to me than the question of the soul in Kierkegaard or whatever it was we had ostensibly been discussing that day (Socrates never stayed on one topic for very long). I felt I had encountered some kind of weft or weave pattern in the world as it was expressed through language, a form as true perhaps in its way as an equation, as the drawing of a circle, as the spiral of a snail's shell. It was not long after this that I attempted to write poetry, those eight-line aphorisms I mentioned before. I would reject philosophy as such as a sole governing principle for my life. I would not reject it entirely. I would simply move somewhat away. Philosophy became a foghorn to me as I travelled in madness and ecstasy and paralytic despair through language. The man in the wind and the west moon. The rising of the moon. Language itself was the truest and strangest mind virus of them all. Language itself a wind. And when I tell you that I was supposed to be some sort of materialist, not a vulgar materialist like the old man who looked like Socrates but nevertheless someone who believed that history unfolded on the basis of the material, of economics and class struggle, and yet I tell you also of death and resurrection and miracles and appear to part ways with the physicists, if I tell you these things and you are troubled by the contradiction or if not by the contradiction then by my seeming unwillingness or inability to solve it, well, I told you my brain was broken for a reason, I was not making it up. I was living in the tumult of a thesis and antithesis without synthesis, a moon and sun in motion around a waiting and stagnant earth.

24.

I had been sitting on the grass in the darkness for some time, thinking and not moving, afraid to move, certainly toward the pond but truly in any direction, afraid as well because for however long I had been sitting there I had witnessed no further changes to the world around me. No moon, no planes, no cars, no people. Only the sound of soft wind in the trees. I knew that behind me somewhere were the willow, the bench, the red sweater, and the row of trees leading to them, and that parallel to that row of trees ran the sidewalk and its street lights. If I could not leave – and I knew I could not leave – then my next-best bet was to go in the direction of the light, to stand under it and see what could be seen, to sit perhaps on the bench if it were not too wet. I stepped carefully through the grass. I felt stones in the grass that I had not remembered feeling as I walked earlier in the day. If not stones – acorns? Pignuts? Eggs? Bezoars? Ambergris? All seemed possible now. I came to the edge of the park that was lined with trees and bordered by the sidewalk – the side facing the concrete buildings with sepia windows. The willow and the bench were near. The red sweater still was where it was and was still red and looked if anything wetter than when I had seen it last. I stood under the light of a lamp, my toes lined up perfectly with the edge of the park, a rough-cut line of grass coming to its end at the sidewalk. The cone of light in front of me was a copper-coloured beam announcing the descent of something too earthly to be an alien, too strange to be an angel. Lucretian atoms in a rain of error and blunder. I breathed in the air of the night and smelled night's cold sweat, the glaze of its brow. Something was about to happen.

And what happened was this: a cloud of unsteadiness jittered into view at the outer edge of the visible, entered the cone of light, and stayed there, folded itself around the bulb so that the ground beneath it was dancing with the silhouettes of capital-B-shaped wings. A hundred moths. Maybe more. I had never seen so many moths in one place. I could not say if this was typical behaviour. I had never heard of this happening, and if there is one thing by now you may say about me with confidence it is that I have tried to be a man who has heard of things. So many moths that I thought – no, I knew – I could hear them, the crinkle of gift paper on the air. Light-brown moths, with bark-like camouflage perhaps, they fluttered in and out of focus too wildly for me to tell one from the next, and yet in a kind of miracle none ever seemed to brush up against their neighbours, the wings passed through the shower of photons up and down without ceasing, never touching. Was it the heat they wanted? The light itself? I did not know then, nor do I now. Just as this street light shone on a small cone of the actual world only, despite all my efforts I myself was acquainted with only a minuscule corner of the world, the rest was mystery, the forms and codes and animal instincts driving the unknown world were mystery, and just as even this visible light was scattered and rendered intermittent by this cloud of moths, so too was the minuscule corner of the world I claimed to know about jammed as if by enemy signals, intermittent, scattered. I used those words already, I know that. My brain was broken. For now, still, yes, if perhaps not forever. I lived in the expectation of the restoration branches, the problem of life disappearing as problem without my being able to say why. But broken until then. I don't have to tell you why. This testament of my vigil in the park will tell you why. Vigil. I had kept using that word, I didn't know why. Something to do with holiness in a secret way. Hidden, catacomb holiness. The moths flapped around. The toes of my shoes stayed stuck to their outermost permissible place in the park. I felt like a cadet doing punishment duty. I swayed a little, like a stake just stuck. I heard the flap of the moths and the oceanic roar in miniature of the shaking leaves and I heard the pregnant near-sound of atmosphere sitting on the chest of the world like a succubus, an incubus, and cutting through all these things like a great ship sliding through the waves with the sureness of the hand of God came another sound, cutting through the waves but then becoming the wave, becoming somehow the sound, the principle around which all other noises were organized. A wave of music, strings I think, an organ possibly, a piano chord kept going on and on by the life support of sustain pedals possibly, garnishings of Moog, garnishings of Korg, garnishings of Roland, studio itself an instrument, a kind of olive press you bundle your sounds into and squeeze as hard as you can, get every last drop – a sweetness to the note, like winter wine, or a kind of angel's keening, and yet a low thrum coming through at the same moment, great whale tremors, earth opening, low bells pealing news of death, ask not, Donne depicted in his own shroud, a doom tone. Both coming through and mingling and building, the doom tone and the sweet keen, red strand over green strand, or orange strand, building to an end that did not seem ready to come, it was incredible the sustain, the reach, the bellow and keen. It did not come with the muffle and sound-bounce of live players, and I mentioned already a studio, this was clearly a recording, but so pure and true to itself that it sounded like it was inside my ears almost, inside my head. I looked out at the buildings, the cubes of frozen sand. The sepia windows stared like pools of tea, like oxidized water caught in troughs. Nothing to indicate the source of the music. I had an idea. I walked backwards into the park to see if the sound got quieter as I moved away or if it still seemed to play out right next to me. Twenty metres, thirty metres, fifty, more, with the trees lining the sidewalk between myself and the buildings now as a buffer perhaps, if the sound was a sound in the world. A hundred, two hundred metres. The lights of the street lamps and the forms of the buildings quite far from me now. And the sound was fainter. Yes. Strong still, but fainter. It was certainly coming from the direction of the build- ings but, at a guess, behind them, from one of the couple of residential streets between the sandy cubes and the main street with the student bars and nightclubs, or at a push from the street with the bars and nightclubs itself, but it did not sound like the kind of thing they usually played in those places. In those places they could still reliably fill the floor with 'Safe and Sound' by Capital Cities. I had heard no other music that could come from a bar. Nor had I heard the shouts to turn it down, the barks of dogs roused from dreams of the chase, that would come naturally if it were played on a residential side street. And in fact I had not heard a dog bark all day. Only bird calls. All too many of those. I walked back to where I had stood before. The sound was louder but the moths were gone. Perhaps all had flown too close at once and died, no moth Daedalus to mourn them, and their labyrinths with them to the end, the criss-cross of instinct and impulse that tangled in their own moth minds. But there was no sign of their bodies if so. The sound was really something now – as if double the instruments, double the pedals, double the garnishings of synthesizers, double the studios, a fat rolling fullness like a hurricane, louder and louder, echoing now off the buildings, off the pavement, even rattling the glass in the street lamps lining the sidewalk. Just as I put my hands to my ears it crested, it broke, it sunk back into the place it had come from, a long fading sustain, thirty, forty, fifty seconds – then, finally, silence. No new song cued up on the secret speaker. No applause, no cheers, no old woman or man saying, 'Thank fuck it's over.' The night was as quiet as before. The sound of a resting atmosphere. The rattle of summer leaves on circling branches. A mighty quiet. Things had happened and may yet be happening – moths had come and gone, and a distant music – but the quiet of this moment gave everything a certain clarity. I was no longer afraid. Fear was for the waiting times, not the times when things were happening. I was a cadet on my perimeter and down the corner at Wellington and Boyne the enemies might come marching, in their red coats or the sash their father wore, and I would say, 'Ireland Boys Hurrah!' with the incongruous accent of a Doric washed away by the Pacific Ocean, the incongruous baptismal record of the Church of Scotland, the incongruous family tree of one who by my aunt's reckoning was 1/32 Irish at best, but no more incongruous in its way than the appearance on an album of that name – I mean *Ireland Boys Hurrah!* – by the Wolfhound, who were Irish Republicans from Belfast, of the Scottish Border ballad 'The Battle of Otterburn,' the song in which the Scottish Earl of Douglas 'roved tae England to catch his prey,' and who in gathering his allies for the ride over the border

> took the Gordons and the Graemes
> The Lindseys light and gay
> But the Jardines with them widnae ride
> And they rue it to this day

Something about this Scottish song had been important to the members of this Irish band and so they had recorded it. After all, Jardines, those of every name who did not come when called and rue it, are everywhere. And so in the face of the marching enemies in red coats or orange sashes it was 'Ireland Boys Hurrah' I would say, it stood for every Ireland that has ever been, of every name and every place in the world where the people with red coats and orange sashes have marched and made enemies, and I was ready for these things to come to pass, to see these people and to say these words, but as I neared the corner of the park at Wellington and Boyne I saw empty streets only, or almost only. For at the very farthest end of this corner was a small form.

I thought at first it was a wallet or a garment. But as I bent down to look I saw the black feathers with ringmaster epaulets of crimson and gold. I saw the tiny seams of its closed eyes. I saw, closer than ever before, the beak that once had sung the song that so long ago in another park had told me I was alive. An obsidian beak, one could say. Or an onyx one. This was Onyx. This dead bird was the one I had been waiting for. I decided it then. Make of it what you will. I admit my logic was loosening, my equivocations of this and that running wild. The workers had left, I thought. All but one. As with the last time I thought something like this, when I saw a flock of them over the buildings, my thought did not cohere clearly with what I saw. The workers had left, save for one who had died, and I could not give the frame to someone who was dead. Let alone sell it. I think I had set aside the idea of selling it much earlier that day, though I cannot say when. In any case we have obligations to the dead even if it is too late to give them the things we would have when they were alive. This is always so. I know it well. Every month a fee of $145 leaves my bank account for the tenancy of a storage unit in New Westminster, within which are boxes containing all the things belonging to my aunt and uncle that I could not take back with me to Ontario and that, so long as I live, I will never throw away. And so, very carefully, I picked up the bird. It weighed almost nothing. The part of me that earlier in the day had seen catshit and feared communicative diseases was gone. Those were no-see-ums, and my concern now was with something I could see. Anyway what was illness to me now? What was West Nile to one who could not leave? As far as I was concerned my obligation was clear. This dead bird was onyx and also Onyx, and the pond too was onyx, and by a chain of words that had turned into images in dreams the pond was also a place of death, and I was or was not involved with death or restoration, who now could say which, and though I had been avoiding the pond for its association with death I now had an obligation, and I was not afraid, something was happening, and so I went onward to the pond, Ireland Boys Hurrah, and I felt myself breaking felled branches, and my ankles rolled over stones, but who cared, and the frame – yes, I had never abandoned it – cut through the air as I swung it in my left hand, and I cradled the bird in my right, and I passed the benches, the toilets, and the baseball diamonds, and sand got in my shoes, and my feet got soaked from the dew, but it did not matter. I had an obligation.

I arrived at the edge of the pond. The banks spread out before me and the dark water shone like a city of silver seen through a window. The moon had not risen and the source of the light was unclear. It was summer as you know and the red and yellow leaves of the pond in autumn had not yet come, but the surface was still nevertheless speckled with variations like a long and contentious will – twigs, green leaves, reeds, lily pads, strange Loch Ness forms that might be logs. I could smell the sodden posy of rotting wood, stagnant algae-eaten stones. Chalazions and sties around the rim of the onyx eye. A goat's eye, I felt now. A rift to eternity like an open grave. I was here at the place I had been afraid to visit and as yet no harm had come to me but I stood at the edge of the still water and felt the wind touch me and knew that the harm could have been done already, all could be over and merely playing itself out forever in diminishment without true final ultimate end. I could have been under the water the whole time, I could be smelling nothing other than myself, the flesh still rising and falling with the current, billowing from my bones like ragged flags from a sunken armada, from every French and Spanish ship that had hoped to smash finally the perfidious Albion, free Hibernia and Cambria and Caledonia from its yoke, Mann and Cornwall too I suppose, all those efforts, two hundred years of them, thwarted almost always by bad weather, as though Satan himself were invested in the health and success of that bloody kingdom by the sea, anyway it could have been my own waterlogged bones I saw protruding from the water, I could be prefiguring the near future or reliving the distant past, I did not know, and a kind of terror presence built somewhere at my back. But I fought it. I had to. Harm may or may not have come to me already, may or may not be about to, but I had obligations to a bird that is often found near water, and here was the water for it to be near. I knelt down with it by a shoreline bracken bush. It seemed as good a place as any. I lifted the leaves and clawed at the earth with my hands until I had a hole a half-foot deep. I committed the bird to the earth under the bracken bush and covered it over. I did not say anything out loud. I closed my eyes and remembered once again the time I had first heard the call of these birds and had thought that the whole green world was singing to me. My harm may or may not have come, but for this bird, this Onyx, harm surely had. I hoped it had not been painful. In truth I saw that my own death was nothing to me, I could handle my own. It was those of others I was not sure I ever truly could.

I stood up, beat the wet earth from my hands. For the first time that night, the frogs were croaking. They must have started while I was occupied by my work. I did not presume they were thanking me. I chose to believe they were saying the things I could not – had carried on for me at the place where words frayed into sounds, sounds into images, images into dreams. I should be thanking them. I looked at my hands. Touching the dead bird had not bothered me, nor had digging in the earth, but our reflexes are strong. I heard in memory my aunt reminding me to wash my hands on the days I had dug for dinosaurs, and so now I had another obligation. It was simply what one did. I must wash my hands.

I remembered only when I had practically arrived at the concrete toilet shack that the doors would surely be locked for the night. I had seen no park employee come to lock it but some things remain true always and one is that after dark the doors of public toilets are locked. I came to the door, I saw the words 'CLOSED FROM DUSK TO DAWN,' and I tell you I was incredibly sad. I had wanted to fulfill my obligation. So on the off chance it might open anyway I pulled at the door handle and without any fuss or alarm it opened and without further hesitation I entered. It was like walking into a copper still of human ferment. The floors were dewy with moisture. Every surface flat enough to register a pen was rebused with jaggy handstyles, skate logo skulls, lizards, wizards, bud leaves, dicks, balls, breasts, a cartoon dog exposing his asshole and expressing to the world by means of speech bubble the words 'GIT SUM,' a grey alien holding an Uzi in one hand and displaying the middle finger of the other, the words 'MIKE SMITH HAS A SMALL DICK,' the words 'BRAD LEDUC IS A GOOF,' and countless other small signets and sigils and semiots too rare and obscure to decipher. I was in a temple to the achievements of the human body and the human mind. Perhaps I could be very happy here.

I had no house and would never. But as I washed my hands with warm, soapy water per instructions I nevertheless took some measure of comfort. If I could not leave, perhaps I could stay here – as long, of course, as the lights did not go out, but I did not think they would. I shut myself into the largest of the cubicles. A fine room for thinking, I thought. This was not my house. It was public, it belonged to everyone, but I was one of everyone, and for the moment I was here and in need of it. If someone else came along we would share. It was no bigger than a crofter's cottage in the old days, but it is a truism that those in the smallest houses are the likeliest to make room for an unexpected guest. Even Keats and Brown had been treated hospitably by such people. 'We lost our way a little yesterday,' Keats wrote from Mull, 'and inquiring at a Cottage, a young woman without a word threw on her cloak and walked a mile in a mizzling rain and splashy way to put us right again.' I wish they had beaten him and taken his money for all he said about them in the language they did not know, but they did not know. It had not escaped me by the way that in Victorian Britain public toilets genuinely had been known as 'cottages,' and that I was a crofting tenant of the mind, and so a new chain of fraying words began, words and sounds and images and dreams, so that this place with its thinking room was a cottage for me to work in, and because it was public I could not be rackrented, and it had not escaped me either that Keats too had once written of his wish to 'build a sort of mental cottage of feelings, quiet and pleasant,' and this was another way he haunted me, he had said things I wanted to say two hundred years before I said them, and this mental cottage in the park was grey concrete and what memories I still had of Aberdeen were of grey concrete and grey granite and grey pebbledash, the flats and the housing schemes, and my ancestors on the tenant farms had lived and died in cottages, sometimes with their animals inside, and they had stalls for their animals in their stone byres, and this place too had stalls, and if a 'stall' was a halt or a slowdown it was no matter. I needed to catch my breath.

But who were my animals? My Onyx bird was gone. I sat on the closed toilet seat and listened through the open-air gaps that passed for windows, shooting slits way up near the ceiling. The frogs I could still hear, like a heartbeat – not mine, a steadier heart, a sleeper's heart, an ascended master's heart, a person not dreaming but just about to. High hot life pulsing like a finger in a door. They must be my animals, the frogs – no, this was wrong. I was theirs. They knew something I didn't. Out there was death and dream and night and the places beyond words, the distant and invisible things. And in here was my temple to the written word. We were working together, the frogs and I, but I did not know how. I wished I could. Beauty is truth is dew on the floor, tang on the air, words on the walls I can't read, dreams I can't remember. Truth is coming on its long lonely march, clackety clackety, poor pilgrim, poor puppet, dancing on its board, and no one even bothered to ask if it was tired. I knew I was. My Onyx bird lay down and died. I buried it under a bracken bush. The Earl of Douglas was buried under a bracken bush too, you know. In some versions. The captain's name was Ned and he died for a maid. My own death was nothing to me, but I came from a people who had spent their lives recounting in song the deaths of others in morbid detail, and it had surely been as hard for them to bear as it was for me, and yet they could not stop remembering it in their songs, they were obsessives, and perhaps it was beautiful and sustained them and perhaps it was nevertheless hell on earth and perhaps the jig dance and onrush would never stop and I still had obligations, many, a long and invisible list, but one in particular, I had to tell one more true story of death, a story I had deferred and deferred and deferred until now and could no more.

25.

Breezes came in through the shooting slits in the public toilet, humming like jug tops and harmonizing with the frogs outside. An aeolian harp. My eyes caught motion in my lower peripherals, down in the left-hand corner closest to the cubicle door. Something stirring. A dead dry willow leaf, curved like a blade or a jai alai xistera, the same basket-woven colour of the latter, honey-tawny, straw-brown, lying on its side and trying to turn over. A tiny click sound as it tried and failed, as the breezes humming in through the shooting-slit jug tops faded in the concrete chamber and could not turn it. A sensitive leaf. I remembered again the contemptuous words of the man who had haunted me, John Keats in his letter from Scotland, from the Gàidhealtachd of Mull, a letter to a brother, Tom, who would soon die of tuberculosis, and I remembered again as well that other letter, the one about the fibres of his brain, the letter whose journey across the world to his brother and sister-in-law I said I would not talk about until later, later, and I see that it is late now, very late, and that I must, it is my obligation, I will do it if I can do nothing else. George and Georgiana were their names. Did anyone warn them how odd their names would look together on a piece of paper, a wedding invitation? But that is beside the point. I have not yet mentioned that at the same time Keats was hit in the eye with a cricket ball, George and Georgiana were in of all places in the world the impossible place of Kentucky in impossible America. George had inherited a thousand pounds, an amount he felt to be too small to start a business in London, and the couple had come to America with the idea that they would farm at the English abolitionist Morris Birkbeck's utopian community in southern Illinois. But they changed their minds, and by degrees we see them become Americans, melt into America, fold into America, leaving whatever commitments they may have had to abolitionism and human freedom aside. By the 1830s George and Georgiana would live in a mansion and own three enslaved people. The couple's initial reluctance to stay with the utopians and live by their own labour, their first turning away down the path of melting into America, has been attributed to their discomfort at the lack of 'near neighbours' at Birkbeck's village, and to George not being prepared for the hard work involved. Some evidence for the latter comes from a new neighbour the Keatses would make in Kentucky, a man who would watch George attempting to chop wood and say, 'I am sure you will do well in this country, Keats. A man who will persist, as you have been doing, in chopping that log, though it has taken you an hour to do what I could do in ten minutes, will certainly get along here.' This neighbour was in fact French, and the son of a plantation owner in Haiti, the country which by 1819 was incredibly, miraculously free – the miracle wrought after so many years of false starts and betrayals and confusions, the miracle of Toussaint and Dessalines – and had no French plantation owners any longer. And so the Frenchman had come to America to make money in another unfree country. He would make it and lose it. He would buy enslaved people and land, go into debt, and sell everything. He would buy a steamboat. He would convince George Keats to invest his inheritance in this steamboat, which would then almost immediately sink. In his letters to America, John Keats excoriated the Frenchman as a swindler: 'I cannot help thinking Mr. Audubon a dishonest man. Why did he make you believe that he was a man of property? How is it that his circumstances have altered so suddenly? In truth, I do not believe you fit to deal with the world, or at least the American world.' Oh yes, I forgot to say. The Frenchman was John James Audubon, later world-famous as the author and illustrator of *Birds of America*. He professed from childhood to have felt for birds an 'intimacy' that was 'bordering on frenzy.'

At some point in the years after I sat in the red leather chair and learned the true name of the bird that had sung to me, I decided to read what the famous Mr. Audubon had said about the red-winged blackbird. In his book he called it the Marsh Blackbird. I read the following:

> The Marsh Blackbird is so well known as being a bird of the most nefarious propensities, that in the United States one can hardly mention its name, without hearing such an account of its pilferings as might induce the young student of nature to conceive that it had been created for the purpose of annoying the farmer. That it destroys an astonishing quantity of corn, rice, and other kinds of grain, cannot be denied; but that before it commences its ravages, it has proved highly serviceable to the crops, is equally certain.

I was unhappy to see the bird slandered like that, but I wanted to know if Audubon had at least found something kind to say about the song that had been so important to me. I read on:

> They frequently alight on trees of moderate size, spread their tail, swell out their plumage, and utter their clear and not unmusical notes, particularly in the early morning, before their departure from the neighbourhood of the places in which they have roosted; for their migrations, you must know, are performed entirely during the day.

He had not found something kind, as far as I was concerned; 'clear and not unmusical notes,' he wrote, and it seemed to me a sentiment not unlike 'clean and not unintelligent' as applied to a poor child by an aristocrat passing in a luxury phaeton. A grudging concession. I felt Audubon obliterating my bird with each new sentence, stealing my bird further and further away from the memory I had nurtured for so long, changing things worse, far worse, than the bird itself had changed things when I saw its singing. I did not believe Audubon when he said my bird was 'nefarious,' you understand. But I knew that generations of adulatory readers around the world *had*. And then I read further:

> The havoc made amongst them is scarcely credible. I have heard that upwards of fifty have been killed at a shot, and am the more inclined to believe such accounts as I have myself shot hundreds in the course of an afternoon, killing from ten to fifteen at every discharge. Whilst travelling in different parts of the Southern States, during the latter part of autumn, I have often seen the fences, trees and fields so strewed with these birds, as to make me believe their number fully equal to that of the falling leaves of the trees in the places traversed by me.

How did he kill so many of what he professed to love? Was this the only possible end for an intimacy bordering on frenzy?

Leaves on the ground; dying, as-yet living leaves, plugged with buckshot and bleeding and coveting breath, raising one or both red-tipped wings in a final spasm of lucid effort, flashing red protest, red banners, the field of the murdered as the steps of the city of Odessa, 1905 red banners dropped in fright or by hands no longer getting any instructions that made sense from nervous systems no longer system, the cruel hooves of the Cossacks' horses, the gun smoke floating out into the harbour and over the mystic waters of the Black Sea, the causeway of the Argonauts, but now only mute uncaring water with no golden fleece at the end of it, one more great basin of salt tears attendant at the demonic ceremonies of the massacrelands, 1905 Odessa and Audubon's Kentucky pasturelands and as a matter of public record all America and Canada disasterlands flying false flags. And I as a child came here from the concrete flats and terraces of the housing schemes across the sea to live with Auntie and Uncle, who had already done the same, all so Uncle could drive a truck until it destroyed him in his mind and body and for Auntie to help in a shop as she had done before, different shop only but otherwise all the same, and for me to acquire an exquisite and perfect consciousness of all this with the language and the frames none of us had ever had before and to truly see everything and for sight itself to destroy me in my mind and body also. People like us were meant to be used up and to die and for God's sake to do it quietly. I never did intend to gae tae a foreign land. Ireland, she meant, in the song. Fennario. The rodeo. Insofar as she *was* the song, she did go, and was changed. The song became a flayed book of blood, red dressings on a ruined face. Destroy all the people in the airy-o. And as I sat in the thinking room of my concrete cottage, or rather yours, mine, and everyone's, and watched the single wing of the dead dry leaf try to turn over in the scraps of the wind and fail, over and over, and the croaks of the frogs echoed among the dark branches I could just see through the shooting slits, I knew a desolation that I felt in that moment could be soothed by no faith, no credo, no special and deliberated meditative sitting, no drug expedited parcel-post across the chilly frontier of the blood-brain barrier, no spirit whose vapours were stoked for a decade in the vaulted silence of oaken bones, no words of love on a scroll from Omar Khayyam, no words of divine assignment from an angel. The frogs were calling in the water and they knew something I didn't and the wind was lapping at the shooting slits and the captain's name was Ned and under the flag that still persisted in the corner of the flag of the province in which I now lived, and which was even more blatant a feature of the flag of the province I had lived in before, a world had groaned in agony and the louche administrators of India and Ireland and the Northwest Territory had known and done nothing as the numbers of the famine and the pestilence dead had risen and risen, it was all by design, they could teach the CIA a thing or two about the murderous stewardship of global empire and as a matter of fact they had, when the Americans were at their most sophisticated they merely aped the devil Britain in its double century of blood. The wings and the leaves. The dying, as-yet living in the desolation. They would keep going but so would the desolation. Until the dance was ended, under false flag or true.

I had leaned the frame against the door of the thinking room. The bottom of the frame bit into the grout of the floor tiles. But the grout was damp and the frame slid down with a crash that echoed weakly in the small concrete chamber, that flat quacking echo small chambers make. I sighed. Now I was very tired. Now I was very hungry. My left kidney was even hurting again. And I saw at last how the frame had been – there was no mistaking it – an incredible burden to me all day. And the one I would have given it to was gone. Perhaps I was stuck with it forever. Perhaps anyone I wished to give it to would die. And as a matter of fact my old theory, practically antediluvian now, at the start of the day, that some tough kids from my lower-middle-class neighbourhood had found it in a rich neighbourhood and taken it, a trophy, a triumph, slung it around the neck of the red hydrant, ring toss, kids playing it, you know the drill by now, anyway this theory that had pleased me so much at the start of the day I now felt compelled to reconsider as I looked at the frame lying ziggurat-side-up on the floor of the thinking room. Perhaps it had been abandoned on the hydrant by someone else to whom it had been a burden. Perhaps it was cursed. Yes, I entertained the idea – the snail ascending the ziggurat stairs in its cold grey robe no benign astronomer come to track the nightly incremental progress of the planets and stars but rather a death-dealing hierophant with a mouth full of curses to mumble out onto the winds far and wide, the coiled wisdom of the shell in fact a trap-laden maze with oblivion at its centre, and the greatest store of malignity inhering always in the heavy and grey and dead yet living wood. I wondered if any of this was remotely reversible. Was that what the frogs were trying to tell me? That it was? I thought again of the pond and its dark upward stare at airplanes or transmigrating souls. Yes, there was a kind of Arthurian symmetry to it, to end my vigil more or less as it had begun, to throw the frame into the dark pond and hope for a hand to reach out of the waters and catch it. Arthur the Welsh king who the English had claimed as their own with help from Geoffrey of Monmouth, a was-he-or-wasn't-he – maybe Welsh, maybe just another Norman franchisee.

I thought of Bedivere in *Le Morte d'Arthur*, the last man alive and unharmed after the great battle, the day of destiny, bidden by the dying Arthur to throw Excalibur into a lake, just as Arthur had received it from the Lady of the Lake at the start. Bedivere goes to the edge of the water but considers it a shame to throw the beautiful and famous sword away, and he comes back to Arthur a liar, claiming he did as he was told but giving the game away by reporting that the sword merely sank into the water without incident. Arthur knows it is a lie, that throwing Excalibur back into the water is an act with magical consequences. He demands that Bedivere go back and do it again, and he does, and the hand of a woman reaches out to catch Excalibur and in time an ethereal ship appears upon the shore – not of the lake but the sea this time – with otherworldly ladies attendant, the true source of Arthur's power summoned by the return of their gift to him, and the dying Arthur sails with them to Avalon. But it is Bedivere's fate that interests me. He no longer has a king to serve. He enters a hermitage and lives out his days in solitude and prayer and the transmission of the parts of the story of Arthur that, as sole survivor, only he could know. A prisoner, in a sense, of memory, a graft from the active and unreflective world of Arthur and his knights to the literate and contemplative one of the monastic orders. It is as though he is put into a computer, into a mother-board, into the great stream of information and its strange dissemination in the texts and the minds of learned women and men. From myth to history. I thought of indebted Monsieur Jacquard and his looms, Ada Lovelace (her name itself a stitched-together thing) and her studies of the brain, the self-taught Alexander Bain with both his looms *and* his studies of the brain. The huge wash of recorded time, graphed space, plotted action. Such heaviness and such sorrow. I breathed out slowly in the thinking room. No, I could not bring the frame to the pond and place it in the water. If I told you that a hand came out to grasp it I would be lying, the truth would be Bedivere's lie, nothing would happen, it would splash and either float or sink like a strange dust mote on the skin of the staring eye, a frame in a lens, and the wood would rot but perhaps still hold the shape of a frame for decades, dying and living wood, and I would have done a strange thing too late, I was in history, under it, I did not live in mythic time. No, I knew what I needed to do. I looked at the sigils and semiots on the door of the thinking room – crude, hopeful, hateful, illegible, derivative, original, all the sacred and profane writings of the bored, the bitter, the witty, the stimming, the set-tripping, hundreds of hands and eyes, fearful, no symmetry. No symmetry. I looked at the coat hook on the door. I looked at the frame. I placed the frame upon the coat hook – gently, like I was placing a delicate sash around the neck of someone who while infinitely deserving of the honour was nervous to receive it. In the moment I did so, the frogs stopped croaking – not all at once, like a video on pause, but rather as though a signal had flashed through every amphibian brain to tell them the next croak they made was their last one for tonight. So the sound died out in a stagger, a syncopation. But it stopped. I raised the frame from the hook for a moment, idly, to discover if the act would set them to croaking again. It did not. There was no going back. Our work together was finished. I returned the frame to the hook. I looked now at the frame on the door, framing the portion of the writings on the door that it could frame. It brought me no peace. Why should it do that? But I liked it there. I liked that the next person who came to think in this place that was everyone's would be staring right at a grey frame with steplike borders surrounding an array of signets, sigils, signs, and semiots of all imaginable origins in no discernible order, and that the longer they stared at the pictograms and rebuses, the more a kind of order would cohere before them, the more a grammar would knit together the symbols according to the grammar of their own lives, the secret grammar of history and time and word and sound and place and space, ideal and material, mythos and logos tumbling together in the darkness, jigging to the rhythms on the folklorist's board, the knowledge of how things do or do not come together formed by a life of trying to make them do so, trying and perhaps never succeeding, the chaos grammars of my brothers and sisters and siblings in broken-brainitude, in madness, in prisons of childhood memory, in endless re-enactments of the first original knowledge of the lack, lack of money, of safety, of a place on which to stand, I swear to you I always thought I could tell these people from across a room, my co-combatants in the unwinnable or perhaps just possibly winnable war. I lied before. It brought me some peace. By looking for long enough it brought me some. I touched the frame again for the last time. The tack of the grey paint was frictionful on the pads of my fingers. I opened the thinking-room door, slowly, and closed it again as though on my child who was sleeping at the end of a story I'd told. I opened the door of the concrete cottage, stepped out into the cool clarity of the night, and closed that door behind me too. I was light now, buoyant. My tenancy was finished. I compare it to a feeling I had felt only once in my life before, when in a fit of misguided ambition I had decided to try out for fifth-grade eight-hundred-metre. I pushed myself so hard to stay close to the much more athletic boy I ran heats against, the boy whose mother had died and who my guardians had always told me to be kind to but who in my estimation did not need anybody's pity, or at least not any more than anybody else, and whose life and happiness I wonder about now. And I pushed so hard to stay close to him that suddenly I lost sensation in my legs. They still moved beneath me, still appeared in contact with the ground. But I felt nothing there, I was half as heavy as normal, I was flying, and it frightened me. I stopped trying to keep up with my opponent. At the finish line I informed the coach that I was quitting track. I had no one to talk to about my body, which I feared, no way of learning about endorphins. But I know now that is what they were. So that outside in the now-silent park the fact that I was flying did not immediately frighten me this time. It was just the endorphins. And as the concrete cubes below me now truly began to look more and more like the shadowy forms of dice, just barely visible in the mingled lights of the street lamps, the windows, and what must certainly be the moon, rising or risen or invisible but sending light anyway somehow like a myth in secret, and as the same commingled lights broke incompletely through the broadleaf trees and left at their feet their shadows, and as the green table sea of the grass was now darkened and velveteen, I saw that at last I could leave, that when I felt something solid underfoot again it would be the moebius-stripped causeway of the invisible bridge of brass, and that walking this bridge to its chief and unmistakable end I would have arrived finally at wherever it is I am now.

Notes

The secondary sources of particular value to me in creating this book included Ian Carter's unforgettable *Farm Life in Northeast Scotland 1840–1914: The Poor Man's Country* (Donald, 1979), Roger Ebert's essay on *The Conversation* in *The Great Movies II* (Crown, 2008), Marjorie Masson and J. F. Jameson's 'The Odyssey of Thomas Muir' (*The American Historical Review*, Vol. 29, No. 1 [Oct., 1923], pp. 49–72), Nicholas Roe's *John Keats: A New Life* (Yale UP, 2012), Jonathan Clark Smith's 'George Keats: The "Money Brother" of John Keats and His Life in Louisville' (*The Register of the Kentucky Historical Society*, Vol. 106, No. 1 [Winter 2008], pp. 43–68), and Silke Stroh's *Gaelic Scotland in the Colonial Imagination: Anglophone Writing from 1600 to 1900* (Northwestern UP, 2016).

Two works of art also provided special encouragement: C. L. R. James's magisterial 1963 historico-political cricket memoir, *Beyond a Boundary*, for its opening image of a park framed in perfect symmetry by a bedroom window, and Luis Buñuel's 1962 surrealist film *The Exterminating Angel*, for its depiction of dinner guests who are unable to leave a party for obscure metaphysical reasons.

Acknowledgements

At Willenfield Literary Agency, an immense thanks to Akin Akinwumi, a true champion of literature, for all of your support and guidance.

At Coach House Books, many thanks to André Alexis for showing me this book in a totally new light with lots of laughs along the way; to Alana Wilcox for your encouragement and acumen; and to Tali Voron, James Lindsay, Crystal Sikma, Lindsay Yates, and Sasha Tate-Howarth for making this book the best version of itself it could be.

Thanks to Natalie Olsen at Kisscut Design for a cover that uses Hugh's description of the light in *The Conversation* to full and glorious effect, and to Emily Cook and everyone at Cursor Literary for bringing Hugh Dalgarno to America.

Thanks to my beta readers, André Babyn, Keijia Wang, and Nina Jankovic, for your thoughtful feedback at an important stage in the process, and to Simon Okotie, Mauro Javier Cárdenas, Jen Craig, and André Babyn (again), for your kind and generous remarks in support of the book.

Thanks to Nathan TeBokkel, botanist, beekeeper, and scholar, for being an ever-ready sounding board whether near or far; to Andy Zuliani, for well over a decade now of meals and conversations; to Matthew Tomkinson, fellow Gumboy and word-smoother, for always inspiring me to keep going; and to Bradley Iles for being excited about a very early draft in a way that made me think I might actually be onto something.

Thanks to my father for encouraging me to write and for introducing me to Coen Brothers movies; to my mother for singing songs, telling stories, and making Doric my 'language spoken at home'; and to my brother and sister for just being so damned fun to be around.

I do not have enough words in my vocabulary to thank my wife, Erica. You have filled my life with a happiness I had not thought possible.

Finally, a humble thank you to all those, living or dead, who have transmitted from memory the songs and stories of the peasants and workers of the world.